THE
HAWTHORNE
SEASON

ALSO BY RICCARDO BRUNI

The Lion and the Rose
The Night of the Moths

THE HAWTHORNE SEASON

RICCARDO BRUNI

TRANSLATED BY HILLARY LOCKE

Text copyright © 2017 by Riccardo Bruni
Translation copyright © 2018 by Hillary Locke
All rights reserved.

Previously published as *La stagione del biancospino* by Amazon Publishing, Amazon Media EU S.à.r.l. in 2017 in Italy. Translated from Italian by Hillary Locke. First published in English by AmazonCrossing in 2018.

Published by AmazonCrossing, Seattle

www.apub.com

Amazon, the Amazon logo, and AmazonCrossing are trademarks of Amazon.com, Inc., or its affiliates.

ISBN-13: 9781503901926
ISBN-10: 1503901920

Cover design by PEPE *nymi*, Milano

Printed in the United States of America

What the white whale was to Ahab, has been hinted; what, at times, he was to me, as yet remains unsaid.

Herman Melville, *Moby Dick*

PREFACE

The orange cat has a secret. The black cat already died many times before. The white cat is the evil one. A strange world on a Tuscan mountainside made of ancient woods, distant legends, and a little village where everyone knows everyone. There, winter is a heavy white mantle, a blanket of snow that seems as if it will never lift.

And a blanket covers the mind of Giulio Rodari: arrested as a suspect in his ex-girlfriend's murder, he can't remember a thing from that night. His memory contains an impenetrable void, a painful amnesia. And there's also an open wound in the memory of the region: they call it Bridge Day, and it's a void that four years ago swallowed the lives of seven people, turning this strange world upside down.

Venomous secrets hide underneath the white mantle of winter. A part of the old woods is about to be wiped out, a committee of dedicated citizens fights to save it, unruly spirits commit inexplicable acts, and a subtle tension runs through the lives of many. But the secrets will blossom when the snow melts, in the hawthorne season.

PROLOGUE

Let's try to lend some order to this mess. We'll start with the bodies.

The first two were in the living room. When the men in black arrived, they could hardly believe their eyes. It took them a good while to get them out of there. They hardly budged. The third was in a small closet, still wrapped up in a carpet. It didn't take a genius to figure out there was a body in there, since the whole bundle was soaked in blood. The fourth was downstairs, in the basement. When they found it, it had already frozen into a block of ice. The fifth was in the woods. A trail of blood spanned from the house to the point where it had come to rest. The sixth was farther away, slouched against a rock, right in the center of a red stain that spread outward in the white snow. Half its face had been blown away, the mouth caught in a strange expression of shock. The seventh and eighth had been buried. One was still in decent condition, considering the circumstances, but the other was already crawling with worms. Eight bodies.

And then there were the other two. When they found them, they were still alive.

PART ONE
THE RETURN

I'm the orange cat. I have a secret.

ONE

Nothing but white. All around.

The carabinieri's dark car winds along the county road. It seems like a mistake, an aberration, in the midst of the bare branches covered with snow, the tranquil landscape wrapped in the white blanket that spreads into the woods. And yet one can sense life there, down below, waiting. But on the surface, everything looks the same. White.

Giulio Rodari observes the monotony, his head heavy from exhaustion, slumped against the window of the patrol car. A few days' worth of beard. Bloodshot eyes. Dark glasses, pale face. A bandage over his left eyebrow covers a wound he doesn't remember getting. One of the many things he doesn't remember. He massages his wrists. His handcuffs are off now, but when he left the prison, they'd had to put them on, for the optics.

"Do they hurt?" asks the carabiniere sitting next to him in the back seat. His name is Scalise, the colonel of the county command.

"A little."

"It'll pass. We won't have to use them again. The press won't follow us this far out."

"How do you know?"

"They have their photos, they'll use the same ones for months. No one will hassle you here. The journalists are doing their writing.

They do it all by phone. They call me more times a day than my wife. They ask the dumbest questions and then record the answers wrong. Anyway, they won't be able to get any more shots of you now, so relax."

Giulio forces a smile. According to the carabiniere, this is good news. But Giulio doesn't bother to point out that, over the next few months, he'll be in all the papers in handcuffs. He doesn't feel like talking now. The painkillers are wearing off, and his headache is back. He hasn't slept for two nights straight, and can't remember a thing from the first night. The void. White, blank. Maybe he killed someone. The deputy prosecutor is sure of it.

"Everything is so white out here," says Scalise. "I love white. It makes everything seem so pure."

"You think?" asks Giulio, without turning around.

"Everyone thinks. Why do you think brides wear white?"

"If you say so."

"Confetti, sugar . . . the best sugar is white, isn't that so?"

"Some white things can be awful."

"For example?"

"A dead man's skin."

The carabiniere nods, unprepared for an answer like that. He looks back out at the landscape, but he won't stay silent for long. He's the type that never stays silent for long.

"I get why you don't like the color white," he says after a few minutes have passed.

"Do you?"

"You're an illustrator. I gave my youngest son a few of your books, you know. The ones about the gnome . . . what's it called?"

"The gnome?"

"Yeah. A mister . . . mister . . . I don't remember."

"Teo the gnome."

"That's it, Teo the gnome. You're really great. I love your work. And I love the stories. Do you write them? You don't just draw, do you? You write the stories too, am I right?"

"Yeah, I do all of it."

Giulio tries to lift his head from the window, but it's too leaden and nods backward against the seat.

"An illustrator like you who works with so many colors wouldn't like white. Maybe you just see white as a blank page to fill. White doesn't contain any other colors."

"That's not true. Blackness is the absence of color. White is the opposite. In a way, it contains all the colors."

"Is that so?"

"It is. That's why it's so scary." Giulio looks out at the expanse of snow gliding by the moving car. "The void is white."

Scalise narrows his eyes and meditates on those last words.

"I wouldn't say white is a scary color," he says, shaking his head.

"That's because you're the victim of a common misconception."

"Me? A victim? How's that?"

"Do you remember *Moby Dick*? There's that whole part about the whiteness of the whale. That's exactly what we're talking about."

"I saw the movie. The one where Gregory Peck plays the captain."

Giulio turns to Scalise. The colonel is the kind of person who never has a doubt in his mind about anything. For some reason he can't understand, Giulio feels compelled to make the colonel waver about something, even for a second, and even if it's about the most insignificant thing in the world.

"Just try for a second to let go of all the things you usually associate with the color white," he says. "Purity, chastity, light. They're nothing but abstract variations on the concept of goodness. Set those aside, let them go. Try to separate white from the idea of good. And now look at it. Doesn't it seem like something else entirely? That albino pallor, the emptiness? Think of something scary, something that really terrifies you. And now imagine it in white. Doesn't it seem even more terrifying?"

Scalise looks out the window again. Maybe this conversation isn't going the way Giulio expected. And questioning something he's so sure of, even the most insignificant thing, doesn't seem like something Scalise would enjoy.

"Anyway, this didn't turn out so bad for you," he says after a few minutes, turning to Giulio again. "I mean, it's nice here, it'll be like a vacation for you. House arrest is never that bad. And as long as your apartment is under search and seizure, you'll be comfortable here. Plus you'll be able to work. I saw you brought all your stuff with you. What is it? Colored pencils? Paper?"

"My materials, yeah. I want to work. You can go crazy in a place like this without something to do."

"You're talking to the wrong guy. Next month I'm going on vacation with my family, and I'd give an eye to be able to lie down by the sea and not lift a finger."

Giulio slouches against the window again, his head growing heavier by the minute. He lets his eyes fall shut but doesn't manage to sleep. He can still see those faces. All disfigured, like in a nightmare. Everything that happened the night before his arrest. Patrizia's neighbor screaming over her body with his enormous mouth, a well that could swallow a person forever. Patrizia. Did he kill her? Was it really possible to kill just like that, without remembering it? To wipe it from his memory like a stain of jam?

"Giulio, you're going to hurt us both." Sometimes in his memory the edges of everything are blurred. Patrizia is an evanescent face against a white background, an overexposed image. There's no context. Patrizia could have said those words to him anywhere. In any place they'd been over the past few months. His amnesia had swallowed him for about four hours, but it's as if the hole in his memory had expanded. A mighty storm upending everything in its path. And the background is white. It's empty.

"You're from around here anyway, aren't you? So it's a bit of a home-coming, am I right?" asks Scalise. Giulio doesn't know how many more times he can stand to hear the "am I right?" that the colonel uses to conclude most of his sentences. His way of posing rhetorical questions as if they were granted affirmations is typical of the kind of person who's convinced they're always right. The kind of person who's incapable of questioning even the most useless and minute and obtuse certainty they have. "Who doesn't like to go home? And you said your mom, Ms. Barbara, is an excellent cook, am I right?"

"They call it Ulysses syndrome," says Giulio.

"What?"

"We spend half our lives leaving home and the other half trying to return."

"Interesting . . ."

"Even if in my case the return is somewhat forced . . ."

"Either way, Ulysses is quite a character. Very astute. Remember the old version, the one with that Greek actor? Beautiful."

"Bekim Fehmiu."

"That's it."

"He wasn't Greek. He was Albanian."

"Really? Funny. Albanian? You think of yourself as quite a cultured person, am I right?"

"You seem surprised."

"Usually when we arrest someone like yourself, it's hard to connect the charges with the prisoner."

"Do you think educated people are more civil?"

"They usually are."

"I thought so too."

"Women are worse than the devil," says the carabiniere behind the wheel.

"You do the driving and mind your own business," says Scalise. Then he turns back to Giulio. "What I mean is that you don't look like the dangerous type, and I'm having trouble picturing it while, well, you get it."

"Is that why you took off my handcuffs?"

"I didn't think they were necessary, but I can put them back on if you prefer."

"I'm just trying to figure this out. Are you saying my arrest is a mistake?"

"I didn't say that."

"It sounded like you did."

"Do you really want to know what I think?"

"By all means." In reality he didn't, but he knew Scalise would tell him anyway.

"I have a few theories myself, you know?"

"I'm listening."

"Back when I was working at another command, I arrested this guy. He was in his sixties, just retired. He was the simple type. The kind of guy who went to play cards all day and took his dog out hunting a few times a year. You know the kind of guy I'm talking about? One day he got home, took off his shoes, turned on the TV, and sat down in his armchair to watch one of those game shows where they win a bunch of money, then he got up during the commercials, took his gun, and blew away his wife and daughter. Just like that. It still gives me chills to think about it. His wife was in the kitchen. He shot her dead while she was cooking dinner. Two bullets. Then he reloaded. Can you imagine? It wasn't just the heat of the moment. He actually took the time to reload his gun. And then he went to his daughter's room, where she was lying on her bed, listening to music with her headphones on. She didn't even have time to jump up. Two shots. Right in the chest. No fuss. Then he called the carabinieri. As we took him away, I kept trying to figure it out. He was the most normal kind of guy. You get me? But then the

8

commercials came on, and he decided to commit a massacre. Insanity, am I right? Who would have ever thought someone like him could have been capable of doing something like that? Do you get what I'm saying? The truth is that there's always a dark room. But do you know what bugs me most about the whole story? What was the answer to the winning game show question? You think the man knew it?"

"I don't know, but I don't get your theory."

"I don't think there's always an explanation for evil. We just have to endure it. And that's what makes it so terrifying. Because as long as we can't explain it, we'll never feel safe."

The barroom is trimmed in light oak. The bar itself, the stools, the tables with their soft chairs, covered with brick-colored velvet, the hand-carved backrests. Circles, diamonds, hearts.

The Gherarda Hotel is perched at an altitude of 1,500 meters, just above the village. Facing the county road, it overlooks a meadow and is surrounded by the old woods. That's how they've always referred to it in these parts, the old woods. Even before the region conducted the census that revealed, at this very spot, the greatest concentration of monumental trees in all of Tuscany.

Barbara stands by the window. Her gray hair hangs loose around her shoulders. She looks in the direction of the meadow on the other side of the street. A white bed.

She clasps her morning cup of herbal tea to her chest with both hands. She lets it cool a little as she takes in its aromas of rose and black currant. The heat relaxes the arthritic joints in her fingers.

"They should be close by now."

Akan's voice behind her. Barbara studies the reflection of his face on the glass, which appears to float in the middle of the meadow. Dark skin, thick mustache.

"Did you turn off the heating on the third floor?"

"It's all off, downstairs too."

"Are you sure you want to stay?"

"We've already discussed that." Barbara turns and looks directly at him. "It's been quite a while since I've seen him, I didn't think . . ."

"You should relax. Everything will be fine."

"But what if he really . . . ?"

"You'll be the first to know."

"I'd like to believe you."

She turns again. The meadow. The woods. The white trees, like skeletons. Down the road, at the bend, a car appears. Barbara rests her cup on a table and walks outside, tightening her shawl around her neck. Akan follows her.

Two teaspoons of instant coffee and one teaspoon of sugar at the bottom of one of the last cups yet to be chipped. She should buy a few more. First task of the day for Grazia: buy new cups. But the day is long, more urgent matters will arise, and the cups will remain at the back of her mind until the next morning.

Grazia pours the water and slowly stirs, observing how quickly the coffee dissolves. She places the empty pot in the sink, along with the dirty dishes from the evening before. The dishwasher is full, and she'll take care of it later; still, she can't help but feel a pang of guilt. Second task: keep the kitchen clean and tidy.

She crosses the dark hallway and stops at Viola's door.

"I made you coffee. I have to go out for a while this morning, remember?"

No answer.

"Viola, I'm going to be late. Can I come in?"

After a few years they came to a compromise: Grazia can enter Viola's room, but only when she's there and absolutely not unless Grazia has Viola's permission.

She knocks again.

No answer.

Viola wouldn't have gone out without saying goodbye.

Grazia opens the door. The acrid odor of stale smoke. Clothes strewn across the desk. Viola is under the duvet. The white cord of her iPhone charger runs from the outlet near the nightstand into her down cocoon. She's fallen asleep with her music on.

There's a notebook by the nightstand with a drawing of a violin key with the moon in the background and a big spider dangling from a spiderweb. Next to that, a succession of chords and notes written out on a staff. A whole world her mother hasn't had access to for a long time.

Grazia picks up a sweatshirt and sniffs it. It reeks of smoke. Last night they played again, and when they hole themselves up in a room together, that's how things end. But for some time now the usual smell seems to have acquired a hint of something new.

She's not bothered by the fact that Viola smokes a few joints now and then as much as she is by the thought that in order to do it, she has to hang out with that half-wit dealer. It must be Solfrizzi, the son of a former classmate and a prime example of how genetic heritage can doom you from birth without relief, benefits, or a reduction of sentence. With his half-wit mother and his half-wit father, Solfrizzi would have defied all the laws of science if he hadn't grown up to be a half-wit too. He's the one who goes off to the city and brings weed back to the village. But the alternative is for Viola to find another source. And that wouldn't be any better, because that kind of incentive usually corresponds to an advanced stage of consumption. Unless Diego, the band's bass player, can arrange something. That guy always has red eyes and looks a bit tired. If only she could find a gram somewhere . . . but she still hasn't had any luck. New priority.

She approaches the duvet and pulls it back.

Viola opens her eyes. This time she'd fallen asleep with all that metal in her face. Through her ears, her eyebrows, her nose, and her lip. Grazia was certain that sooner or later she'd get used to the piercings that riddled her daughter's face, but she hadn't yet.

Viola squints up at her and takes off her headphones. "What?"

"I brought you coffee. I have to leave early this morning."

"Put it there."

She grabs the duvet to pull it up, but Grazia holds it back and stops her.

"Maybe you should shower before you go out today."

"What are you talking about?"

"You reek of smoke. A lot." She rests the cup on the nightstand. "We'll discuss this tonight."

Viola sits up and clasps the cup. "Diego's the one who smokes when we play. The room is tiny. Of course I stink."

"I could run a urine test, you know."

"Are you seriously threatening to bring your work into this?" Viola sips her coffee.

"Try not to put me in that position," says Grazia.

"Bye, Mom. You're going to be late."

"We'll discuss this tonight."

Viola shrugs, looks up, and smiles. Grazia knows that body language. It's her way of saying "Fine, no problem," when saying it aloud wouldn't sound convincing enough.

Grazia brings her face close to Viola's. She plants a kiss on her forehead. She sniffs her hair.

"Take a shower," she repeats as she leaves, closing the bedroom door behind her.

Her daughter spends too much time at home alone. After seeing the dirty plates in the sink, Grazia is already awash in a second wave of guilt. Since the day has hardly begun, there's room for another, which is surely on its way.

Grazia pulls her hair into a low ponytail. She takes her hat from the rack next to the door and puts it on as she descends the stairs to the door of the building. The golden flame. She zips her jacket with its carabinieri logos up to her chin and opens the door. Parked in front of the building is a car from the carabinieri station she runs. Sitting behind the wheel waiting for her is Donato Esposito, or Esposito Donato: there are several interpretations and theories regarding his name.

"I've been in these parts before," says the driver of the car that is bringing Giulio back to the Gherarda. The carabiniere gestures toward the road on the right that ascends to the summit. "Four years ago, the day of the tragedy, when that bus . . ." He's still talking when he notices that the chief is staring at him.

"My aunt was on that bus," says Rodari.

"Seriously?" asks Scalise.

"Seriously. Bridge Day. That's what they call it around here. It's a little ironic, since that's the day the bridge ceased to exist."

"I came two years later," says Scalise, "but I remember seeing it on the news."

"Me too," says Rodari. "I tried to come, to get someone to drive me—because I don't drive—but the road was all jammed with emergency vehicles, and they made us turn around. I only managed to get here the day after it happened."

"A real tragedy," says Scalise.

"The kind you were talking about, Colonel. The kind that have no explanation."

Viola emerges from her chrysalis, wearing panties and a tank top. She surrenders to the air's impact, allowing it to give her goose bumps, and then uses the shudder through her body to wake up the rest of the way.

In the bathroom she stares into the mirror, checking that all her piercings are still in place. The hair on the sides of her head is starting to grow out; she'll have to run the razor over it soon.

"Cheer up, we have a long fucking day of work ahead of us."

And she makes a punk face in the mirror, giving herself the finger and sticking her tongue out as far as it will go.

"What's the new book about?"

Scalise is one of those people who make the use of headphones essential for avoiding a conversation.

"I'm not quite sure yet."

"Did I tell you that my kids have a few? My youngest is getting to them now."

"Yeah, you said."

"When I found out it was you, I wanted to tell my kids, but then I thought that given the circumstances . . ."

Giulio turns to face him. He looks for signs that betray his Martian origins. He wants to ask him if by chance he has fallen asleep lately next to a huge pod, like in the *Body Snatchers*. Maybe people like Scalise really are aliens who have come to Earth with a set of behaviors designed in a lab, speak like they're in one of those live soaps where none of the actors bother to study their lines.

"Because of the fact you were arrested, I mean . . . ," Scalise says. "Because maybe, well, under different circumstances, you might have signed one of my copies, right? My kids—" But a sneeze prevents him from finishing his sentence.

"Bless you, chief," says the driver.

"Tha . . . than—" And he sneezes again.

"It's freezing out, chief. If you want, I'll turn off the air-conditioning."

"God, please no," says Giulio.

"No worries," says Scalise. "No heat. Noted. The artist here has already said he gets carsick without air-conditioning. We'll warm up at the hotel."

"Around here they say to put a chestnut in your pocket," says Giulio, feeling guilty that everyone has to freeze just because he gets carsick.

"A chestnut?"

"Yeah, it stops you from catching a cold."

"Oh right, a chestnut! Now that you say it, I think I read that somewhere."

"I referred to it a few times in my gnome stories."

Scalise sneezes again.

"Maybe the next time you come you can bring one of your books," says Giulio, "so I can sign it. You can always tell your kids we met some other way."

"You're very kind. I'll do that." He pauses before continuing. "Can I ask you something? Because there's one thing about your story that has me thinking."

"What's that?"

"Do you really not remember anything? I mean, you've been accused of murder and you don't remember a thing. Partial amnesia, they called it. From drinking, if I'm not mistaken. Funny thing, and it happened to you once before. You asked me if I think your arrest is a mistake. But I have a question for you: What do you think? In all your forgetfulness you must have some theory about who the killer is, right?"

He was correct. According to the defense, the amnesia was from drinking. Giulio had only drunk alcohol once before. He was a kid. And that time, like the second, he awoke with a black hole in his memory. But that's just a theory. The prosecutor will use another. Amnesia provoked by a removal mechanism over what he had done.

"Sorry, Colonel," says Giulio, "but my attorney said I can't discuss it."

"Of course. Pardon me, it was my curiosity speaking."

"We're here, chief," says the driver. "That's the Gherarda Hotel."

Giulio turns. The car slows to a roll. His mother is walking outside accompanied by a corpulent man with a mustache. It's Akan, the Kurd, a castaway on the mountain, who has helped his mother since she found herself alone. Giulio looks at the Gherarda. He tries to determine the last time he was here, but he can't.

"Magnificent place," says Scalise, through a completely stuffed-up nose.

TWO

The bus stop is located in the square at the entrance to the village. At the shelter, colorful down jackets, clouds of smoke, someone who talks and laughs too loudly, a backpack flying into the middle of the street.

Viola took the back way and slipped into Bar Fuga, or The Escape, a name that reflects her current plan. It's practically at the intersection with the street. From the counter, she can see the square, but the angle and the glass ensure a degree of protection. And it's better this way, because at the shelter, among the others waiting for the express bus to the city, is Minetti, and if that brat spots her, she could have problems. Viola can just imagine it: their teacher calling roll, Minetti innocently saying something like "Weird. I just saw her this morning. At Bar Fuga, I think. Maybe she missed the bus, poor thing . . ."

The fact is that she needs time, because the songwriting is going slow, and at this rate they risk not being able to record. Because Lilith has an expiration date. Their breakup has already been decided, and it's approaching fast.

Arturo, the drummer, is having a breakdown over graduation. This is March and final exams are in sight. And that's not all. For September, his parents are already house-hunting in a city a half a day away by train so he can attend the same university as his father, who has already planned for him to graduate in pharmacy. His destiny is written just a few feet away from the bus stop, a few numbers down from Bar Fuga, in letters that remind Viola of a cough syrup label: NOVELLI PHARMACY. He can't escape it. Arturo isn't bad; he has a good relationship with the tom-tom and sometimes manages to get a nearly tribal sound out of it. Among other things, he's the owner of the agricultural annex turned practice room that has served as Lilith's home base. But he's one of those who play out of passion, not necessity. One of those whose fate is written elsewhere, a future with no sharp turns, a bank account at the ready, a shiny, polished car to drive into town on Sunday afternoons, and his drum kit for those occasions when he needs to blow off steam, never to realize that all his possessions are worth as much as a sandcastle before the tide comes in.

Diego, the bassist, is capable of a deep conversation. He understands music. He's always on YouTube, coming up with stuff that's trending all around the world. His issue is that he's increasingly stoned, in the sense that he smokes joints like they're Skittles. One after the other. He's been known to nod off in the practice room. His parents work at the health spa, not far from the village. His mom is a masseuse, and his dad works the storeroom. It's not much, but sometimes they'll get a free pass to the thermal baths. His surname, Chessa, won't be written over the entrance to a pharmacy anytime soon—at least not until they legalize medical marijuana. In the end maybe he'll turn out to be one of those types who prefer to listen to music, perhaps sitting at the foot of an old, worn-in sofa, with a rum and coke at his side and a half pipe of the Old Toby, his name for weed, apparently from *The Lord of the Rings*. This is probably also why his beard is so overgrown lately, and why he started using a pipe to smoke weed, and why, at every practice session, to which he invariably arrives late, he announces that "a wizard is never late, nor is he early, he arrives precisely when he means to." But even he has a plan for when school is over: to go abroad and live with his cousin for the summer to work in his ice cream parlor. Officially, the reason is to have an educational experience in another country, which nowadays is worth more than a diploma. The fact that the ice cream parlor happens to be in Amsterdam is incidental.

The members of Lilith have been playing together for years now. But the group is about to break up. It had been a tough decision, but after everyone announced their plans for life after the Galileo Institute, they all agreed that the distractions wouldn't have done justice to the band's good name. Before they call it quits, however, they have a job to do, something important. Their song. There can't be a group with a name and a story, no matter how short-lived, without a song of its own. But practice days are hard to come by now, and it's more and more common for them to play two gigs in a row. Which is why, since they have another job to do before tonight's rehearsal, Viola decided to take the day off. As she waited for the bus to carry off Minetti and the rest of them, she took her cappuccino, with its dusting of cocoa powder prepared by Gerri, and slipped into the bar's dark room, where the last pinball machine resists in a corner, besieged by the slot machines that one by one have replaced all the video games that once stood here.

No one is sitting at the slots yet, but soon the room will start to smell of vinegar breath and days-old sweat.

Lining the wall, like a small shrine, are the archery trophies Gervaso Torloni won before he closed himself off behind the bar for good. In the photos, Gerri still has hair, twenty pounds less belly, and a smile that must have diminished over the years, fading like the name of the bar on the sign outside. The 1999 regional championship gold medal rests between two photos that commemorate an awards ceremony to be remembered.

It's exactly the sort of thing that induces anxiety in someone like Viola. It's the worst horror film she could watch. It's enough to look at the poor guy who just made her cappuccino and know how life can crush you if you spend it in the wrong place. And how anxiety overcomes you. The fear of not making it out in time. Knowing that before you go there's at least one thing you have to do.

Viola slips a bobby pin into her bangs so they don't fall into her eyes, revealing the buzzed lower half of her head. She banishes her ugly thoughts, fishing a token out of her jeans pocket. She slides it into the pinball machine. With her fingertips left exposed by her open-tipped wool gloves, the ones she also uses to play when the practice room is too cold, she grips the controls. And the game begins.

The background is inspired by the Ninja Turtles. Raphael has gone, however: the lever representing him has collapsed over time, and knowing how to use it requires a certain affinity with the machine. But Viola knows how to move the ball, and in a few minutes she's activated Master Splinter, who gives her a bonus. Cowabunga. After the first game, the music clicks on. And the bar door slams behind the person who just walked in.

"You left the car on an empty tank." Viola recognizes the voice of Gerri's wife, Katerina. Six feet of blonde imported from the East who, according to the bartender, had managed a restaurant at some resort. It turns out that when the ski slopes are closed due to lack of snow, somebody still might wander in for a spritz, but the stroke of luck Katerina hoped to have had with Gerri proved to be rather different from what she'd imagined.

"Hey, I don't even remember the last time I drove the car." The stroke of luck Gerri thought he'd had with her had sadly been put into perspective over time.

"Exactly. You never fill it up. I always have to do it when I need the car. Make me a coffee. They postponed my massage. Can you believe it? They sent me a text this morning an hour beforehand to say they're opening late. But I say, does no one around here know how to work? Back home this kind of thing would never happen. Anyway, this coffee sucks. You need to change the machine or I'll open a tab at another bar that doesn't poison me every time I sit down. Give me a fifty, I don't want to get out of the car to pay with a card when I get gas."

Leonardo shoots the ball into the hole, and Master Splinter's whiskery face lights up again. Cowabunga. The front door slams, Katerina's heels fade out, and the pop of the cork on the sparkling white that Gerri opens behind the bar announces that, for the bartender, the time has come to open the ceremonies, and accompany his disappointments by getting as wasted as God commands.

THREE

"I'd stay here in a second, boss." Donato Esposito is a twenty-four-year-old boy. He keeps his uniform perfect, his hair looks like it's made of Legos, his shave is impeccable, and his nerves are always wound up from being overworked and invincible. "I mean, if they confirm me for more time, I'll call my wife, make her join me, and have her popping 'em out in no time."

"Sounds like a plan." Grazia is in the passenger seat, in the car issued to the carabinieri station under her command. She's still thinking of Solfrizzi, who probably sells weed to her daughter. She knows where he lives; she could wait for him outside his house and lock him up on a whim. "Stay away from Viola or this is what happens every night, you hear me?" That could work. Or maybe something more in the style of Clint Eastwood is in order.

"I want at least five. I'm one of three, all boys. I want three boys and two girls. But I'm a little worried about the girls, because when they get older you have to deal with the boyfriends, and I think I'll be a jealous father, jealous of anyone who gets too close to my daughters . . . you get me, boss?"

"Yep. That's the way it goes." And maybe that idiot goes around bragging that he sells weed to the Marshal's daughter. That's what they call her: the Marshal. Maybe they do it out of respect for her femininity, with her being a woman, and a mother. Anyway, it sounds like the title of one of those old Alvaro Vitali movies.

"Five children, boss. So no matter how bad it turns out, at least we can have our own soccer team. What do you think? We could—" The car slips in the snow.

"Careful!" Grazia grabs the door handle. "If you want to set up house around here, you have to learn to drive in the snow, because there's only one plow in the whole province and it doesn't run more than once a week. You have to go slow, in a low gear, and definitely never hit the brakes like that."

"I apologize, ma'am."

"And I told you not to address me so formally when we're alone. We're not Fantozzi and Filini, for God's sake."

"Okay, boss. I apologize."

"Go slow. The Gherarda Hotel is coming up, let's try to make it there in one piece."

As they approach the hotel, the car from the provincial police carrying Giulio Rodari, the man accused of murdering his ex-girlfriend and hiding her body in a jealous rage, appears around the curve. Aggravated homicide and concealment of a corpse. Grazia already knows. He had been another one of her classmates, like Solfrizzi's father. Giulio, though, had been a good guy. Which makes the whole story seem a bit absurd. Someone like him losing his head that way. But he did have stalking complaints against him. Witnesses too.

The cars arrive practically at the same time. This will make Scalise happy, since it gives the impression of extreme punctuality and coordination. Barbara, Rodari's mother, is standing outside the hotel, along with the Kurd who works for her. They've closed the winter season early so they can accommodate Rodari and handle things with a measure of calm.

The driver for the colonel of the provincial police gets out of the car and opens the door for him. Scalise adjusts his uniform and drapes his coat over his shoulders. Grazia and Donato walk over to greet him.

Rodari is the last one out of the car. The others all notice that they're staring at him and look away in unison, while Grazia only notices after it's too late and turns to observe Barbara. She's already thought about how a mother might feel in all this. Her eyes are glassy, perhaps frightened, as she approaches her son, embracing him. And now she can't hold back her tears. Grazia only realizes after the fact that this will make her cry too. It's a mother thing . . . but it's a sign of weakness that she shouldn't have displayed in front of Scalise. She takes out her handkerchief and blows her nose, trying to dab at her tears without being too obvious.

"Let's go inside, I just baked a cake," Barbara says, wiping the sleeve of her jacket across her eyes.

"A cake? Great!" says the driver who accompanied Scalise, before receiving a glare from the colonel.

"Come on, you can't say no to a good cake," says Barbara.

"Especially one of the Gherarda's cakes," Grazia adds.

"So go get your cake," Scalise says.

The snow muffles their footsteps as they approach the entrance.

As soon as Akan opens the door, a big orange cat leaps out.

"Beautiful cat, my compliments," says Scalise. "My wife is a cat lover. We have two, but I've never seen one that big."

"We have three," says Barbara. "They belonged to my sister, Amanda."

Akan waits for everyone to enter, looks to the sky, which is dense, with a foreboding pallor, and closes the door.

It's the day of shortcuts. Viola puts on her helmet and calculates that the shortest route to her destination passes by the Gherarda—the hotel where her mother went this morning to see that guy who killed his ex and who is staying there until the trial. So she has to take another route and make sure to hide her scooter in a place where it can't be seen from the road.

She walks the path as she puts on her heavy gloves over her open-tipped ones. She doesn't anticipate any issues.

Turn the key, press the button. She gives it some gas, and the wheel skids underneath her. But for someone who has learned to drive on these roads, it's no problem. Nerves of steel, no hard braking, and so on.

After a few minutes the scooter is already climbing the old road, the one no one takes anymore because it's blocked farther down. Everyone knows why, but it's one of those things people don't like to talk about. And this makes her nervous. Because sometimes she has the impression that people behave like this when they want to forget about certain things. And in the end it's the people who are forgotten. Everyone has the right to be happy, but that's the jerkiest way to go about it.

When she arrives at the fork, she stops. Everything around her is white. To the left the road slopes upward, and from there she can stop and go on through the old woods by foot. To the right the road goes down to the bridge.

The bridge that no longer exists. The void in its place. A void that, four years ago, swallowed the lives of seven people. Michele was among them. The fourth member of Lilith.

Rodari went upstairs. He said he needed to shower and lie down for a few hours. The four officers are sitting at one of the bar tables, and each has a plate with a slice of apple cake.

"It's a fairy tale," says the driver of Scalise's car. "But you shouldn't close the hotel. The season is good this year, you can still ski in March, the lifts are open, and . . ." Too late, again, he notices the commander.

"They say when it snows during the days of the blackbird, the snow stays on the ground until late April," says Barbara, who understands the situation and is trying to help the indiscreet carabiniere.

"The blackbird?" asks Scalise.

"The last days of January," says Barbara. "According to tradition, they're the coldest days of the year. Legend has it that a lady blackbird once spent them in the shelter of a chimney dirty with soot, and ever since then the females have been darker than the males."

Scalise seems to be struck by intuition. "Your son wrote about it in one of his gnome books, right? I'm sure I've read that."

Barbara smiles. "We closed a little early," she says, turning to the driver, "so we could dedicate ourselves to some matters that have been pending for a long time. And it just so happened to come in handy, with regard to my son's affair. He wouldn't have been able to stay here if the hotel were running."

"Obviously," confirms Scalise, glaring at the driver, who shoves a piece of cake into his mouth and slowly chews. "I saw the forecast: it's going to snow in the next few days," the colonel resumes, when the silence gets too long for his taste. "You're not ever scared of the isolation? I've heard the roads get blocked with snow."

"We have a snowmobile," says Barbara. "Akan knows how to drive it. Thank goodness for him. I can't even drive the car. I have an old Ford that belonged to my sister, but without Akan, it never would have left the garage."

"I'm sorry about your sister. Your son told me what happened," says Scalise.

"Thank you. Anyway, I don't think we'll be going out much. We want to focus on the tasks at hand so we can make up for the lost weeks in the summer season, when this story will be behind us." The carabinieri remain silent. "I know, my timeline is optimistic. But I think the deputy prosecutor will soon realize that she's mistaken."

"I hope you're right," says Scalise. "Meanwhile, you'll have all of the local officers at your disposal. I thought I'd see them all this morning, but obviously the others felt the duty to remain on the job. Isn't that right, Marshal Parodi?"

It takes Grazia a few seconds to realize the colonel isn't joking.

"The others?" asks Donato, a moment before realizing it's better to stay quiet.

"The others, of course. What's wrong with that, Marshal? I thought it was a given."

Grazia rests her fork on her plate, wipes her mouth with her napkin, and tries to find the best words for her response.

"Colonel," she says, "there are no others."

"Yes, I see they aren't here, Marshal. It's good that they're so dedicated to their work, and I'm not one to get my panties in a bunch, but this is my first time up here and I expected to meet all of you. Don't worry, just let them know I'm grateful for their constant attention to their duties in this delightful, remote corner of our province."

"Look," says Grazia, "I think there's been a mistake."

"A mistake?"

"Yes, Colonel. It's not that they're not here right now. It's that they don't exist. Esposito and I are the only ones manning the station."

Silence.

"Anyone want another slice?" asks Barbara. Grazia smiles at her for trying to break the tension.

"How is that possible?" asks Scalise.

"Marmora got his transfer and went back home to the Marche. D'Arrigo didn't get the transfer he put in for, but he was sent to Palermo. Chelli applied for a mission abroad, and he's completing the prep course. Friguglia is on sick leave."

"How sick is he?"

"I don't know. He's been sick since I was assigned to the station. Maybe he has issues answering to a woman commander."

"Don't be ridiculous, Parodi. I'll address this myself. But why didn't you report the situation?"

"Maybe they never passed it along to you, Colonel, but I've been sounding the alarm for a while now."

"Of course, I imagine. Who doesn't complain these days? Isn't that right, Ms. Barbara? I'll bet even you had to make a few mistakes before you learned how to make such an exquisite cake, am I right?"

"Even colonels can mess up sometimes, huh?" chirps the driver.

Grazia captures the flash of absolute anger across the colonel's eyes. The driver doesn't seem to realize that the return journey will be the longest and most wrenching of his career. She realizes that she shouldn't concern herself with Esposito's plans for staying or his intentions to reproduce.

A sudden noise catches everyone off guard. It seems to come from the wall, maybe from the ceiling. A metallic sort of cry.

"Pipes," says Barbara. "It happens. One of the things we have to fix. I think my son is trying to shower."

Grazia hopes Barbara doesn't start crying again, because then she'll start too. She hates the way she can't help but feel for everyone and everything: it makes her feel fragile, and as a woman in uniform she is at risk of embarrassing herself in front of her superiors. Scalise wasn't the one to put her up for her job. Nor does she think he ever would have.

FOUR

There is a clearing at the foot of the cliff called the Sasso del Corvo, or the Crow's Rock, after its elongated shape that's reminiscent of a beak. And there is a small cave, just there, where they say that a murderous highwayman has been hiding for some time. It's not very deep, but deep enough to house voices, legends, stories, folklore, and local hearsay about satanic masses and immigrants gone missing. Sometimes there's a big owl that flies around these parts. There are also those who say this place lies at the exact center of the old woods, where the forces that inhabit it are most concentrated. Spirits. According to ancient pagan beliefs, which date back to before the construction of the village church down below, when people born in these parts die, their souls take up residence in the woods, waiting.

Viola is sitting on her backpack, leaning against a large rock emerging from the cover of snow. She's holding an iPhone set on record. She holds it straight out in front of her and moves it all around, as if she were trying to pick up a signal. Sounds. Voices. The breath of the woods, they call it. Maybe it's just the wind rustling the dry beech branches. Maybe it's just a load of crap, suggestions that awaken the old stories they heard as kids. But the iPhone's recording app signals something: it's recording a sound. Even if Viola can't hear it, something out there is producing a sound. That's what the old stories refer to. And it's the imperceptible sound that she needs for Lilith's song.

She's been here for an hour, give or take. She's recorded a bunch of small files of a few minutes each.

She hits pause and props up the smartphone against the rock.

Her eyes are tearing up, which happens to her often in these parts. She wipes them with her fingerless gloves, which reveal her fingernails, painted black. Her skin is pale, and the dark makeup on her eyes and lips makes her look even more pallid.

She looks around at the still landscape as she fidgets with seven silver earrings on her left ear.

The day is perfect for recording the breath. Now she has good material to work with. There's little time to spare, because before the end of school, before their exams and all the rest of it, Lilith will break up. They even decided on the date: June 21. Summer solstice. Lilith, the wind, and the rain. It will all end with spring.

Viola takes the phone and checks her calls. Nothing from her mother: it's all going smoothly.

She opens WhatsApp to write a message to Arturo.

I got some good material, can I come mix?

She places the phone back against the rock. She digs into her pocket and pulls out her pouch of Old Holborn blue, places the tobacco in a rolling paper, which her agile fingers roll quickly, her tongue passing along the edge to close it. Viola lights the cigarette and exhales a mouthful of blue smoke that dissipates in the frosty air. Her sadness has passed, leaving the strange sense of comfort that this place grants her in a way that few others do.

A message notification.

My house is your house, my parents are out. See you tonight.

It's time to start compiling the song.

Giulio is sitting on the edge of the bed. The hood of his bathrobe covers his head. His eyes are fixed on the floor. This is his old room, in the separate part of the hotel his family used as their residence.

"Giulio, I don't want to see you anymore. You scare me, do you understand?"

They're sitting at a table near the concession stand in the park. Patrizia is wearing her usual sweet perfume. They're only at the beginning of the crisis. They've just sat down; she hasn't even sipped the spritz they brought over. The ice melts as the water fizzes. After she tells him she's afraid of him, she'll get up and leave. Giulio will stay, observing her pendulating strides. He'll feel a lacerating sensation as she walks away, as if that motion were tearing her out of him. His body is hit with an electric jolt, the need to destroy everything in his sight. The table, Patrizia's spritz, his alcohol-free lager, the little bowl of potato chips, the one with the olives, and all the rest of that sore thumb of a concession stand that looks like it belongs in a park on the moon.

He needs to breathe. Slowly. He needs to see a doctor to get some strong medication. He's unwell. Really unwell. And this is just the beginning.

Sitting on the edge of the bed, his eyes are focused on that concession stand. And everything that came after. The nights spent outside Patrizia's apartment. The r-r-ring of her phone into the void. The messages he sent, those cursed check marks that turned blue when she read them, and so why didn't she respond? *It won't kill you to answer me for once, bitch.* There it was. The breakdown of language. The first sign of his emotional unraveling. Sitting on the edge of the bed, he stares into the abyss that swallowed him.

Is there a cure?

In this room in his mother's hotel, the floor is wood. The planks were arranged at regular intervals. From the exact center of each one begins the next.

On the day they went to the park, the carabinieri arrived at the concession stand and restrained him. Patrizia had only been gone for a few minutes when he lost his mind. The bar manager is wielding a broom in an attempt to defend himself. The other customers have gathered around him. A couple of tables have been flipped over. Pigeons peck at the potato chips among the pieces of glass scattered on the pavement. Even passersby have stopped to look at that crazy guy.

"The bar manager accepts compensation and withdraws his lawsuit, sir, but you need to calm down."

The carabiniere isn't wearing a hat.

The bathrobe is damp.

The wood planks are all parallel.

Giulio raises his head. He looks around. What happened? This had been his room, years ago. Opposite the bed there is a desk, and above it are shelves with books. A whole shelf is taken up by the complete collection of *The Fantastic Adventures of Teo the Gnome*. He cannot believe he ever managed to write so many. Those old country stories, legends about the woods he heard from his aunt Amanda, the witch.

My name is Theophrastus Grimblegromble, but you can call me Teo, if you please. I have a red beard and a nice green hat.

The concession stand in the park was his tipping point. The spritz glass with the melting ice, the last thing he recalls being intact.

Then the rest came.

The abyss.

"Sir, a complaint was lodged against you pursuant to article 612-bis, do you know what that means? Persecutory acts. Stalking. She's not messing around now."

To be a gnome, to be able to disappear.

And then, toward the epilogue, the final chapter of the tragedy.

"Sir, what happened the other night?"

The void. White. He hasn't a clue what happened. He has a hole of at least four hours and a cut on his eyebrow and no idea how it got there. Whenever he tries to explain, the listener has that expression. The expression that says they don't believe a single word he's saying.

"Sir, do you know where I can find Patrizia Alberti?"

FIVE

The day will be long. Like everything else. Grazia walks into the minimart to buy sandwiches and drinks. Ever since there have been only two officers at the station, in practice, their shift is a single and eternal one.

She walks along the aisles, among the biscuits and the fruit juices, and her mind wanders from the dirty dishes in the sink to Viola, who is surely smoking weed; to Rodari's surveillance, to which she has been added; to the list of other things a squadron of six should be dealing with.

When she passes in front of the newspaper stand, she looks at the first page of the local paper. The headline is Rodari's arrest. "Children's Book Author Accused of Homicide." There's a photo of him, perhaps taken from online, holding a book with a gnome on the cover. He looks stunned. When they were kids, in class, he drew constantly.

"The last thing poor Barbara needed," Grazia hears someone say. Beyond the pasta section is the food counter. The voice belongs to Fioralba, the owner of the minimart. Grazia stops, scanning the newspaper headlines, in an attempt to eavesdrop.

"Anyway, that guy was always a little off." The voice belongs to Mirna, the wife of Eugenio Falconi, the mayor. "He says he doesn't remember a thing, I read it in the paper. But that's a strange kind of amnesia if you ask me. And if it really did happen, can he claim he's innocent? How does he even know?"

"He never came back to visit his mother in all these years," adds Adele, her inseparable companion with an olive-green Panda four by four, and her partner in Buraco Rummy.

The chime of the bell warns everyone that the door has opened. The detergent shelf blocks the newcomer from view. In any case, the voices fall silent.

"You wanted some bread, Mirna?"

"Just a sliver, dear, that'll be more than enough."

Dorina comes out from behind the detergent shelf. She's looking for something in her bag. She pulls out what looks like an acoustic device and places it behind her ear. Only then does she notice Grazia and smiles, embarrassed, before disappearing behind the pasta section to join the others at Fioralba's food counter.

Grazia keeps listening. Because she knows them and doesn't want to miss out on any useful tidbits. Adele's cousin, Dorina, is Barbara's dearest friend, as well as her Buraco partner. In the countryside everyone knows the rivalry that divides these two sets of friends. And between Adele and Dorina, in particular, there's some old dirt that—if Grazia remembers correctly—involves an inheritance from years back. It almost seems as if Dorina came in for the sole purpose of interrupting their ugly gossip about Barbara's son.

"Dorina, darling, how are you?" asks Mirna.

"Splendidly, dear."

"How nice to hear that," says Adele. "What about Barbara?"

"Busy, I'm afraid," Dorina says.

"'Busy' sounds like the word, darling," says Mirna. "And what about her son, has he arrived? Eugenio says they brought him up this morning."

"I haven't spoken to Barbara yet this morning, but if Eugenio says so . . ."

"When you hear from her, please tell her not to worry about the game. If she wants, we can postpone, and if we can't do it at the hotel, we can play at mine for once."

"No problem, Giulio is in a separate wing of the hotel, in the apartment where he used to live as a boy. We can play at the bar. Barbara will probably appreciate the distraction."

"I thought since it was house arrest—"

"Don't worry, Mirna. No one will arrest us for this."

Grazia skirts the pasta aisle and enters the scene.

"Marshal, good morning," says Fioralba. "I didn't hear you come in. The usual sandwiches?"

"You're just the person we needed, Marshal," says Mirna. "We were just wondering if we could still go to the bar at the Gherarda, since Barbara's son . . ."

"The bar is officially closed," says Grazia. "But Rodari is staying in another wing of the hotel, so it should be fine. Not even the police would dream of impeding the great Buraco tradition."

A burst of laughter warms up the minimart, loosening the ancient hostility between the two adverse fronts. But it's just a temporary truce.

SIX

Lilith's practice room is set up in an alcove. The Novellis of the Novelli Pharmacy have more than one. But this one is exclusively at the disposal of Arturo's whims, so he can play his drums without frightening guests. The walls are soundproof, and the inside looks like a NASA command center.

Computers, amplifiers, connectors. Arturo's drum kit is a wall of tom-toms.

Viola has turned on the electric stove, and the air is warming up now. Not enough to take off her woolen gloves, which cover only the palms and backs of her hands and allow her to work on the computer.

She's already downloaded the recordings she made with her iPhone, and now she's using a program that links them all together. The software confirms the presence of a sound. Viola connected the laptop to the system and raised the volume to the max, but she still can't hear a thing. There's a sound, but it's silent. It could be an ultrasound, something that the human ear can't grasp.

She's prepping the base tracks for Lilith's first and last original track. And this is the first element, the first track. Maybe no one will hear a thing, but the breath of the woods is still the starting point for the whole piece. And while the program develops it, Viola puts on her headphones to get the second element from another file. A recording.

She made it with her old phone a few years back, but the new software enabled her to clean up all the unwanted noises. A tedious job. One of the many causes of the dark circles that appear under her eyes every morning.

The file name is a date: 09/09/2010.

Her fingers swipe the track pad, and the pointer stops a few millimeters from the icon with the white triangle. She can almost feel it, but she doesn't click it yet. Viola tries to fidget with her earrings, but her headphones get in the way.

"I heard you in church last Sunday. You played something before Mass."

Viola has long hair and the face of a twelve-year-old, still free of makeup. She's gone over to Michele's house because she had to bring some baking sheets back to his mother. She's already rung the bell a few times, but no one has answered. She goes over to the window and sees Michele through the curtains. He's sitting in front of his keyboard. He's wearing headphones, so he can't hear her. But after coming all this way under the summer sun, she has no intention of turning back with the empty baking sheets, which her mother was intent on sending back that morning. It takes her a while to get his attention, but in the end he notices her, takes off his headphones, and opens the door.

He's older than she is. He's already a few years into high school.

He smiles and invites her in. He has the gentle ways of an old man. He takes the trays, brings them to the kitchen, and asks Viola if she is thirsty. Her throat is parched from the heat, but the only thing she can say is how she had heard him play before Mass. And she realizes at that very moment how much she had hoped his mother wouldn't be home, just so she would be able to talk to him.

"Do you like music?" Michele asks.

"A little."

"Do you play an instrument?"

"I wouldn't say that."

"That's a shame."

Michele approaches the keyboard, takes his headphones, and puts them on Viola's head.

He's about to start playing but stops and turns to her again.

"It's an old song," he says. "It's called 'A Whiter Shade of Pale.'"

Viola closes her eyes. She always closes her eyes when she listens to music. She seems to be able to see it. Now it's as if the notes coming out of the organ were bright streaks, yellow and red, appearing and chasing each other in the dark. It's the music she'd heard in church. She only opens her eyes again when the song is over. She realizes she's smiling like a little girl. To shift tone she removes the headphones, resuming her serious, mildly sullen expression.

"What is it?" she asks him.

"A group, an old one."

"They're not bad."

"They're not bad at all."

"But isn't church the place for more . . . sacred stuff?"

"I don't know any of it. The priest asked if I'd play the organ some-times, and I go to church because they have a fantastic organ. That's all. Why do you go? Are you a religious type? Do you pray and all the rest of it?"

"I've never given it much thought. I guess I go sometimes because I like to hear you play."

Michele seems like he's thinking. As if he were considering an idea that just popped up in his mind. From this close up he looks so cool. If it weren't for those thick glasses that make his eyes look like two black dots and that wrinkled shirt hanging open over his white tank top. There really is something old-mannish about his mannerisms, his way of being. Viola realizes she's staring at him and can't stop from blushing, like the girl she is.

"Would you like to learn to play the guitar?" Michele asks.

"Me?"

"There are only two of us in this room."

"Oh right. The guitar? I don't have one."

"I do. I mean, I have more than one. Let's say I have one I can lend you, so maybe we can play something together. You can accompany me."

After a couple of minutes, Michele bounds up the stairs to the basement with an electric guitar in his hand. The neck is wooden and the body is black. The things Viola will later learn to call pickups, the devices that capture the sound of the strings, are made of steel. It's wonderful.

"It's a Fender. David Gilmour has one like it," Michele says.

"Oh."

"You know who David Gilmour is, right?"

"Of course. He's a guitarist."

"Maybe I'll lend you a few CDs."

Viola can't take her eyes off the guitar.

"Now. To play it you have to hold it first," Michele says, handing it to her.

It's heavy. She didn't think a guitar would weigh that much. She rests the body flat on her lap and plucks at the strings with her left thumb.

"Don't tell me you're a lefty . . ."

"Is that a problem?"

"I'll have to restring it. Let's do this, come back tomorrow, same time, and I'll have it ready for you, okay?"

"Okay."

"Will you be serious about learning, or are you going to waste my time?"

"I don't have anything better to do."

Michele smiles, realizing this isn't exactly what she meant. Not in that way, at least. He walks with her to the door. She's about to leave but can't until she turns back to clarify something.

"Do you like apple muffins?"

"Yes, yes I do. Why?"

"Because I can't afford to pay you for lessons, but I know how to make apple muffins and a few types of cookies. I can also make cakes, but they never turn out so well."

"Apple muffins will be just fine."

Viola lifts her fingers from the computer track pad. The pointer freezes. The triangle play button is still there. But every time she listens to that file, she's overcome with emotion. She needs to breathe a little first.

Her guitar is here, leaning against the wall, still in the case. She hopes the drop in temperature overnight didn't affect the pickups, but leaving it was the only way she would get away with working here this morning.

She unzips the case. Here it is. The same as ever. The same as the first time Michele ever showed it to her. He only realized afterward that he wouldn't be able to use it after he restrung it. So, after a few lessons, after she gained his trust, he had allowed her to take it home with her to practice. He had other guitars, or so he said. For some strange reason, he seemed to think it was really important to teach her to play it.

"You can keep it," he told her one day. "That guitar has a great desire to be played."

Viola rests it against her leg, inserts the cable, and turns on the amplifier. And her fingers slide along the strings into the opening arpeggio of "Stairway to Heaven."

"Why do you always listen to music that's so . . . ?"

"Old?"

She can tell Michele has been waiting for her to ask that question for a while. They've been playing together for a few months now. And in fact, all the songs that he has taught her are older than the two of them put together. They're in the living room now, where there's a wall that's completely occupied by the stereo system, including a record player, and a full wall of records and CDs.

"Yeah. I mean, I love all the songs we're playing, but I was curious . . ."

"It's the first records I heard when I was little. My father had them. They're all beautiful songs. Once you learn to play them, you'll never stop. The songs they make today aren't like that. You get bored before you know it."

"I don't know my dad." The words just come out of her, like that, for no good reason. "That is, I know his name and where he is, but we've never met."

"You're a little down today."

"A little."

"So let me teach you a song called 'Wish You Were Here.' And you can dedicate it to whomever you'd like."

Viola rests her guitar on its case. The computer has finished processing the breath of the woods. It's time to input the second track of Lilith's first and last original song. The file is ready. Her fingers touch the track pad again, and this time they click the triangle-shaped icon.

09/09/2010

Play.

"I'm going to play you something I wrote." It's the first time Michele has confessed to writing a song, but it's something Viola has long since suspected. "It's not really a song yet. Let's call it a work in progress."

"Oh stop, just play it for me. I want to hear it."

Michele plays the song, a slow blues in a minor key. It's almost hypnotic.

Viola closes her eyes again. The song surrounds her now as it leaves Arturo's system, closing the gap in time between now and the day Michele played it for the first time. She's no longer ashamed of her girlish smile, which now opens across a changed face, pale, made ghostly with heavy black makeup, and piercings that sprout from her lips, nose, and eyebrows.

"It's beautiful."

"It's just a melody now. I have to develop it."

"Do you mind if I record it on my phone? I'd love to have it."

"Sure, tell me when you're ready and I'll play it again."

Lilith's first and last original song has its second track.

SEVEN

The large wood-fired oven is located behind the Gherarda, looking out over the woods. From there a path goes down to the valley. The oven is rarely used, so they have to let the fire warm the stone walls before it can be used. Barbara adds a bit of wood to feed the flame that she lit with the long kitchen matches. She has to prepare for the Evening of Bread, a tradition from times of old.

The air is cold. Akan shoveled the snow away from the sides of the oven to make it accessible.

Barbara reaches her hands inside to feel the heat of the flames. She's not alone. The orange cat jumps from the ground to the flat stone. He's the largest of the three, the most gluttonous. He felt the heat. He's come to soak it up.

"You're out here too?"

The cat slinks in front of her, rubbing his tail against her face.

"Maybe it's better if you go back inside. It's cold out here, don't you think?"

As soon as the door opens, the cat slips in and bounds up the stairs. Barbara goes back to the barroom to make another cup of tea and warm up.

"You've changed a few things around here."

She turns and freezes. Giulio is sitting at a table with a coffee cup in front of him. He's changed the bandage on his eyebrow. He's wearing his gray jacket from ski school that she left in his room. His city clothes aren't well suited to the mountain climate. He's shaved, and he looks better than before. But his eyes are still red.

"You scared me to death," Barbara says, shaking out her shoulders.

"Sorry. I couldn't sleep."

"Did Akan make too much noise?"

"No, it wasn't that."

Barbara sits at the table with him. "What changes were you referring to?"

"Nothing big, I was just saying. There was a photo over there. From New Year's Eve, if I recall. We were all here: Dad, Amanda . . . I came down to check it out, but it's not here anymore."

"You're right. It fell and the frame broke. I need to fix it."

"Maybe one day—"

"Giulio, when are you going to tell me what happened?"

Outside the window, the meadow lies under a blanket of snow.

"I don't know what happened. I was out of my mind, I drank a lot. I only remember a few images. And they aren't good ones." He smiles as he fidgets with the spoon in his empty coffee cup.

"You shouldn't have been drinking. But it will all come back to you, you'll see."

"I don't know if I want that."

"Of course you do, because I'm sure you didn't hurt her."

"Of course I hurt her. In so many ways. I made her life a living hell. Because I wanted her to suffer, you know? I wanted her to suffer with me. It's all so confusing, it's like a part of me I didn't know existed just took over. Whenever I go over it in my mind, it feels like I'm thinking about someone else. That time I broke into her house at night and started screaming like a madman . . . I don't want all that to come back to me."

"Do you want another coffee?"

"Yes, please."

Barbara takes off her jacket and drapes it over a chair. She wraps her warm wool shawl even tighter. She takes a cup, fills the coffee machine, and presses the illuminated button. The aroma of Arabia blend quickly follows.

"It's supposed to snow tomorrow," says Barbara. "Might be the last one of the season."

"The deputy prosecutor is coming tomorrow afternoon," says Giulio. "They want to question me."

"I know, Grazia told me. She's the one guarding you, did you know that?"

"We'll need to prepare a room."

"I've already thought about that. You'll be in the dining room, we can stay downstairs in the basement."

"For Buraco?"

"Of course not. Buraco is on Wednesday, tomorrow is Tuesday."

"So who's coming tomorrow?"

"We formed a committee."

"A committee?"

"Didn't I tell you? We found out a company bought a tranche of the old woods that for some godforsaken reason doesn't fall within the protected area. They're going to build a waste treatment plant."

"In the middle of the old woods?"

"Right in the middle."

"Can they even do that?"

"The commission has to decide." Barbara brings the coffee to the table. "Apparently, they're going to meet in a few days to vote on whether to issue the permits. The crazy thing is that to bring that stuff out there they'll have to widen the roads for the trucks. Insanity, don't you think?"

"And so you formed a committee."

"A committee for the defense of our woods, of course."

Giulio opens a sugar packet and empties it into the cup. He had grown unused to all that white out there.

"I'm sorry I didn't come back very often."

"That's one way to put it."

"All right, almost never."

Perhaps this isn't the time to make him face certain issues. Barbara checks the clock on the wall.

"Let me know if you need anything. Akan is going out to pick up some eggs. He said he wants to make you tagliatelle."

"Mom . . ."

"What."

Giulio looks out the window. "It's as if it's all covered in snow."

EIGHT

The only sound that survives at Bar Fuga is the music from the slots coming from the other room. The girl, Viola, is gone. She seemed to be in a hurry. Gerri hopes she didn't hear this morning's spat with Katerina, but in vain. He knows she did. Just like he knows that people in the village have started whispering about him. He knows because that's how things go. He fills another glass and gulps it down, though today it tastes more bitter than usual. Gerri's forty-five today. They say a time comes for everyone, sooner or later, when you're the only one who knows it's your birthday. And usually that's not a happy day. The most important thing to remember is that it only lasts one day. But people say a lot of stupid things. Gerri feels the weight of the truth that if life were a football game, he'd be at the end of the first half, sitting in the locker room, tired, with an overwhelming disadvantage and the depressing awareness that his opponent has more legs and more breath than he does. He messed up the game plan. Got the wrong day, the wrong game. It happens, the championship is long. The door to the bar opens. The lumberjacks. They've been freezing their butts off, and a round is in order. Today, he offers drinks on the house. Why? Because it's the bartender's birthday, and this year he's found a way out of cel-ebrating alone. The referee blows the whistle, or maybe it's just another damn slot machine. Fact is, the field awaits him, the second half begins. There's a game to turn around. Cheers.

"The story of the Kurdish man who was shipwrecked on the mountain."

Giulio is standing in the kitchen door. Akan is at the workbench. His shirtsleeves are rolled up, and his hands are coated in flour. He's preparing the dough for the noodles. He looks up, sees Giulio, and smiles.

"Whenever you want to write that story, you have my permission."

"And reveal the Gherarda's greatest secret?" Giulio asks, entering the room. "That the guardian of the secular tradition of wild boar ragù comes from the other side of the Mediterranean?"

"From the cradle of civilization."

"You never take the credit you deserve for all this work, infidel." Giulio approaches him, rolling up his sleeves. He notices the pot on the stove where Akan's ragù is simmering. "I think a good Christian sampling is in order, a pious swipe, if you will . . ."

"The bread is still in the bag," Akan tells him with a nod as he resumes kneading.

Giulio approaches the bag. He takes out the loaf.

"You disappoint me, Akan. You have that wood-fired oven out there and you go and buy bread—"

But as he takes the loaf, he reveals the newspaper underneath it. His photo is on the front page.

"The wood-fired oven isn't warm enough yet," says Akan. "It'll be ready for tonight. It's the Evening of Bread, remember? A lot of people are coming, you'll see. Too bad you can't . . ." But Akan's voice seems to come from far away. From a place where everything is still whole.

Giulio looks at the newspaper. He's reading the piece about him. His story with Patrizia. When it started, when it ended. Everything is there. The stalking charges, the messages he sent her, the nights he spent outside her apartment, the harassment. All of it.

"Don't read that." Akan interrupts the movement of the dough. "It's a load of nonsense."

"But it's my nonsense."

Akan approaches him. He wipes his hands on a cloth. He takes the newspaper out of Giulio's hands and puts it back where it was.

"I weathered my storm, Giulio. Now you have to weather yours."

Giulio studies him. The Kurd's face is lined with wrinkles, his skin dark. Sometimes he has the eyes of someone who has stared death in the face and lived to tell the tale. Giulio purses his lips and nods. Weather the storm. He hopes he's ready for it.

He grabs the bread and reaches for the serrated knife.

"Did someone around here say something about a pious swipe, or was I hearing things?"

NINE

"Do you think they'll send someone?"

Donato drives the patrol car. He has to practice. Grazia is sitting next to him with the bag of sandwiches on her lap. The encounter with Scalise didn't go well for him. There was no opportunity to discuss his future. But if they just sent some reinforcements to the station, he might be able to put in for a day to go see his wife.

"I don't know, maybe they can send someone else because of Rodari." Grazia is thinking of something else entirely. Her daughter smokes weed and maybe even brags about how she makes a fool of the Marshal.

"How many times do we have to pass by the hotel?" asks Donato.

"I don't know, we'll pass by when we have the time and I'll record it. If someone has a problem with it, we'll let them tell us."

The car arrives in front of the hotel, and Donato turns off the engine.

Grazia doesn't get out.

"Should we wait?" asks Donato.

"You have somewhere to be?"

The phone rings. Grazia picks it up and passes it to Donato.

"Carabinieri," he says. "What? To GeoService? What? Blood? But . . . Okay, okay. We'll be there in a few minutes."

"What happened?" asks Grazia.

"That was the GeoService office. They found the head of a fox stuck on a pole and something written in blood across the door."

"We'll wait a few minutes and then go."

"A few minutes?"

"Are you sure you don't have somewhere to be?"

Viola's scooter peeks around the curve. She parks it in front of the entrance to the hotel and crosses the street toward the patrol car.

Grazia lowers the window. "Everything okay?"

"Fine."

"Thank Barbara for me. I'll see you tonight."

As Viola walks toward the Gherarda, Barbara waves at Grazia from the window.

"Now that Rodari is under house arrest," says Donato, "is it okay for Viola to be eating with them?"

"Officially, Rodari is confined to his room in the other wing of the hotel, and there's no reason to go verify that, right? Besides, he's only a suspect in the murder, he hasn't been officially charged, so I don't think he's so dangerous at the moment."

"I'm just saying because—"

"Barbara is a friend, I can't take care of my daughter because we're up to our ears, and I'd like her to have one good meal today. Any other questions?"

"No, boss."

"Perfect. Now, then, if you don't have any other questions, we can go and see about this fox head stuck on a pole."

"Sure, boss."

The patrol car pulls away.

Viola drops her backpack on the living room sofa next to the fireplace. Right behind it is the rack of Gherarda hunting rifles. It's funny to think they can shoot for real. Whenever she leaves her backpack here, she can't help but stop and consider it.

"Remingtons. Hunting is a religion around here."

Viola turns. She didn't think she'd find him right there in front of her. Her mother had told her that he was staying in another wing of the hotel, more or less separated from the rest of it. And instead, Giulio Rodari, the man under arrest because he apparently killed his ex-girlfriend and stashed her corpse somewhere they still haven't found, is standing in the living room. "They were my father's. He was the hunter in the family." Viola is quiet, searching for something to say. "Even my aunt knew how to shoot, she had killer aim. But I take after my mother. I wouldn't be able to catch a wild boar in the crosshairs from a foot away."

"Hi," says Viola, not knowing what else to say.

"Hi. I didn't mean to scare you. I saw you here and I wanted to say hello."

"I . . ."

"You're Grazia's daughter." He looks like a kind person. His hair is disheveled, he's wearing a fleece with a ski lift tag, and he looks like he hasn't slept in a century. He's carrying a plate of noodles and a glass of water. "I wanted to see if you looked like her."

"Yeah." Viola wanted to add more, but she couldn't think of anything to say.

"I'll let you go, sorry again." He starts up the stairs, but Viola is curious.

"So do I look like her?" she asks.

"A little," he says, turning back. "When we were your age, we were close friends. Now that I have to stay in my room, I sometimes feel like I'm back in those days. I had a David Bowie poster on my wall, only now, whenever I turn to look at it, it's gone. Sorry, I don't know why I'm telling you these things. I'm a little out of it." He turns again to leave.

"We play 'Heroes' . . ." She stops him. Again.

"Who's we?"

"I'm in a band."

"Beautiful song—really. *We can be heroes just for one day* . . ."

"You don't look like you'd be a David Bowie fan."

"What do I look like?"

"More the classic rock type."

"Is it because I'm holding a plate of noodles with ragù and a glass of water?"

"Maybe."

"Room service is on vacation and I . . ."

"Of course, you're under . . . that is, I mean . . ."

"I've been arrested, yes. House arrest. Strange concept, don't you think? In the sense that either you're arrested or you're at home, right?"

"Come to think of it . . ." Viola hates it when she says "come to think of it," because she can never find anything else to say after that. But she knows that she shouldn't be talking to this guy, and that if her mother finds out she'll freak. So naturally she can't help but talk to him.

"All right, I'll let you go. I shouldn't be in here, much less talking to you. The court order lists all the parts of the hotel where I can go, and this is absolutely off-limits."

"I read one of your books." Rodari looks surprised, but maybe he always does when someone tells him they read one of his books. "That is, not now, a few years ago. When I was younger. It wasn't bad, the story of the gnome. It was good, seriously. Your drawings are great. I draw sometimes too. My mom bought it for me, the gnome book. She told me about you, that you went to school together and all that."

"Thanks for telling me, it makes me very happy to hear that."

"I liked the fact that the gnome can disappear because the woods protect him. Disappearing into the woods has always been my dream."

"Mine too, sometimes." Rodari seems a bit sad now. Maybe she shouldn't have said anything about disappearing into the woods to someone who has been accused of making a woman disappear. "Be well," he tells her, before climbing the stairs. And this time, Viola finds no good excuse to stop him.

THE SPIRITS OF THE WOODS DON'T FORGIVE

These are the words written on GeoService's door. But they weren't written in blood. The person who found them just assumed that was the case after he saw the fox's head. For Grazia, all it took was getting a few steps closer until she smelled the paint.

The office is set up inside a wood and plastic prefab cabin located near the site where the plant is supposed to be built. It's still empty, but if they approve the waste storage and treatment permits, the employees will begin to arrive.

"I pass by here about twice a day, in the morning and in the afternoon." The lumberjack who reported what will be officially described as an "act of vandalism" recounts the discovery. Next to him is Eugenio Falconi, the mayor of the village, the second person who heard from the lumberjack. He's a short man who wears a cowboy hat. Next to him is Aurelio Magliarini, who goes by Maglio, the owner of Magliarini Forestry Services, who was the first to be notified of the finding by his employee.

"We maintain the cabin," explains Maglio, "by agreement with the owner. We shovel the snow, stuff like that."

"It's a serious offense," says the mayor, "and who knows what it's all about."

"It seems pretty clear to me," says Donato. "These are the offices of the company that wants to build a waste treatment plant in the middle of the woods, and these *Spirits* don't have any intention of forgiving the damage the decision will cause."

"You mean if the decision causes damage," the mayor replies. "The permits won't be authorized, son. I mean, they killed a fox. What kind of environmentalist goes around decapitating foxes?"

"Marshal, if there's nothing else," says Maglio, "we have to get back to work."

Grazia checks the ground. The animal's blood has pooled at the base of the long pole. It's paint, even here. She takes a picture with her phone.

"What if it has something to do with old Peter's story?" asks the young lumberjack.

Grazia turns to him and catches Maglio's gaze, silencing him.

"Who's old Peter?" asks Donato.

"He was a wanderer," says Grazia. "From northern Europe—I don't know where exactly, some German forest. He lived in the woods. He claimed to be a diviner. But then he disappeared, probably during that flood four years ago. An overlooked death, since it happened around the time the bridge came down. No one has seen him since."

"But there's nothing to be sorry about," says Maglio. "He was some hobo who lived in the woods. It's no one's fault if something happened to him."

"Did they ever find his body?" asks Donato.

"No, it's one of the many mysteries about this place," says Grazia, staring out into the old woods.

TEN

I'm the orange cat. I have a secret.

It's not important, though. Not as important as what happened four years ago. I was lazing on the windowsill, the one that looks out onto the meadow. It's my favorite place, because there's a radiator right under it, and I love the warm air. And then from the kitchen there's the smell of things to eat, and I love to be there to smell them. I love it all. They say I'm fat, but it's just how I'm built.

That day, however, the kitchen was closed. Actually, I think it was the first and last time I didn't get a single whiff of food. Everyone knows the story. There was a time when they used to gather every week to tell it. They said it was their way of not feeling guilty because the faces of the people who are no longer with us begin to fade with time. You come to forget them. It's normal. A cat knows.

So for a time they would meet here and remember what happened. In those afternoons there were always cookies and pastries that left crisp crumbs on the floor, and everyone, when they saw I was there, would give me a bite and a rub.

There were seven people on that bus, including the driver.

And they all died.

The problem, according to what they said when they gathered here and offered me all those treats, was the rain. Too much rain. But rain falls, and not even people, who can build these warm homes with radiators that give off the heat I like so much, have ever invented a way to stop the rain. So it seems to me that blaming the rain for raining is a little like blaming fire for burning you because it's hot. In reality, you're the drunk who got your whiskers too close to the flame. Anyhow.

The real problem, which became clearer as they gathered together with that woman, the one everyone is looking for now and who—according to rumors—Giulio killed because he went crazy, the real problem, as I was saying, was the state of the bridge. Because the water flowing beneath it had eaten at the ground that had been supporting it for a long time. But even in this case, I mean, is it the water's fault for eating the earth? Is it possible that they can build such beautiful houses, with radiators that give off the heat I like so much, and still not understand that water eats the earth? It's like the story of the fire and the drunk who burns his whiskers. Maybe the problem is they don't have whiskers. And even the few who do, I dare say, wear them so short that they're completely useless.

So the rain falls, the water eats the ground. The fact is that when that bus crossed the bridge, that bridge went straight down as if it had been built with snow. And seven people lost their lives.

At first, they talked about it constantly. As if they couldn't help it. There were those seven photos always on display. They sang sad songs together, candles lit, with all the photos. They were mourning their dead. They mourned Amanda, the witch; Michele, the church organist; Alberto, the plumber who lost his license because he kept all the water in pipes; Teresa, the seamstress and the wife of Maglio the lumberjack; Goran, who worked in the woods and in the evening met with the other people at the train station who spoke his language; Carmela, who knew all the secrets of chocolate; and Ferdinand, who drove the bus. And they say cats don't have a good memory. Anyhow.

Sometimes they spoke about Peter, that nice old man, Amanda's friend, who would always give me a scratch under the chin where I really like it. No one has seen him for a long time, and everyone thinks the rain washed him away too, right where the bridge came down and the river ran over its banks and into the woods. He lived in the woods. He was looking for water. So he said. Funny thing: let's imagine that he found too much water, as it very well seems. They never put a photo of him with the others, because he wasn't on that bus. They left him alone and apart even in their memories. But at the end of the day, where he is now, I don't think it makes a big difference.

In short, they've all moved on a good bit from those days. It's like the rain. It's not that all the drops stop together. But at some point you look around and it's not raining anymore. And it was the same with them. At some point, they looked around and everyone had stopped crying. So, with time, all those nonsense discussions about how it had rained too much, about how the river had eaten the earth and all the rest of it, in short, all those discussions are over. They only met when that woman came back and spoke about her lawyer things. And I liked it when she came because they would meet here and I would arrange myself in my favorite spot, enjoying the warm air rising from the radiator that I like so much, and from time to time someone would offer me a treat.

But, as I understand it, things didn't go the way that woman wanted. In the end it came out that no one was to blame, and then they stopped coming. Anyhow.

Now they seem to have started again. But they don't talk about the bridge and the bus that went down. They don't mention those seven people. They don't even talk about old Peter anymore. They talk about this plant thing in the woods, which nobody wants. But in any case, when they come, I get back in my favorite spot and hope that someone will offer me a treat.

But sometimes I wonder. What could have happened to old Peter? And who knows what became of that woman?

They say we cats sometimes feel things before they happen.

And I have the feeling something is about to happen.

PART TWO
AMNESIA

I'm the black cat. I've already died, many times before.

ONE

The lawyer is wearing a gray suit, a white shirt, and a blue tie. Giulio studies him as he pulls the files from his soft leather bag, which he placed on the dining room table where they're sitting. It's a worn-out bag, too worn for a lawyer who's no older than forty. Maybe it's a family piece. Superstitious people tend to cling to these things. His name is Alberto Colletti. His shave is perfect, with a good douse of aftershave, minty breath. His semiautomatic smile reveals a row of sparkling teeth.

"Well, well, well," he says after putting all the files in front of him. "It's my duty to inform you of a couple of things, Giulio."

"Is this the part where you tell me that people who lie to their lawyers tell the truth on the stand?"

"You should write legal thrillers instead of children's stories. No, no. We're in the real world, where no one cares about the truth. But I do have to inform you what can happen if you do get officially charged. We are still in the preliminary investigation phase, so maybe this will all go away, but we need to have a plan in case it doesn't. A regular trial for murder and concealment of a corpse could easily come with a life sentence. If you decide to confess immediately, collaborate with the investigators, indemnify the victim's family, etcetera, etcetera, we may get some great deals out of it, including a sentence reduction by at least a third. If we then go for an abbreviated trial, we would get another sentence reduction of an additional third. And if we could make the case for partial insanity, which is not impossible, since you have a stalking complaint lodged against you, we could get a further reduction. From life to twenty-four years, twenty-four to sixteen, sixteen to, say, eleven. You could do five on the inside and then get out on good behavior, maybe do some community service."

"Five years in jail for killing a person?"

"This is best-case scenario. On the one hand, this, on the other hand, life. It depends on how we decide to move."

"There are a lot of personal things in the newspaper. How did they find out about them?" Giulio asks.

"You read the paper?"

"Akan buys it every morning, then my mother hides it under the sofa."

"It's the prosecutor. They're rummaging around in every corner of your life and passing any info they find to the press. It's how they turn up the heat and push you to confess."

"Do you think I killed her?"

The lawyer is taken aback and doesn't bother to hide it. He reclines in his chair and assumes a more relaxed position, as if he were accepting that the conversation was shifting to a more personal level.

"You've already admitted to the stalking. Calling in the middle of the night, messages with an unmistakable tone. You threatened to kill the victim more than once."

"Patrizia. Let's call her by her name." Giulio stares out the window. A light snow has begun to fall.

"As you like. You threatened Patrizia in front of witnesses, and you admitted to doing it. The night she disappeared you drank a lot of alcohol, which causes you to have partial amnesia. But you remember going over to her apartment, you remember almost tearing her door off the hinges. You remember attacking the neighbors, who told you she wasn't there. You don't remember how, exactly, but you managed to get yourself to the place where Patrizia was drinking with friends and colleagues. You knew she would be there because you knew where she hung out. And then you proceeded to act like a lunatic with the security personnel until she came outside to get you out of trouble. The people who were with her say she came back inside and said she couldn't leave you in that state, because you had been drinking and it was something you couldn't do, and she said she'd bring you home. They all told her not to, for obvious reasons. One of them offered to go with her, but she said no and called a taxi. And that's the last time anyone saw her."

"Who offered to go with her?"

Alberto checks the files. "Maccari. Leonardo Maccari. Another attorney. He works at the same firm." He continues reading, then snaps the file closed. "But that's irrelevant."

"He's the tennis player."

"What do you mean?"

"Tall, blond, broad shoulders, he plays tennis every Tuesday and Friday evening, usually from seven to eight."

"Did you stalk him too?"

"Patrizia was seeing another man. I saw her with someone. I only tried to figure out who he was."

"Why?"

"Because I'm a controlling maniac."

"Exactly. And since you haven't been charged for it yet, let's try to keep that between us, okay?"

"He's a prime candidate."

"Who? What do you mean?"

"The tennis player."

"Christ, Giulio."

"Why did you close the file?"

"Because there was nothing else to read."

"There was something written about Maccari, but you didn't read it."

"Nothing in there is relevant to us right now."

"It was him, wasn't it?"

"Stop it."

"Give me the file."

"I'm leaving."

"The fuck you are! Give me the file."

The lawyer surrenders, flinging the file in Giulio's face with a huff. Then he gets up and walks over to the table where Giulio's mother has left a pitcher of juice.

Giulio reads quickly. His eyes skip from one page to another.

"They didn't write it down. There must be another file like this. Where is it? Didn't they give it to you?"

Alberto returns to the table with a glass full of blood orange juice.

"Let's talk about the footage of the attack now."

Giulio drops the file and grants a truce. "All right."

"It was picked up by the surveillance camera at a credit institution ten minutes from your apartment. The attorney is still waiting for Patrizia's phone records to check her calls, but especially what the towers picked up. Anyway, after she left your apartment, Patrizia must have decided to walk home. And after ten minutes she reached the camera. Giving you enough time to go back downstairs and catch up to her."

"Have you already written my sentence?"

"The camera is positioned in a narrow street and only captured a reflection of the scene in a window. So the image quality is poor. You can still recognize Patrizia, but not her attacker. He's basically a shadow that jumps out and kills her, without a doubt. He grabs her from behind with one arm, she squirms, then the attacker gives a hard tug, and it's pretty clear that he breaks her neck. Patrizia's body goes unnaturally limp. The attacker drags her away and disappears from the frame."

"Am I the attacker?"

"As I said, the attacker isn't recognizable. He's more or less your body type. Six feet tall, strong build. But a lot of men look like that.

The video isn't going to put you in jail, it's the fact that you knew where Patrizia was and, as you said before, that you're a controlling maniac. And I assure you, that could help us a lot in a psychiatric examination if we need to go for a sentence reduction."

Giulio gets up from his chair. He recognizes the anxiety that's overtaking him. It's like a movie with long, missing parts. White. The streets that waver and the lights that blur. The hedge, the one he crashed into, the dirt on the ground. The quickening breath, the feeling that his heart is about to explode. Patrizia's neighbors. The bar, with its red and blue lights and that loud music, the voice of Lady Gaga. The heaters warming the people outside, where they could smoke. Moving headlights, the smell of plastic and vanilla, maybe a Little Trees air freshener. It could be the inside of a taxi. Patrizia's face, the expression of pity. The bed is unmade. His headache. The disgusting taste of alcohol. The vomit that climbs his throat. Pain in his face and blood in his eye.

Giulio approaches the window. His face is reflected in the glass, the bandage on his eyebrow. Outside it's snowing. A terrible white that conceals everything. Meadows, flowers, rocks. Everything is under it. Everything is covered by this continuous, monotonous, uniform, stifling expanse of white.

"You didn't answer me," he says to the lawyer.

"I don't remember the question."

"Do you think I killed her?"

Alberto Colletti is quiet. Giulio looks out at the white, but he can imagine his movements. The attorney takes a deep breath as he leans back in his chair and looks up at the ceiling, exhaling loudly as if he were stretching.

The noise coming from outside the house is that of a car engine.

The carabinieri's Alfa Romeo is approaching. In it is Annalaura Lorenzon, deputy prosecutor of the republic, head of the Giulio Rodari investigation.

TWO

In the barroom, the voices of the various members of the Committee for the Defense of the Old Woods mix like a dough reminiscent of a good piecrust.

This is what Barbara is thinking, about how you need a good piecrust to serve as a base for the sweet apples, the cheeky cinnamon, the whimsical whipped cream. She listens as their conversations merge into a single background hum.

The plant will destroy the forest; not a soul will remain; the young people are all leaving; we won't sell the land; what's on the agenda?; what will we leave to the younger generations?; but this is hazelnut flour; I didn't know we had an agenda; we sabotage them like they did in Val di Susa; I heard the committee in defense of the holm oak always has an agenda; I don't think you can sabotage a construction site with a parachute; there is still a little bit of that cake left; look, in '77 I led the occupation of the Bruschi movie theater myself; I don't think it's hazelnut flour, dear, I think it's pistachio; the younger generations are already old; I'm just saying that if we had an agenda it would be more—how should I put it?—official; there should be Environmental Protection data somewhere—there's always Environmental Protection data; we'll light fires and organize lookout shifts in the woods; you think I can't tell the difference between hazelnut and pistachio?; this whole agenda thing is getting out of hand; look, during the war my father did the same thing with the Germans.

The deputy prosecutor didn't like it that the committee was at the bar.

"You said the place would be closed, ma'am," she told Barbara when they met.

"Barbara, dear . . ." Barbara turns, Dorina is next to her, touching her shoulder with her hand, with the gentle touch of an old friend. "I'm sorry to distract you from your thoughts, but Fralassi keeps going on about this agenda business, and if we don't start the meeting soon, Rosi will have planned an armed takeover before lunch."

"I'm sorry. I'll handle it."

Barbara waves her hands to draw the attention of the other committee members. "All right, friends, we're starting now."

The piecrust thins. The background noise fades out with a few final notes.

"Let's see how you plan on doing this without an agenda," commented accountant Fralassi, taking a seat with an air of defiance.

Lilith is back together. The practice room is already toasty from the space heater. Arturo is doing a stretching exercise he saw Mike Portnoy do in a video shot backstage at his Dream Theater concert. Diego's eyes are red—almost scarlet—and he reeks of marijuana, the explanation. He must have gotten carried away with Old Toby. Viola connected her laptop to the system so the band could listen to the two tracks of their first and last original song.

"Do you have a title yet?" Arturo asks, continuing to shake out his arms as if he were preparing for a freestyle boxing match.

"I'm working on it. It's going to be an instrumental piece," says Viola, looking out through the small window at the falling snow.

"No lyrics?" Arturo asks.

"No, just music."

"That's, like, so in line with our progressive approach," says the drummer, who is already dripping with sweat.

A snowflake comes to rest on the windowpane. Viola studies it for a few moments until it melts into a tiny droplet that remains suspended on the glass.

"Do you know what they say about snowflakes?" Viola asks.

"I don't," says Arturo, wiping at the sweat on his arms.

"No two are alike, but they all have the identical proportions of a perfect hexagon." Viola touches the glass with her fingers. "A bit like the moments that make up a life, don't you think?"

Arturo closes his eyes and considers it.

As they remain silent, meditating on snowflakes, Diego continues to obsessively pluck at the first two strings on his bass in an attempt to tune them.

"I think he's on a loop," says Arturo, looking at him. "Hey, Diego, try the electronic tuner, the one on your phone, remember?"

Diego smiles, takes his phone, and plays with it for a while.

"Do you think he can play like this?" Arturo asks.

Viola turns and looks at the bassist. She smiles. "I've seen him play in worse shape than this."

Diego plays with his phone. Arturo wipes his sweat with the towel that he always leaves next to his drum kit.

"The first time through we'll play it straight," says Viola, "on the second I'll enter with an arpeggio, on the third you start with the tom-toms for two rounds, for the fifth you come in with Diego. Got that, Diego?"

Diego smiles at her, phone in hand.

"I think he needs coffee," says Arturo. "Or we could rub his head in the snow. It worked that other time."

Katerina is sitting in an armchair with a warm compress over her eyes. Her pants are rolled past her ankles, and her feet are bare, propped up on a towel, her emerald-green toenail polish still fresh. Marica is working on her hands.

"Well, that one's always been a bit strange," Katerina says. She's talking about Rodari, the ongoing topic at Beauty Island Beauty Center—Hairstyling and Well-Being. There's a copy of the local daily paper, the *Tirreno*, resting on the table, the front page taken up with an image of the alleged murderer.

"But how did they know each other?" Marica asks.

"Her mother was from here. Right after the bridge collapsed, she came to talk to the victims' families because she wanted to be their attorney. If they could prove the bridge came down due to negligence, they would have been able to get a ton of money. Attorney stuff. So she met him too, because his aunt was on the bus."

"The newspaper said his aunt never took that bus."

"When your time comes . . ." As she says it, Katerina touches the iron table next to her.

"Emerald for your fingernails too?" Marica asks.

The sound of an incoming text distracts Katerina, who turns to the table. With her free hand, she removes the compress over her eyes, takes the phone, and reads. The sender is Sara.

Let's try to meet tomorrow afternoon. I need to show you something I got for you. Kisses—you know where.

Katerina quickly closes the text, but she can't conceal her smile of contentment.

"An admirer?" Marica asks.

"Just a marketing text."

Sara does not exist. Sara is a married man who showers her with attention and has a plan for them both. A plan that she likes, because if it works, she can finally leave this place that's so pathetic it makes her long for where she came from. Sara is a man who is about to make a lot of money and who has promised her a new life in Santo Domingo. He's already shown her the house in Sosúa Bay, with palm trees that line the Caribbean beach kissed by the Antilles sun.

"What about your hands?" Marica asks.

"Emerald on those too."

THREE

Deputy prosecutor Annalaura Lorenzon is sitting across from the suspect.

Colonel Scalise called Grazia to attend the interrogation "as head of the suspect's surveillance under house arrest." Scalise sometimes speaks like a police report. Grazia has the feeling that he only does it with her, because he's not entirely at ease with a woman marshal. As soon as they entered, he took her aside, assured her he was dealing with the "organic problem that he verified and of which I was only recently notified," and then advised her not to mention it to the deputy prosecutor because they're not "arguments inherent to the investigation activity to which the prosecution is party."

Giulio looks tired, despite having tried to make himself presentable. He's wearing a jacket that's a little too big, and his hair is disheveled.

Grazia looks at him, trying to be discreet. She can recall how he looked in high school. It's strange, how she hadn't thought of him for so long, and yet she used to have such a weakness for that dazed boy who drew strange things. Elves, warriors, sorcerers, beautiful women who lived in imaginary worlds. He filled entire notebooks. One day he had given her a portrait: her in a fantasy heroine costume. Back then she never wondered where she'd be in twenty years. It seemed impossible that she would become a woman, a wife, a mother. Two out of three in the end isn't too bad. But the last thing she could have expected from life was that she would be feet away from Giulio Rodari, overseeing his surveillance as a suspect under investigation for murder and the concealment of a corpse.

And in fact, now she's in charge of an entire empty police station, with a daughter who probably smokes weed with someone she might even be sleeping with, a house that's always a mess, those cursed dishes in the sink every morning, no social life, no relationship on the horizon. She's forced to be in this room by a superior who is embarrassed about working with a woman while her life slips along toward the wrong side of forty. Amen.

"Marshal Parodi, everything all right?" Lorenzon's voice seizes her and brings her back to the Gherarda dining room, converted for the time being into an interrogation room.

"Excuse me, ma'am . . ."

"As I was saying, could we have a summary of your surveillance activities?"

"Of course, ma'am. I can email it later."

"It's not ready?"

"Not at the moment."

"I understand." The deputy prosecutor's last glance before diving back into her files is directed at Scalise.

"Okay, Rodari, let's get to it." The deputy prosecutor adjusts the glasses on her nose. "I'll quickly cover some information, you correct me if necessary. So then." She takes a sheet of paper scrawled with pen and begins to read. "You and Patrizia Alberti met in 2011."

"Not exactly," says Giulio.

"What do you mean?"

"We already knew each other, of course. She lived here for a while."

"Did you already have a relationship?"

"No, but out here in the country—"

"Everyone knows everyone, I know. But that's not what interests us here, Rodari. I'm referring to your relationship, understand? In any case, we say that in 2011 you met again and that you already knew each other in passing due to the fact that you both come from the same town. How's that?"

"Continue," Giulio's lawyer intervened, clutching the knot of his tie.

"The occasion of your *new* encounter was the calamitous event that transpired in your local community that November. The collapse of a bridge that killed seven people traveling on a bus. One of the victims, Carmela Giomi, was a cousin of attorney Alberti's mother, which is why she decided to represent the victims' families during the preliminary investigation, with the intention of lodging a civil suit. A suit that could not take place, since the investigation was shelved, as the investigators couldn't find any objective case for liability."

"Twice," says Giulio.

"What's that?"

"The prosecutor shelved the case twice. After the first time, the judge accepted attorney Alberti's request"—this is the first time Giulio has referred to her in this way—"and ordered the prosecutor to reopen the investigation."

"Which led to nothing, right?" asks Lorenzon.

"Does this have anything to do with the investigation at hand?" Giulio's lawyer asks.

"Right now, no. Not at the moment." The deputy prosecutor begins to read again. "Since Giulio Rodari and his mother, Barbara Tantulli, also lost her sister, Amanda Tantulli, in the accident, they both agreed to be represented by attorney Alberti."

Only one week had passed since Bridge Day, as the newspapers had begun to call it. Giulio was looking out the window in the small waiting room of the law firm that contacted him. It was raining. Raindrops all along the windowpane. The door opened behind him. Patrizia.

"Hi, Giulio, thank you for coming. Come on in."

"Is that right?" Lorenzon's voice.

"What was that?" asks Giulio.

"Are you listening to me, Rodari? You do know what we're talking about, here, today, do you not?"

"My client is very shocked, ma'am, please take that into account." Alberto Colletti's voice is calm, relaxed. The deputy prosecutor doesn't like him, it's obvious. Giulio has the feeling that Lorenzon isn't so opposed to the idea of a man killing a woman and a woman sticking it to him, and that all these little men standing between her and this story are just annoying obstacles that she wants to swat out of the way.

"Let's resume, if we all agree," Lorenzon says. "Could we say the occasion of this meeting was the beginning of the relationship between attorney Alberti and the suspect?"

"Ma'am," Colletti says.

"Excuse me. Between attorney Alberti and Rodari. A relationship that went on for four years, but not in the form of a stable domestic partnership"—the deputy prosecutor seems to say it with a good amount of reproach—"and that attorney Alberti decided to end in August of last year, just before going on vacation in Greece with some colleagues."

That night they had gone out for a pizza. They had decided to sleep together at Patrizia's. Giulio had a couple of DVDs. They had just left the restaurant when the abyss opened at his feet.

"Do you mind sleeping at your house tonight?" Patrizia asked.

"What's wrong?"

"Sometimes I have the impression that you don't listen to me. That you live in a world where reality doesn't penetrate. Giulio, what were we saying before?"

"You're going on vacation with your friends."

"Giulio, I was saying we need to take some time."

"I don't get it."

"I want to be alone for a while. I don't know if I still believe in us."

"What are you talking about?"

"I'm talking about the same thing I've been trying to talk to you about for a long time and you keep ignoring me, Giulio. Look, I'm sorry, really, you're a great person . . . oh, sorry, I never thought I'd say that. The fact is . . . well, I don't know exactly. I don't think I need to have a specific reason, maybe it will take time for us to understand why it didn't work out. But I need to not see you for a while. And if you can go to my place and get all your things while I'm in Greece, that would make everything a lot easier."

Patrizia returned from Greece two weeks later.

When Giulio sees her name come up on his phone, he decides not to answer. Not right away, at least. He needs to be able to explain the difficult concept of emotional blackout that he's still sorting out. It came to him so suddenly, as he was in her apartment collecting his toothbrush, pajamas, bathrobe, instant coffee, some sweaters, a pair of trousers. He could fit it all into one bag. That was the thing that freaked him out. That their entire story could all come down to one bag and be carried away just like that, without the slightest disturbance. The fact is that every thunderstorm has a first drop of rain. As soon as it hits the ground and fragments into so many smaller drops, it already contains the potential of the destruction that will follow. The little bag, leaning against the front door. Giulio felt something like a calling. He turned. The apartment was perfectly in order. It was as if he had never been a part of it. Patrizia continued to call his cell, knowing sooner or later he'd have to answer. He needed to explain to her that at first he only intended to leave a sign of his presence, something that couldn't be deleted so easily, like a white eraser across a pencil stroke. But then something happened. The raindrop. The blackout. The apartment devastated, only fragments of which remain in his memory. As if Giulio Rodari had left those rooms, leaving behind another Giulio Rodari to destroy everything in his path. "Maybe you should talk to that Giulio," he whispered, watching his silenced phone, with the display of Patrizia's smiling face in that picture they took during a weekend in Paris when she had accompanied him to deliver a job. "I know it seems strange, love, but it's like it wasn't me," he continued to whisper to her image on the illuminated display. "It's like it was a totally different person."

"Rodari?" Lorenzon's voice. "Attorney Colletti, do you think your client could deign to give us his attention? It's not like we're here telling bedtime stories, you know? I'm sure we all have better things to be doing."

"Sorry, ma'am," Colletti says. "I think it's best if we take a little break. Maybe they can bring us something to drink, what do you say? Giulio, are you with us? Can we get something to drink?"

Grazia looks at him.

He seems detached. Sometimes it seems as if he were somewhere else. Is this what happens, then? Does a person flip a switch and become a monster? One flick and an infinite darkness takes over? Did he really kill Patrizia? The attorney sitting beside him shakes him, doing everything he can to keep that priggish smile on his face. Giulio looks like he's coming back from a long, arduous journey. The deputy prosecutor is staring at him with stone-cold eyes.

"Sorry, I was distracted," he says, looking around as if he were lost.

The station phone vibrates. Grazia pulls it out of her pocket. It's Donato. "What's up?"

"Hey, chief, remember that fox?"

"What fox?"

"The head they found at GeoService."

"Donato, I don't think now is the time to—"

"It was already dead, I think."

"You know, we're in the middle of an important interrogation here and I—"

"I was at Bar Fuga, and there were these guys who were talking, and one of them said something about wild animals crossing the road, how they get disoriented by the snow. And he said that just the other night, on his way home, he hit a fox. He got out of his car to check that it was actually dead. That animal's abdomen was cut open like it had passed through a meat grinder. He ended up moving it to the edge of the road so that no one would have an accident trying to brake on the ice if they saw it in the way."

"Very interesting, Donato. Draw up a report. In the meantime I'll be here . . ."

"So the Spirits of the Woods didn't kill the animal, per se, but they used it to demonstrate how man can harm the creatures of the forest when he's too distracted. This changes our approach to the investigation, don't you think?"

"Donato, seriously, there is no spirit in the woods, and I don't think we need to launch an investigation for a prank with everything else we have . . ."

"What I mean to say is that I don't think they're evil."

"Are you listening to me? What were you doing at the bar? Did they make you drink?"

"The guys gave me some kind of strange hot chocolate."

The Fuga's famous chocolate liqueur, a kind of baptism by fire for newcomers. An alcohol content that would down an elephant.

"Donato, where are you going?"

"I'm coming to you. I realized I need to talk to Scalise personally."

"No! Negative, go back to the station."

"But I think—"

"That's an order from your commander, Officer. Go back to the station."

That damned fox was the last thing they needed.

FOUR

The committee meeting is particularly animated. Maybe it's the cinnamon that excites them, or the tea they've consumed by the gallon, most often with a dash of rum. Outside it's snowing.

Mayor Falconi is like all politicians: only concerned with his own interests; yes, but he promised he wouldn't authorize the project; yes, but besides that, are we ready to organize an armed resistance or not?; Mayor Falconi can only object in the presence of well-founded security reasons—it's written right here; here? where?; in this thing I got online; a resistance armed with what, specifically?; if you got it online, it could be a buffalo for all we know; yes, but then why isn't the mayor here?; he's afraid of being seen with us; I say we appoint a security committee to deal with enemy attempts at infiltration; there's still some tea left; when we occupied the Bruschi theater . . . ; oh, stop it; I'm serious, they gave me a citation for that stupid theater; there's no more tea, but there's still some rum; we should go to Brussels; you're delusional; if there's no agenda next time, I'm not coming; the EU is in Brussels; they can stop them; I found the Environmental Protection data online.

Barbara isn't here. She's sitting with them, next to the window, and she's caressing the orange cat, who is purring at her, but her mind is in another room. She had wanted to attend the interrogation, but the deputy prosecutor wouldn't allow it. And she didn't insist that much, since Lorenzon was already so annoyed by the committee meeting. That woman is a very rigid person.

"Barbara, as hostess, would you like to be the committee spokesperson? We're thinking of appointing officers so that we can have a defined organizational chart." Having abandoned his dream of having an agenda, Fralassi has moved on to the distribution of roles, proposing himself as secretary.

"Where have you been?" Gerri's back in his place, behind the counter at Bar Fuga. The lumberjacks are back in the woods, and the bar is deserted. The incessant music from the slot machines penetrates from the other room. The slots are hungry. They want tokens and loneliness to swallow with their multicolored and smiling faces. The old bar floor is a slurry of melted snowdrops.

"I was at the spa, like I said," says Katerina, sitting at a table. "Do you think it's too dark?" she asks, examining the emerald polish on her nails.

"You left here three hours ago."

"So? What is this now, are you clocking my time?"

"I wish you'd give me a hand around here sometimes."

"Why?" Katerina looks around at all the empty tables. "Too many customers? Look, give me a prosecco, keep yourself busy."

"Why don't you get it yourself?"

"So that's how it is. You brought me to this country to make a kitchen maid out of me? You want me to skip the ball to become a servant, eh?"

"You did all your dancing in a strip club."

"Fuck you, Gerri." She gets up and leaves, slamming the door behind her.

Gerri guzzles another glass of cool white wine. To swallow that "fuck you," however, he'll need another. He sends it down, smothering those forty-five candles that lit in his stomach and burned like hell. He enters the slot room. The music seems to grow louder. On one screen, a smiling watermelon invites him to play. But Gerri came to look for something else. His birthday gone unnoticed has triggered something. A mechanism that turns back time, and one that's increasingly difficult to escape. When it happens, there is nothing he can do but cash in and see how long he can stay on his feet.

Here it is on the wall, his picture from so many years ago. Regional archery champion. Minus twenty pounds and a failed marriage. He liked being an archer. Watching the arrow go exactly where he sent it. Being at one with it. Feeling a little like Kevin Costner in *Robin Hood*. Then his focus changes, and the glass covering the photo reveals the image of the present day. He hadn't even noticed he'd been crying. Defeat burns. No victory can ever make up for the pain of certain losses. He can't even remember the last time they had sex, he and Katerina. The fact is, she likes it too much to have gone without it all this time. And he has a growing suspicion that she's doing it with someone else. That's what they're saying around town—he'd bet on it. They said the same thing about his father. But this shouldn't have happened to him. To the young archer, this wasn't supposed to have happened.

"It's really a great song, Purple." Diego calls Viola by her Italian name in English. His eyes are still red and glassy like two colored marbles, but he looks like he's starting to come out of it.

"The first time I heard it, I knew right away that . . ." Viola's voice wavers, and she has to stop. With an infinite delicacy she passes the cuff of her sweater over the Fender plate, wiping away the invisible particles of dust. "I know it's weird, but I want Michele to be in this song. It's important. This guitar was his."

The presence of Lilith's fourth member is a nearly palpable void. In reality, Michele has never been part of the band; Diego and Arturo barely knew him.

"It's not weird, Purple," Diego says. "I like playing with him. And I'm sure he likes to hear it too. If he really is in the woods with everyone else, I think he'll enjoy your arrangement."

"Oh, he's in the woods." Viola's eyes are glassy. Whenever she talks about that boy, she gets choked up.

Diego nods, smiles. "If it's okay by you, Purple, I want to try a few variations to bring out a few passages. Send me the file so I can listen to it when I have more time."

"Send it to me too," says Arturo as he passes the towel over his hair. He can sweat like a fiend in the span of fifteen minutes. "It wouldn't be a bad idea to double up on a few passages for more thrust. Give it a more progressive sound. Don't you think?"

"Go for it," says Viola. "I have to work on the guitar solo now. I have to record two different tracks."

"So how will we perform it live?" Arturo asks.

"Live? I didn't think we were going to play any more live shows. We only have three months left together. We have to finish this song, record it once and for all, and upload it to YouTube. That's my focus."

Three months until the end of Lilith. The last ninety days, more or less, of the band that got them through their teenage years.

Viola checks the time. "It's still too early for the other thing," she tells her friends.

"I have a few sandwiches in my bag," says Arturo. "We can wait here. In the meantime—"

Before he's done speaking, Diego interrupts with a riff from "Seven Nation Army." His eyes are half-closed, his head bobs, and he looks like a wayward antenna that's swirling around to avoid losing a signal it just captured from outer space.

Viola smiles. She wants some distortion in the song. She presses the pedal, looks at the red light on the overdrive, and touches the strings of her Stratocaster.

Arturo has the expression of a Maori warrior. He extends his arms, spins his drumsticks between his fingers. He waits for the right moment. When it arrives, he nods to the others and pounces on the drums.

The White Stripes song explodes.

FIVE

"So, so, so, we're coming up to the night of March eleventh." Deputy prosecutor Annalaura Lorenzon has resumed browsing her notes. During the break, she had stepped out to smoke a couple of cigarettes. She lit the second one with the butt of the first. Grazia observed her through the window. Her coat was draped over her shoulders, and she was on her phone the whole time. Grazia sent a few messages to Viola, to warn her that she'd be late, but her daughter hasn't responded yet. She'll have to make another dinner alone, and she'll probably smoke some more weed. Grazia should be there with her, to talk about what is happening to her, but Esposito can't stand in for the Marshal. She checks the time again, but her phone falls to the ground as Scalise turns to her. Grazia smiles and apologizes as she picks it up. "The night from which," continues the deputy prosecutor, "as is evident from the statements you already issued, you recall nothing. Or has something come back to you, by chance? For example, how did you get that cut?"

Giulio touches the bandage on his left eyebrow.

"My client has a problem with alcohol," says Colletti.

"Well, Counsel, here we've arrived at the crux of the matter. Could you specify what kind of problem it is and if there's any documentation of it?" asks Lorenzon.

"Rodari can't tolerate alcohol," Colletti explains, looking through his worn leather briefcase. "He never could, because he never drank it. These are very personal matters, however, and I'm not sure if my client . . ."

Giulio nods.

"Okay," Colletti continues. "Rodari lost his father when he was nine. A car accident—drinking and driving."

The memory of that day has a specific color. White. His father hadn't come home. The phone call. The carabinieri's car coming to take his mother away. They'd found him. The car had been buried in snow.

"You know what happened, right?" his aunt Amanda had asked. She had the poufy hair and black eyeliner of a rock 'n' roll chick. "You'll have to be strong, but you're already a little man, I can tell. Would you like a slice of cake? And after the snowplow comes we can go for a little spin, okay? Let's just do what we want. We can get in the car and drive, without knowing where we're going, see where the day takes us. How does that sound?"

"The trauma from his father's death is why he never drank alcohol. So his issue didn't reveal itself until one day, at a party, when he agreed to drink for the first time in his life. He was twenty-five years old. The next morning he knocked on the door of a farm to ask where he was. During the night he had traveled twelve miles. But that memory was reconstructed later, with the time and help of a psychologist. Because Rodari didn't remember a thing about that night. In technical terms, it's called *lacunar amnesia*. There are articles and studies about it that I look forward to producing as soon as possible, following the appointment of a psychiatric consultant. It's the opinion of this defense that on the night of March eleventh, the same thing occurred, as a result of, let's say, a conspicuous intake of alcoholic substances, due to my client's emotional state. This evoked the same reaction that he had before, in his body, leading him to be completely removed from what happened that night. I certainly don't need to remind the deputy prosecutor that the burden of proof is not up to this defense, and that it's the prosecution that must corroborate its accusations against my client, including drinking alcohol, leaving his house, following attorney Alberti, attacking her, killing her, and then finding the lucidity necessary to hide her body and conceal any evidence that could be attributed to such criminal acts."

"Don't get too excited, Counsel," snaps Lorenzon. "It's yet to be determined if he concealed all the evidence."

"There's no evidence to conceal because—"

"Says you, not me. However, I don't think anyone can deny us the great pleasure of a psychiatric opinion. So we'll defer the matter to the preliminary judge and see how we proceed. In the meantime, however, so I have a little more information, could you tell me, Mr. Rodari, anything about what you remember about that night? Do you remember, for example, your confrontation with Alberti's neighbors?"

"In part," says Giulio. "I remember trying to break down her apartment door."

"But you had had a set of keys to that apartment, in the past."

"I still had them. But Patrizia changed the lock."

"And why was that?"

"Because I entered without her permission and I—"

"Excuse me, but what does this have to do with anything?" asks Colletti.

"Counsel, we're just trying to clarify this point, but if you prefer we can bring your client straight to the judge in handcuffs."

"I tormented her, it's no secret," says Giulio. "She filed a report against me. Stalking. I went to her apartment in the evenings, I sent her messages nonstop, I followed her. I made her life a living hell."

"And this you remember because you were sober, evidently."

"Madam prosecutor, excuse me, but—" Colletti tries to intervene.

"Look, Counsel, allow me to point something out. When you spoke of this presumed—what did you call it?—*lacunar amnesia*, you said that Rodari, who was twenty-five at the time, spent the whole night walking. He didn't just stare at the ceiling until it passed, or am I wrong? So the fact that he doesn't recall what happened on the night of March eleventh, because he decided to get wasted, doesn't mean that he spent the whole night tucked away in bed, waiting for his hangover to pass. Because before the time lapse of which he alleges to have no memory, he did a whole series of things that are relatively indicative of his state and his intentions with regard to the victim. And if you interrupt me again while I try to clarify this point with your client, we can bring him to the judge and let him try. Have I made myself clear?"

Colletti loosens the knot on his blue tie.

"I'd drunk a lot," Giulio continues. "I was trying to knock down the door, and that's when the neighbors came out onto the landing. The Castagninis. I knew them because I spent a good amount of time at Patrizia's. They told me she wasn't home, or something like that anyway. I started shouting that they needed to mind their own business, and I think I may have scared them."

"You said, 'Mind your own fucking business or I'll kill you,' or so says Mr. Castagnini," the deputy prosecutor cites, reading from a sheet in front of her. "Do you remember that?"

"I may have said something along those lines."

"And that's not all you said. You said, 'I'll kill the lot of you, first her, then you, and then I'll kill myself.'"

"A plan he didn't follow through on, obviously," notes Colletti.

"What does that have to do with it?" asks the deputy prosecutor.

"He said he was going to kill himself, but he didn't."

"So?"

"So I'd say it changes the value of the neighbors' testimony regarding his plans."

"We'll leave it to the judge to determine that, Counsel. Now, let's proceed. Please, Rodari, go on. With whatever you remember, of course."

"Patrizia always hung out at the same place, The Garden, so I went there. On the way, I think I stopped off for a drink in a couple of bars."

"If you can remember which ones, maybe we can reconstruct your trail and call them to verify your story," says the deputy prosecutor.

"I'll try."

"Go on."

"When I got to The Garden, I started to scream."

"According to the security officer, you said, 'Let me in or I'll kill you.'"

"It's possible."

"And then what?"

"Then everything blurs. I remember Patrizia's scent, her perfume. Chanel No. 5, like Marilyn. She loved that fact. Advertising in general has that effect. I remember the taxi, I think, a disgusting vanilla Little Trees air freshener. Plastic. My unmade bed. My pillow. Patrizia's voice, insisting she wanted to call emergency services. I heard her talking angrily to someone on the phone. The last thing I remember is seeing the bottle of antidepressants on the bedside table and trying to remember how many I'd taken."

"You were drinking with your medication?" asks the deputy prosecutor.

"My doctor prescribed them to treat my obsession."

"Go on."

"That's more or less everything. The next morning, when I opened my eyes, the carabinieri were there. Someone had called them because Patrizia never made it back to the bar. And she wasn't at home."

"It was Leonardo Maccari, do you know him?"

"The one who called?"

Colletti brings his hand to his forehead.

"Do you know him?"

"The tennis player . . ." Giulio looks to his attorney. "You knew about him, right?"

"Giulio, I . . ."

"I need a new attorney."

"Giulio, let it go . . ."

"My lawyer hid this information from me."

"Rodari, calm down," says the deputy prosecutor. "What do you mean? What information?"

"If Patrizia had a relationship with this person, I need to know about it."

"Maybe we need to suspend—" Colletti says.

"It was him. Don't you get that?" says Giulio.

Grazia can't move. She's glued to the chair. Rodari seems like he's out of his mind. Maybe it's better if Viola eats out of a can at home for the time being.

"He followed her, and when she went back downstairs, he attacked her," says Giulio.

"His motive being . . . ?" asks the deputy prosecutor.

Giulio stops. Grazia can read the expression in his eyes. It's as if he had suddenly hit a wall.

The deputy prosecutor checks the time. "Let's stop here," she says. "We'll be back soon, in the next few days. I have to evaluate a couple of things. Do you really want to appoint another lawyer?"

Giulio doesn't answer. His eyes are empty again, lost in a blind alley.

"We'll let you know," Colletti says.

The deputy prosecutor collects all the files into her bag and leaves, followed by Scalise, who gestures to Grazia just before he walks out the door.

"I recommend, Marshal, that you assign extra surveillance to your men." Her men. *A total denial of reality,* Grazia thinks as she nods, hoping that Donato is no longer feeling the effects of the chocolate liqueur and that he's forgotten about that absurd story of the fox and the Spirits of the Woods. "Keep me apprised," Scalise says, turning to leave.

SIX

It's the Evening of Bread. The large stone oven, lit from the day before, has reached the ideal temperature. It stopped snowing a few hours ago, and the inhabitants of the village and the surrounding countryside have arrived, each with a bowl or cloth full of yeasty dough.

Akan has lit the fire under the grill next to the oven, because the Evening of Bread is a ritual that can go on for a long time and the waiting should be diminished. As usual, in the beginning, there was only a bit of bread with olive oil, garlic, and salt, but then everyone brought something with them and the grill was quickly filled with sausages, ribs, bacon, and even some hamburgers, offered by the most considerate guests, who are convinced that Akan is an observant Muslim who doesn't eat pork. In fact, religion is not among the things that he has managed to save from his own wreckage. Such a pity.

The voices start to blend with layers of laughter and traditional songs, refreshed between glasses of red wine.

Barbara is standing by the oven, her face red from the flames that leap out every time she opens its iron door. Every now and then she looks at Giulio's window in the other part of the hotel. His light is on.

"I find it shameful," says Dorina, standing beside her, after a long silence. She seemed to be meditating. The Evening of Bread should bring with it only good thoughts, but she obviously couldn't resist.

"What?" asks Barbara.

Dorina doesn't answer. "It's shameful is what I think," she repeats.

Barbara puts her hand on Dorina's arm and gestures toward her ear. Dorina snorts, looks around as if preparing to commit an unthinkable offense, and with the speed of a weasel, she slips in her hearing aid.

"Now," says Barbara again, "what is it that's so shameful?"

"These people. When it comes to the committee, we can't even get ten people. When it comes to fraternizing with sausages, they all come running and never leave."

"Dorina, haven't you been attending the committee meetings?"

"What do you mean?"

"We can't agree on anything as it is, and there aren't that many of us. Can you imagine if all these people showed up?"

"The truth is, they're all ignorant. Most of them wouldn't notice if they built a nuclear power plant in the middle of the woods. Just a few trees would be enough to fool them into thinking nothing has changed in their lives. And the cycle of grilling and hangovers would continue."

"Have you been talking to your daughter?"

"Why?"

"Because whenever you've heard from her, you're always in a sour mood."

"She mentioned that loan again," admits Dorina. "I think she wants to go through with it."

"Are you worried?"

"Wouldn't you be? The only thing I can offer as a guarantee is my house."

"Everything will be fine."

"Did you hear about that retirement home? The one they opened on that farm? You can live there if you turn over your apartment to them. But I don't think they accept apartments that guarantee another mortgage."

"How long have you been thinking about living in a retirement home?"

"I'm not thinking about it, but if I needed to do it, my pension and savings wouldn't be enough."

"You know what?" asks Barbara, reaching for two glasses of wine and handing one to Dorina for a toast. "To hell with the banks, Dorina. If anything happens, you can always come and stay here, give me a hand with that chestnut tree, the best one in the mountains. What do you say?"

Dorina smiles. She clinks her glass with Barbara's. They drink.

"A toast, how beautiful!" It's Falconi, the mayor.

Barbara turns. Next to him is Mirna, wife of the first citizen and her eternal rival at the Buraco table.

"Welcome," says Barbara.

Mirna places her cutting board next to the oven, removes the cloth, and takes the dough in her hand. Barbara opens the iron door and positions the bread with the spatula. She checks the other loaves: she retrieves the one that's ready.

"Assunta, I believe this is yours."

A huge woman with a rib in her hand approaches. She takes the bread, wraps it in a cloth, and slides it under her arm.

"Next year, I'll bring the nice black *mazzafegato* sausage my brother makes," she says, throwing the bone to the ground next to the oven, where the big orange cat is waiting. The bone barely touches the ground. The cat snatches it and scurries away.

"Don't give him any more, that cat is so fat it's scary," says Barbara.

"At the committee today someone was hoping you'd be there," Dorina says to the mayor.

"We were busy, dear." Mirna speaks up before her husband can even open his mouth. "We went to town to pick up a new electric oven."

"The committee will be meeting again in a few days," Dorina says. "We wanted to know how things are going."

"Dorina," says Mirna, "don't you find it a bit like asking a doctor to visit you after hours? I mean, Eugenio is the mayor, and he has so many things to do that maybe you should go visit him in town instead of asking him to go out of his way for your committee."

"That committee exists for our woods."

"Do you think it's the only one, dear?"

"Oh, it's all right," says the mayor, smiling under his cowboy hat. "We all care about our woods, and I know this whole thing will blow over in no time. And Barbara, I promise you next time I'll come and explain everything to that committee of *ours*. But tonight I want a nice glass of that wine and, if I can get to it, a nice hunk of bacon on a piece of bread, what do you say?"

Akan serves the mayor as Mirna's dough transforms into a crusty loaf.

Barbara moves over a few steps. She looks up. Giulio's window. The light is still on.

"Is there room for me?" Adele appears next to Mirna and places her dough on the stone floor by the oven. "I couldn't find a place to park, so I had to walk fifteen minutes to get here. A glass of wine wouldn't hurt."

Dorina greets her cousin with a smile so strained it looks like her face is frozen. Barbara hands her a glass, and Mirna mimes a toast with hers. Now that her companion has joined the group, the Buraco quartet is complete.

The mayor notices the friction in the air among the women and edges closer to Akan, who is adjusting a slice of bacon on the grill with some tongs.

"Thank goodness it stopped snowing," says Falconi.

The Kurd smiles at him with his mouth full. In the other hand he's holding some bread sandwiching a sausage.

He's drawing. Giulio Rodari is wielding a pencil again, but not for his next Teo the gnome adventure. He's trying to reconstruct a picture only with the elements he can see in front of him. If it were just any illustration, it would be perfect as usual. But Giulio needs it to be something more. He needs it to be true.

After what happened at that party, when he lost his memory, he managed to recover it by redrawing the faces of his friends and the journey he made later that night. Piece after piece, almost everything returned to its place. There are always holes, but sometimes he's convinced that they shrink over the years. Now, however, he doesn't have that kind of time. He must remember. If he really killed Patrizia, he won't even try to defend his actions. But he needs to know what happened. He has to silence that deadly mixture of anxiety and terror that has been eating him from within.

His mother has hidden away a lot of things from Bridge Day. She tucked them all into a green envelope. There were pictures of her sister in the newspaper. A piece of her sister is still inside of his mother. That's always how it is when a twin dies. And they were truly identical in a lot of ways. Sometimes they had entire conversations between them without even opening their mouths. Maybe if he could find those clippings, it would jog his memory. There were interviews with Patrizia in there, photos of her. All of it from the days they first met.

He knows where the envelope is. He goes to get it.

Grazia and Donato are inside the patrol car. They're nearing the GeoService office for special surveillance duty arranged by Scalise.

Apparently, the company called the command ranting about a lawsuit against unknown parties for acts of vandalism. So Scalise asked *someone* to go over and take a look.

"I don't know if he's messing with me or if it really did get that far," says Grazia. Donato is sitting next to her, but this time he's in the passenger seat. He still has a lingering headache from the chocolate liqueur he got from the lumberjacks at Bar Fuga. "I mean, I told him how things are. And then he keeps talking about my *men*, he tells me to send *someone*. To do what? Monitor a shack?"

"Boss, do you think I'll ever be able to explain my situation to him?"

"Donato. Did you hear me? I told him we're only two people, and he keeps talking to me as if it was no big deal. As if I had all the staff in the world available. Or is he totally out of it? That would explain why they sent him here after his Rome assignment. Or maybe this is his way of telling me that the issue at my station is my problem alone and he has no intention of raising a finger for it. You know we have to do night shifts too, right? Do you remember what happened the last time you didn't sleep for three days? You were so hyped up on coffee your hands were shaking. We're useless in that state. I don't even have five minutes to talk to my own daughter. And she smokes weed, did you know that? I know. I need to talk to her, but instead I got sucked into an interrogation that ran all afternoon and now this and in an hour we have to be at the Gherarda again. Do you want some real advice?"

"I don't know, maybe this isn't the right time—"

"Leave this place. I'm serious. Get out of here."

"That would be a shame, since—"

A noise.

"Did you hear that?" Grazia asks.

They get out of the car.

"It came from behind the shack," says Donato, standing up straighter.

They turn on their flashlights. Hands on their guns.

"Is there anybody there?" says Grazia.

Again.

They circle the shack and point their flashlights.

A black cat is licking its paw next to a fallen stack of wood.

"What are you doing here?" Grazia asks. She removes her hand from her gun and walks toward the cat. "You gave me a pretty good scare, did you know that? Look—"

"Boss, over there!"

Donato points into the woods. A green light. Just a flash, then it vanishes.

"What the hell could that be?" asks Grazia.

"An ignis fatuus," says Donato.

"A what?"

"An ignis fatuus. I read about them online. They're common in haunted forests."

"Haunted by what, exactly?"

"Don't pretend you don't know what I'm talking about, boss."

"You don't seriously believe there are spirits here, do you?"

"I believe what I see. And what I just saw may have been an ignis fatuus."

"All right, let's go check it out."

They walk into the woods.

"There's no one here, Donato. There's not a single footprint in the snow."

"There it is again," says Donato.

A green light flashes in the direction he's pointing.

"Anyone there?" shouts Grazia. "This isn't funny."

They walk in that direction. The green light appears again. But it's even farther away now.

"There it is again—there," says Donato. "It looks like it's moving away from us."

Grazia looks at it. She turns back. It's dark in the woods, and it will take a while to get back to the patrol car by the light of their flashlights alone.

"I think this looks like something else, Donato."

"What's that, boss?"

"Like we're two suckers."

They've gone deeper into the woods than they intended. It's pitch-black, and the beams from their flashlights don't reach long enough for them to follow their own tracks. When they finally make it back to the clearing where the GeoService office stands, what they find, for Grazia, is no surprise.

Where the old scrawl that Maglio's lumberjacks cleaned had been, there has appeared another, also in red.

THE SPIRITS OF THE WOODS WILL NOT ALLOW IT

And under the writing, a drawing of a giant deer head. It has a demonic look to it, with drops of paint dripping from the horns, resembling blood.

"How did they manage to draw it in so little time?" Donato asks.

"They had one of those stencils that graffiti artists use," Grazia answers. "Looks like they didn't have any dead foxes on hand this time." She approaches the deer head. She takes a handkerchief from her jacket pocket and dabs at the paint. She looks at the handkerchief: the red really looks like blood this time. "They were organized. Ignis fatuus and all."

Giulio opens the wardrobe in his mother's room. He finds the green envelope where his mother put all the clippings from those days. But there's something else under the envelope. It's another envelope, containing the photograph that had been hanging on the wall of the bar. The frame is intact; there's no trace of the damage his mother referred to. Perhaps it represents one of their last happy days, when they were all still together. A New Year's Eve at the Gherarda, back in the early eighties. His father, as he recalls, died not long after. In the picture, he has a huge mustache and is wearing a tight waistcoat. The inevitable cigarette in one hand and an arm around his wife's shoulders. Barbara, in an evening dress, an arm around her husband's waist, and a hand resting on her son's shoulder. Giulio in the middle, smiling. He's just a kid, with long hair and huge teeth. Amanda is the only one who isn't looking at the camera. She's sitting at the table, smiling, with a glass in her hand, looking over to her right as if she were greeting someone. She's posed that way to cover the left side of her neck, where she has a scar, a burn she got when she was a little girl from a fallen pot of boiling water. Giulio can remember his mother's story about that episode. Amanda was cooking the eyes of a cat. She had found it in the street, dead, and she knew—Barbara didn't remember how—that she could gain superhuman night vision if she made a potion out of its eyes.

She had been a witch as a child.

Teo the gnome says that time is just an illusion, because things that seem so long ago can still touch you, right on the heart. The gnome sometimes says things that can't be included in a children's story. Because children don't have a sense of time. They already know it's just an illusion.

My name is Theophrastus Grimblegromble, but you can call me Teo, if you please. I have a red beard and a nice green hat.

His aunt Amanda was the first person to tell him about the gnomes.

"When you can't remember something," she told him one night, "ask your gnome friend to remind you."

Patrizia's scent is overwhelming. It's one of the last nights they spent together. Giulio tries to deny it, but he already senses her distance. Something's wrong. She's moving away from him. He hugs her tight to him, with all his strength. He clings. Beyond her is the abyss, and he doesn't want to fall into it again.

"Let me go. You're hurting me."

Patrizia turns. She looks at him. There it is, her face, right in front of his.

Giulio feels he could do it now. He could give life to that portrait he was attempting before. He's about to close the wardrobe and go back to drawing when another envelope catches his eye.

He opens it. There's a document inside. It's a preliminary letter of intent.

His mother is selling the Gherarda to GeoService.

SEVEN

Adele parks her olive-green Panda four by four in its usual spot, next to the old fountain in the little square. It's still the Evening of Bread, and the streets are echoing with the voices of revelers. Motorcycles roar over the noise. They will persist until dawn. Hooligans. Kids who want nothing more from life than to get wasted and make a scene.

She turns the key in the wooden door. The houses are old, no one wants to buy them, and they aren't worth a cent. Because they're too narrow and can't be widened without knocking them down and starting over. She's spent years envying one of those newer homes down in the valley, built not long ago. The terraces, the large windows, the wide and luminous staircases. She passed by the Carli Agency and looked at the ads. In one of those modern homes, someone might have been able to take Marcello out for some air. But it's all about to end anyway.

She climbs the narrow stairs, arriving at the narrow door.

"I'm home," she says. Even her voice seems narrower, here inside.

She turns on the foyer light. Entering the kitchen, she flicks on that light too and rests her freshly baked bread on the table.

"It came out so well, a delight," she says, pulling off a piece and tasting it. "When it's still hot like this, it's the best thing in the world."

She takes off her coat and leaves it on the chair.

"And you should have seen Dorina, how pleased she was. And I believe it. With the habit she has of taking things that don't belong to her, of course she took the opportunity to swipe herself some supper, living alone and all, the old cheapskate."

She enters her bedroom and turns on the light. Adele hates darkness and always turns on all the lights.

"She's deaf as a bat, always wearing that hearing aid and thinking people don't notice. She tries to hide it."

Marcello, her husband, is sitting in his wheelchair, facing the window.

"I can't believe that lazy Romanian. She hasn't spun you around once all evening."

Adele approaches, takes the chair, and deftly swivels it around. Marcello's face is frozen. Twisted in a grimace. His mouth is open, a filament of drool clinging to it. Adele dries it with the wrinkled napkin on his legs. He's been like this for years. Adele forces herself each day to forget how many. She doesn't want to know. She doesn't even remember the last real words they exchanged before the imaginary dialogues that she has been carrying on since then, trying to interpret what he would say if he were still here with her.

"I'll put on some TV for you, what do you say? Let's see if there's one of those westerns you like so much. But don't think I'm going to let you sit here all night in front of the television. Night is made for sleeping, and you know it, my dear sir." Adele searches for the remote control. "What did you say? Were there a lot of people there? Yeah, there were. When it comes to eating and drinking for free, they appear like mushrooms." She finds the remote control and turns on the TV. She searches for a movie, putting the volume on low. "I know, I know, you never go out and you want to know the word around town . . . but what do you want me to tell you? The people around here just go on and on about the same old things."

"And did you talk about that thing?" Marcello doesn't ask.

"I didn't have the chance, but anyway, there's not much to say. It will all go as planned, you'll see."

"Are you sure?"

"Of course I'm sure. I wouldn't say so if I wasn't. You ask all these questions, as if you don't trust me."

"I trust you."

"Well, that's good, because if I hadn't found out on my own that your father left that little piece of land in the woods, I don't know how we'd get out of this mess. Out of this old, damp house that makes my bones ache."

"You really are on the ball."

"I know, I know, don't worry, sir." Adele caresses her husband's face. It's as hard as stone. His eyes are motionless, fixed in a strained and unnatural stare. "You don't have to worry about a thing, you know that, right?"

"You know what's best for everyone. I trust you."

Adele hears the noise emanating from her husband's belly and, soon after that, the stink of shit.

"You couldn't at least warn me?" she says. "I would have put that thing on you."

"I couldn't say anything in time. I was thinking about when all this will end, and I'm a little excited," her husband doesn't answer.

"Do you think the Romanian can take care of it tomorrow? I have a terrible backache tonight."

"Don't worry, Adelina. Of course I can wait. Go to sleep in your room, I'll watch some TV and nod off."

"Good night, then."

"Good night."

Adele looks at him again as she closes the door. Marcello is motionless, with the blue light of the TV flashing against his contorted face.

Before going to sleep she goes to the bathroom. She opens the medicine cabinet. There is a box with a padlock. She carries the key around her neck. Inside is a syringe, at the ready. As soon as that thing is done, she can leave this place forever. Get away to somewhere warm, far from here. Far from her cousin. But she has no intention of leaving Marcello alone in his condition. Inside that locked box that only the key around her neck can open is a loaded syringe that will allow her to bring her husband with her, wherever she goes.

Forever.

EIGHT

Grazia dropped Donato off at the station to rest for a few hours on the cot so he could cover the morning shift. The last hurdle of the day is the ride to the Gherarda, and she can do it alone, before returning home.

She stops in front of the hotel and turns off the engine. At this hour, Viola will already be asleep. She'll have to find another time to talk to her.

She rests her head back on the seat. She tries to relax, gather her thoughts. To review and reprioritize her commitments as clearly as possible now that she has a moment to think.

She looks toward the Gherarda and sees a cloud of smoke rising against the glow from one of the outside lights. There's someone sitting on the stairs to the hotel. She can just make out the dark profile, which seemed to be as much a part of the hotel as the nearby pile of wood. He's wrapped in a blanket. It's Giulio. He lifts his arm and waves at her. Grazia gets out of the car and approaches him.

"Are you trying to freeze to death?" she asks him.

"I suppose I shouldn't be out here," Giulio says, blowing out the smoke of the cigarette between his fingers. "Because of the ordinance, or whatever the hell it's called."

"That's right. According to the ordinance, you're actually considered a fugitive right now. But if you give me a cigarette, I promise I won't report you."

"They're Akan's," says Rodari, handing her the pack of Camel Lights. "He hides them in the sideboard behind the cans. He says he doesn't smoke. And I quit ten years ago, so I get to deny taking them. You know how it goes."

"I stopped eighteen years ago when I got pregnant. I win."

Grazia sits beside him. Maybe he's a killer, but maybe not even he really knows for certain. Does it matter?

"It's a good reason to start over," says Rodari.

"Do you remember the time you drew me?"

"The warrior queen."

"You actually remember."

"It's not like I fried my entire brain, you know."

"Sorry, I didn't mean it that way. I heard that—"

"Nothing to do with the case tonight, okay? Just two old classmates hanging out on a stoop after last call, sneaking cigarettes."

"We sneaked cigarettes back then too, and I always stole them from you."

"On Saturday night we'd go to Ghino's for pizza. Ten thousand lire for a ham and mushroom pizza and a beer full of foam."

"Ghino's, where the food is bad and the prices are better," says Grazia, as if she were reciting an ad.

They smile. They smoke. The night envelops them.

"And I also remember eating here at the Gherarda," says Grazia. "In the summer when the woods belonged to us. Some nights seemed endless. Do you remember the bonfires?"

"It's strange, back then I wanted to leave here so badly, and instead it was the best part of my life."

"You can always come back."

"Yeah, if I don't end up in prison for the next forty years. But I don't know if the Gherarda will be here by then."

"Where's it going?"

"It really does seem impossible, these woods without the Gherarda."

Grazia feels the caress of smoke in her throat and feels that sense of abandon from so many years before.

"Doesn't it seem strange to you?" asks Grazia.

"What?"

"The two of us, here. More than twenty years have passed, but it feels like we just spoke yesterday, at the end of summer holidays."

"They say old classmates have that effect on each other."

"Do you think kids nowadays are anything like how we were back then?" Grazia asks.

"Are you talking about your daughter?"

"Is it that obvious?"

"I don't know, I don't have much experience in that field."

"Her father was a married man." She wants to tell him. And the moment is odd enough to be the right one. "When I realized I was pregnant, he said he'd pay for the abortion, he'd take care of everything. I thought about it a little. And every time I look at Viola, I feel guilty for having let it cross my mind. For having had those moments of uncertainty that could have made her not exist. I feel guilty for the instant that my fears could have won out. And now I can't even find ten minutes to talk to her. Does that seem normal to you?"

"I don't think there are many normal things in life, after a certain point."

"That's a good one. I'll use it later."

"Do you remember the Calabrian?"

"The math teacher?"

"He always said we were a generation of degenerates. Because we were born in the seventies when everyone was doing drugs."

"My God, it's true . . . he had that horrible face . . . and his accent was so thick you couldn't understand a word he said . . ."

Giulio hunches over, crosses his eyes, and curls back his lips, baring his teeth. "Degenerates, I say!"

Grazia can't stifle her guffaw. Her laugh is peculiar, noisy. Giulio looks around guiltily, as if they might wake someone up. Grazia puts her hand in front of her mouth, as if she would make less noise that way.

They laugh awhile longer, as the moment of warmth between them slips away.

Then they finish their cigarettes and say goodbye.

Giulio lingers for a few minutes to watch the patrol car pull away. The cigarettes have made him nauseous. He reaches out, grabs a handful of fresh snow, and puts it in his mouth to calm his stomach. In the book he read about quitting smoking, it said that nicotine is water soluble and can be flushed out of the system by drinking a lot of water. The guy who wrote the book is long dead from lung cancer.

Why didn't anyone tell him about the sale?

Sitting on those steps, he thinks of the storm he has to face, as Akan called it. He thinks about the preliminary letter of intent that he found by chance, looking for something else. He thinks about the few times he returned to the Gherarda in all these years, and he thinks about how he knew it was there, how he knew that returning here was one of those things he'd never want to give up, knowing about Ulysses syndrome and his inevitable return journey. He thinks about that white space in his memory, amnesia like a thick cover of snow hiding something terrifying.

NINE

I'm the black cat. I've already died, many times before.

The first time, I didn't make it one freaking year. All those beautiful white lights racing toward me and I flung myself at them to see what they were. I still remember the blow. It took me days to come back to life.

The second time I died it was because of that damned wild boar. Cats don't attack wild boars. Wanna know why? Because no cat has ever survived to tell the tale. But that horrible beast, stupid as a river stone, was convinced that he could snuff around with his ugly snout just beneath the tree I liked to climb so much, because there's a pointy-beaked bird who always makes its nest up there. I already had my claws in her by the time she tried to get in between me and her eggs. That day I climbed the tree to find myself a snack, and when the boar passed under me, with its sweaty and stinky neck, I had an overwhelming desire to sink my claws and teeth into it. You should hear how those nasty beasts howl when they feel pain. Then he bucked like he was possessed until he threw me off, stabbing me with one of his tusks. But do you know what? I climbed that tree a few more times, and I ate my eggs whenever I felt like it, while that wild boar hasn't shown its ugly snout around here again. I like to think it learned its lesson or that it ended up in one of those pasta dishes that the man with the whiskers at the Gherarda likes to cook and who offers me a little snack from time to time.

Not long ago I was perched in my favorite tree, licking my whiskers and watching all those fat people stuffing their faces around the fire. And my associate, the one with the orange coat, didn't miss the opportunity to put on a few pounds himself. I was a little triggered because I hadn't had the chance to swipe at anyone all day long, especially since everyone who knows me keeps me at arm's length because they say I'm looking for a fight. Go figure. So as soon as I saw the squirrel, I pounced right away. Not because I was still hungry. But because I love to hunt. Chase, catch, and mangle. Nothing makes me feel more alive.

I chased that damned squirrel all over creation, but in the end it jumped from one tree to another and escaped me. At that point I realized I'd ended up right in the middle of the old woods, and that's not the kind of place you can wander without your wits about you. So I tried to rest a little behind that cabin, on top of the wood stack. I always go there when I want to sit and be still. That old man was always there. A big, tall vagabond who walked around in the woods with that strange tool in his hand. Anyway, I was there when I saw them coming. All black clothes from head to toe. In short, people who do things in secret. I think they're damaging things. So I like them. They were about to do something fun, but at some point the car came and they had to stop. They stuck around for a while, hidden in the trees. Then they seemed to have an idea, and one of them left. But they made a big noise. So then I knocked down some wood, and those two idiots who got out of the car thought the first noise was me too. The woman, Viola's mother, approached and said I scared her. You get the picture. Then she stretched out her hand, and I just knew she was about to do one of those annoying things like pass it over my ears or some crap like that. That's when the green lights appeared. I don't know what they were, but I don't usually like green. So I stayed where I was, because I was curious about what those guys in black were up to.

When those two people who got out of the car walked into the woods to follow the green lights, the others came out of the trees and started to get the cabin all dirty. With the color red that I love so much more than green. Because it's the color of blood.

When those two people who got out of the car came back, they didn't realize that the people dressed in black were still there. They had just hidden among the trees, but their clothes were so black that only a cat—a black one at that—could see them. They stayed there, frozen, waiting for those other two to get back in the car and leave. Crazy stuff. Then they circled back around again for good measure.

My associate—not that tubby cat with the orange coat that will rub against anyone for a crumb of cake, but the other one—says strange things are happening here. That crazy old man I liked has disappeared, and no one knows what happened to him. There are these strange guys dressed in black who go around at night doing strange things. And there's something else. My associate, the one with the white coat, sometimes says strange things, and it's not that he knows exactly what he's saying, but he does say that something stinks around here and that something terrible has happened and that, if his whiskers aren't deceiving him, something else is going to happen too.

And he says he'll tell you about it.

PART THREE

REVELATIONS

I'm the white cat. I'm the evil one.

ONE

The morning is cold. A thick fog blurs with the snow, erasing the boundary between earth and sky all around. The huge beech in the middle of the Gherarda's meadow is as white and motionless as a skeleton. A wood and ice sculpture looming over anything else in view.

Barbara's eyes rest on it as she drinks her morning tea, standing in the entrance to the Gherarda. The aroma of rose hips and black currants. She had risen early to gather the silence and put it away for the raucous days to come. Her heavy coat zipped up to her chin, her shawl, her soft woolen gloves warmed by the cup, softening her stiff fingers.

Soon, the snow will be gone and the meadow will begin to bloom again.

She drinks the last sip, places the cup next to the door, and walks around to the back, by the oven. She faces the chimney: no more smoke. She collects the ash inside the oven with an iron trowel and places it on a kitchen cloth that she pulls out of her coat pocket. One, two, three, four trowelfuls in all. She refolds and knots the cloth so the ash can't escape and goes back inside.

When she passes the barroom door, she smells coffee.

Giulio is sitting at the table with a cup resting in front of him. He doesn't seem to have slept much. His eyes are still sunken.

"Up already?" she asks.

"Are you doing that for her?"

Barbara looks down at the cloth with the ashes in her hands.

"It's strange, you know, but sometimes I have the feeling she's talking to me."

"That's not strange. I don't think. But you shouldn't feel obligated to do all this. The oven, the ashes, and now you'll go into the woods and you'll pour your four fists, one for fire, one for wind, one for the earth, one for water. And you'll do other meaningless things because that's what we do when we don't know how to handle the void people leave behind. For example, I talk to a gnome."

"Maybe you should talk to an actual person."

"I took the green envelope. I thought I wanted to help myself remember."

"But now you're not so sure?"

"No, no I'm not. I don't know if it's such a great idea for me to remember this stuff."

"You didn't hurt her, Giulio. You don't have to be afraid of that."

"Is that what Amanda said?"

"Don't be ridiculous." Barbara places the cloth with the ash behind the counter and goes to sit next to him. "If you could remember what you did that night, you could help your attorney prove it wasn't you."

"And what if it was me?"

"It wasn't."

"Did you ever hear about that guy who got up during a commercial break on TV to kill his whole family with a shotgun?"

"Is this something you heard from the gnome?"

"No, the colonel of the carabinieri told me on the ride here. The gnome is more naïve. He thinks you can shut out the orcs."

"You can't?"

"I found the photo that was hanging over there. The frame is fine." Giulio seems to be studying it in his mind. "Is there anything you'd like to tell me?"

Barbara smiles, softens her eyes, and nods. "I know. The frame is fine. You can get used to some things, others you just pretend not to think about. And then there are others still that call for more effort. Sometimes you just need to be able to turn away from them."

"That's not what I wanted . . ."

"Don't worry. Listen, why don't you work a little? Don't you have that deadline? Try to use the gnome for something useful. I'll ask Akan to make a roast for lunch. Hello? Are you there?"

Giulio takes her hands, still in the gloves. It's been a long time since he's held her hands in his. They're hard, knotted. For a moment, Barbara feels a wave of shame at how time has reduced them, and she almost withdraws. But then she receives the gesture, smiling.

"Gnomes are creatures of the woods," Amanda once said, many years before. "And the woods take care of them. So when they're in danger, it protects them and helps them to disappear."

TWO

"All I'm saying is that some people should mind their own business."

Aurelio Magliarini, otherwise known as Maglio, the son of Giovagnolo, who was the first head lumberjack in the area and master carpenter in a glorious bygone era, is leaning on the counter at Bar Fuga with his first spiked hot chocolate of the day. Beside him there are the other lumberjacks on shift, ready to climb into their van and drive ten miles into the forest to saw through tree trunks.

The subject of interest isn't yet in the newspaper, which is still publishing Giulio Rodari's face on the front page. In this one, he's handcuffed and being escorted from prison. He looks overwhelmed. The caption promises new, succulent revelations about the case. But they're discussing something else that happened in the countryside today. The new fact has already circulated and rebounded. A monstrous deer with bloody horns and a threat written along the entire facade of the GeoService cabin.

"Of course if they left it to you, there wouldn't be any trees left," says Vannone Ghinozzi, owner of the Ghino di Tacco restaurant, named after the brigand of whom he is a descendant, even though his claims in this regard are somewhat nebulous. For the past few years, his son—a two-hundred-fifty-pound boy known to most as little Francesco—has looked over the restaurant while his father prolongs his mornings by visiting Bar Fuga for a friendly debate.

"All right, Ghinozzi. Maybe we should all come work for you, what do you say?"

"When your dad used to do your job, my friend, he only had five men and they worked all year round. Now you use more workers to do the same cutting faster, but you send them all home when it comes time to sort out the trunks."

"You don't know what you're talking about."

"Oh, but I do. You want to do what your dad did, but you want to make more money at it, so you cut corners. Simple."

"Go fry up some mushrooms at your restaurant and relax. When my dad owned the company, everything cost less and he didn't have to lose his mind trying to make sense of where and when he could and couldn't cut. I have five workers sitting at home, and until they see a paycheck they won't be coming to eat in your restaurant. And if things keep on like this, there will only be empty houses left. As if there weren't enough around here already."

"So you realize you're just like those guys who want to destroy the forest. The people around here used to take care of the woods because it was their world, not because they were looking for cash. And so now we're opening our doors to those guys who want to bury mafia trash in our woods. Don't you get it?"

"And now we have the mafia to worry about. People like us never end up building waste treatment plants like that, you know? There are people who are trained to do certain things. What kind of knowledge does a chef have? All I know is that you use oil for frying and then you dump it in the bucket behind the restaurant. That pollutes the countryside too, you know that?"

"Behind the restaurant is where we'll dump your head. Look—"

But everything is interrupted when Katerina makes her entrance. Blonde hair loose over a pink cropped down jacket, jeans so tight they look like a second skin, immaculate white cowgirl boots, and a Prada buckle seemingly designed to be seen from a spy satellite.

In a few strides, to the tune of the ticktack of her heeled boots, she arrives at the counter. The only concession she makes to the others is a smile that slips away without much conviction.

Her dark-green fingernails scrape at the register's keys that open the cash drawer. She shoves a pair of banknotes into the pocket of her jeans, with a rise so low that her lace panties peep out, taking the breath away from all of the men who witnessed it. She closes the drawer, and in the resonance of its ding, the door to the bar slams shut in her perfumed wake.

"She's up early this morning," says Ghinozzi.

Gerri forces a smile, but the reality is that he would like to chase her and drag her back to the counter by her hair. *I'll show you what hair is good for on someone like you,* he thinks. And then he'd add a nice "ugly slut" if it weren't for his childhood spent in school camps at the Camaldolese monastery. Instead, he follows her with his eyes, through the glass door of Bar Fuga, and watches as she approaches her white Alfa Romeo Giulietta and opens the door. And it occurs to him, for the first time in years, that an archer never loses his aim.

"You see, Marshal, GeoService would like to clarify this, and I've made myself available to do the clarifying." Scalise's voice is affected and theatrical; on the phone it's even more obvious. Reminiscent of Vittorio Gassman, the actor. As she listens, Grazia sees him standing next to the speakerphone, upright as a general looking out toward the enemy camp before battle. "Crimes against private property are never tolerated well by the community. And the last thing we want is a disgruntled community, for which reason this mission will remain our preeminent concern." Pre—what? What on earth is he saying? "Therefore, dispatch all your men without delay." Everyone? Really, Colonel? "And give this matter your utmost attention."

"What about Rodari's surveillance?"

"Secondary, Marshal. Absolute double priority. Do your best, Marshal Parodi. The force is counting on you."

Grazia gently places the phone on the table and looks around, half expecting to see someone come out from under a table and ask her to smile for the audience watching at home. What was that show called? Ah yes, *Candid Camera*. Scalise is that type. The kind of guy who the comedian on Channel 1 used to impersonate, back in the days of Teo Teocoli.

The phone display lights up. The battery is dying. She opens the drawer, but the charger is gone.

Donato has just left the Fioralba minimart with his bag from the deli counter: two half-filled baguettes with sausage and pistachio, one can of orange juice for him, and a soda for the boss.

The plow hasn't passed yet. A car that's been spinning its wheels is stuck in the middle of the road while another guy is instructing the driver on how to best get out. Donato knows them both and is trying to remember their names when he hears someone behind him call his name. He turns and finds himself facing Falconi and his cowboy hat.

"Hello, Mayor."

"Are they still stuck?" Falconi asks, pointing to the car. "This snow-plow thing is a disaster. We need more of them here."

"We do . . ."

"And what about the investigation, those vandals, anything yet?"

"Well, they didn't kill that fox."

"What do you mean? It cut its own head off?"

"Remember—" But then his phone rings. "Sorry, just a second. Hello?"

"Donato, I have to go home and get my charger. You get all the men assembled in the meeting room, and I'll see you there to discuss the new, absolute double priority."

"Boss, what men? Are you okay? Have you been talking to Scalise again?"

A scooter hurtles down the county road. The snow doesn't faze its driver. A skull sticker on a black helmet. A backpack with purple writing: PURPLE RAIN.

Dorina walks along the edge of the road in her boots lined with rabbit fur. She has a new pair that she bought last year, but she's never worn them, because the old ones are more comfortable now that they are molded to her feet. And she likes the fact that an old thing can be better than a new one.

She's removed her hearing aid; she doesn't need it now anyway. She hears just fine without it. Like she told the doctor, she only wears it as a precaution.

Today, she's going to the Gherarda on foot. The mist is parting for a timid sun, which, according to the weather forecast in the paper, will grow radiant within a matter of hours. The front page also had a photo of Giulio in handcuffs. But it's best that she forget all this for now, or at least for a while, because it's Wednesday, the day she cannot lose her concentration. The day of the duel.

Buraco day.

But first she has to go tell Barbara what she heard at the Fioralba minimart. Because it's good to know what kind of company you're keeping.

"I'm taking the car today, if you don't mind," says Adele. Marcello is turned toward the window again. His face is frozen, a prisoner of his grimace. The Romanian already came to clean him up, and she'll be back soon to finish the housework. "I have Buraco, remember? Today is Wednesday. It's still Wednesday. When you're waiting for one day to come, time passes so slowly, don't you find?"

"Yes, Adelina, it's just as you say."

"You don't mind if I leave you alone a little longer today, do you, darling?"

"Of course not, I have my trusty old TV to keep me company."

"I'm stopping by the pharmacy for some candy to take to the Gherarda. Do you need anything?"

"Don't worry, the Romanian will take care of everything, she'll be here in a few minutes. You go, though. Don't stay here, otherwise she'll stand around talking to you and she won't get anything done."

"See you later, then. Don't wear yourself out too much."

Adele goes down the stairs, exits the door, and looks up to the window from the street. On the other side of the curtain, she can just make out her husband's frozen face, deformed like plastic melted by the sun. She raises her hand and waves at him with a smile, happy to be living in that world where her husband can still see her and talk to her.

Grazia enters the house. The wicker basket is in front of the washing machine. In her bedroom, she moves the nightstand away from the wall and unplugs the charger from its socket.

She slips it into her pocket as she passes by Viola's bedroom door. Viola's bedroom.

She knows she's not allowed to enter. Not unless Viola is inside. It's the law that governs the life and good relationships in the house.

However.

The door isn't locked. And the law was established before her private life fell into an abyss of twenty-four-hour shifts. And if her daughter is a druggie, she has to find out as her mother first before she catches her as the police. And it won't be the first time she conducts a search without a warrant.

Her daughter's room is an anthology of different ages. The bookshelf is lined with stuffed animals from when she was small, Winnie the Pooh and Tigger, old cassette tapes, books, notebooks, diaries, CDs everywhere, DVDs, tangles of wires. Her drawing notebooks. She was good. On the wall there's a poster of a rock band that looks like a bunch of satanic serial killers, and another old poster with the animals of the forest. On the bedside table there's an old edition of *Spoon River*, the poems of Masters. She reads it often. Maybe they remind her of the boy who gave her the guitar. Maybe she thinks she can hear his voice in those poems, talking about life without the anxiety of having to live it. Viola lost a friend who was dear to her, and her mother sometimes has the impression she didn't do enough to help her "work through the loss," as the psychologist who came to the country after Bridge Day said. This is what happens with survivors of a disaster. And it's as if all the inhabitants of the countryside were just that: survivors.

In front of the nightstand are the boots she uses for her hikes and a backpack with a drawing of a huge spider at the top. It makes quite the impression. The boots are wet. She must have been in the woods again. Strange. They're very wet. She must have returned not long ago. Grazia moves the backpack to open the drawer and hears that noise.

At first it's just an instinct. An idea that crosses her mind without taking a precise shape. Then it comes together. Viola draws very well. Viola was just in the woods.

Grazia takes the backpack. She puts it on the bed, noting the placement of the objects inside so she can reproduce it exactly after her warrantless search.

And she finds it.

A can of spray paint.

How did it take her this long to realize? Everything is becoming clear. There is even a final detail, crystal clear and right before her eyes. It's in the poster, the one with the animals of the forest. Grazia approaches it, spray paint still in hand, as if she were transported by some mystical force.

There's the owl, there's the wolf.

And there's the deer. It doesn't have the demonic expression she saw on the other one, but other than that, the shape is identical to what the Spirits of the Woods drew.

THREE

The gnome says that sometimes the best way to find something is to stop looking for it. So Giulio shaved, put on his fleece, cleaned his desk—putting the envelope with the photographs and newspaper clippings from Bridge Day on the nightstand—and organized his drawing notebooks with his sharpened pencils.

The new history of the gnome involves a house on the tree, a father who has to leave, a child who gets lost in the woods, his brother who looks for him, and a father, the same one as before, who eventually returns. The stories of the gnome always have a circular structure. They offer the comfort that everything will make sense in the end.

Giulio takes the pencil and starts with the tree. The gnome says that trees have deep and solid roots, not like people, so it's best to start there. The tree has a hole, and looking out of the hole is an old owl. The gnome likes old owls. And there are two big branches that support the house, which has a staircase that goes down to the ground. Butterflies? A few, blue and yellow, maybe? Baby birds? Up high, on the left, a mama bird flies by with her three little ones behind her. A squirrel? Why not, running on a branch, perhaps, with its inevitable acorn in its claws. Patrizia? I don't know, I remember I was very angry from the shame she made me feel when she left that bar and took me home instead of insulting me and having me arrested. Did you bring her home? I was clinging to her, in my bedroom. That's where I was clinging to her. The image is clear, reflected in the mirror. Now I see it. It's like the gnome says: to find something you have to stop looking for it.

"Get off me, you're hurting me," says Patrizia, who had dragged him up the stairs and into his apartment. Now it's clear.

Giulio looks at the owl's eyes as they look out at him from inside the large tree. They seem to smile. He drops the pencil, walks over to the bedside table, and picks up his mother's envelope. He dumps its contents onto the bed and searches for the clip with Patrizia's photo. Something is returning from the land of oblivion.

"Get the fuck out or I'll have you arrested." The security guard at the bar where Patrizia is. Giulio can't stand, but he does scream that he's going to kill everyone there. She follows him out. The taxi, the stairs of his apartment. He grabs her, clings to her, so he doesn't fall. He doesn't want to let her go.

"Get off me, you're hurting me," says Patrizia.

"Leave, then. Why are you even here?"

"You're ruining your life, Giulio. Why have you reduced yourself to this?"

"You should know, you had your part in the spectacle."

"This is the last time, Giulio. The next time I'm calling the police and you'll really be in trouble. They could arrest you, you understand? I don't want to live like this anymore. Why are you doing this to me? You shouldn't have stooped to this, you shouldn't be drinking, it's dangerous. I'm calling emergency services."

"No."

"Stop it."

Giulio is about to say his no again, but he falls to the ground. Patrizia helps him up and drags him onto the bed. His pillow. His head aches, and he presses his hand to his forehead, blood on his fingers.

"I scratched you with my ring, I'm sorry," says Patrizia. Then she lowers her voice as she speaks with the emergency operator. Her voice moves away, is gone.

Giulio looks at the mirror. The wound on the eyebrow, there it is. It was Patrizia, yes, but not because he was attacking her. It's not a trace of his aggression and a woman's desperate attempt to defend herself. It was just an accident.

He needs a splash of cold water. He goes to the bathroom, turns on the tap, and rinses his face. As he towels off, he sees the carabinieri's car pull up under the window. Just the boy, this time. His shift. He goes back to the bedroom. Stop looking for it, says the gnome.

The room is too hot. He wants to let in some fresh air, ventilation. The window faces the opposite side of the road, where the woods behind the Gherarda begin. Giulio opens the window. A cool breeze enters. There's a timid hint of sunshine, somewhere, reflected on the icy snow. Giulio inhales, filling his lungs with cold air. And suddenly, the big orange cat leaps inside. It must have climbed up the ladder. It circles the room and then chooses one of the pillows on the bed.

"Go right ahead, sit down."

"Um, Rodari," whispers a voice from under the window. Giulio turns and looks for it. He finds it. "Give me a hand, Rodari. I'm in trouble."

Katerina is back home after her trip to the perfumery. She's pulled off her white cowgirl boots and socks, and now she's resting with her feet up, her emerald-green toenails on the table in front of the TV. There's a show on with a crazy lady who can't throw anything away. She saves everything: boxes, bags, packaging, everything. She lives buried in the house in the midst of that useless stuff. She's going to die from suffocation.

Before stretching out on the sofa, Katerina opened a packet of smoked salmon that cost twenty euros per ounce, a box of miniature toasts, salty butter, and a bottle of Carpenè Malvolti. She'll be leaving soon, and she has to relax, especially because anxiety is terrible for her skin.

She watches that lady buried in her own home and thinks of the sun shining in Sosúa Bay, lined with palm trees along a Caribbean beach kissed by the Antilles sun. That's how it was described on that website, so it must be true. He won't be a highflier, but at least he knows how to take initiative, and he won't die buried in useless crap in a sad and shabby bar like other people in this shithole.

Álvaro Soler's voice bursts from the gold-plated iPhone resting on the glass table.

Yo quiero que este
Sea el mundo que conteste
Del este hasta oeste
Y bajo el mismo sol

The name that pops up is Sara, and the profile picture is a kitten playing with a daisy.

Ahora nos vamos
Si juntos celebramos
Aquí todos estamos
Bajo el mismo sol

Before she answers, Katerina takes the remote control and lowers the volume on the TV.

"Hello? My love! This afternoon at your place? Are you alone, my little puppy? Do you want to do dirty-dog things to your little bunny? Do you have a surprise for me? You know how much I love surprises . . . And listen, how much longer do I have to wait? . . . He's strange, he keeps looking at me funny, I think he's going insane . . . I can't even think about it, it disgusts me to even imagine it, he always smells of booze, he sweats like a pig . . . My love, I want to get away from here with you. How much longer? . . . But can't you get them to give you all that money first? . . . Well, hurry, then. I'm afraid I'm going to die buried in all this crap . . . Okay, I'll come to your place this afternoon . . . I thought of a game I could play with you . . . No, no, you have to wait."

She turns up the volume on the TV, takes a slice of the Scottish salmon, and places it on top of a miniature golden toast. The lady who filled the house with all that crap is crying now, saying how she no longer wants to live that way and wants someone to help her throw everything out. But it would be better if she just burned down the house and moved somewhere else. Actually, it would be even better if the lady went up in flames with the house. Who comes up with these shows?

She crunches on the toast and changes the channel.

Barbara is doing inventory in the pantry with Akan when she hears the doorbell. It's Dorina.

"You won't believe what I just heard at Fioralba!"

"What?" Barbara asks, preparing a barley coffee with orange rind for her friend.

"Rachele, can you believe her? She was there all yakety-yak with Ms. Panciardi, talking about Giulio. I heard them loud and clear." She takes off her coat and drapes it on a chair. Barbara checks her ear. She's wearing her hearing aid—for the better. It's the day of Buraco, and when she doesn't wear it, it can be embarrassing to ask her repeatedly whether she wants tea. "They said he has his aunt's genes, can you believe it? They said, 'Of course he went nuts, it's all Amanda's genes.' But they stopped right away, mind you. As soon as they saw me, those two vipers."

"People talk, Dorina. They always have. And those pictures in the paper don't help."

"So you got the paper, then?"

Barbara hands her the cup of barley coffee with orange. "You shouldn't distract yourself with this, Dorina. I don't want to lose to Mirna and Adele, not today."

"But did you hear her last night? 'We were busy. We went to town to pick up a new electric oven.' I detest that woman. And then, did you notice how much she went on about her husband? 'Eugenio this, Eugenio that, Eugenio is the mayor and he's soooo busy.' I can imagine. Sometimes I think she does it on purpose. When she's with us. I think she loves being the one who has a husband."

"What a horrible thing to say, Dorina!"

They look at each other in silence for a moment. Dorina tries to hold back. Barbara gives up first and bursts into laughter.

Underneath the window there's a man wearing a black helmet.

"Who are you?" asks Giulio.

The guy takes off his helmet. It's the girl, Grazia's daughter, the one from the other day at lunch.

"It's me, Viola," she says.

"Are you lost?"

"The patrol car is here."

"Did you rob a bank?"

"Have you any tea and sympathy? If he sees me, he'll tell the Marshal and I'll be in for it. Last thing I need right now."

"Bad situation, worse than mine."

"Can you help me up?"

"I don't think so. Remember? I'm on house arrest."

"I won't tell anyone."

"And I have stuff to do."

"I'll stay out of your way. I have stuff to do too."

The girl pulls her phone out of her jacket pocket and checks the time.

The phone.

"Do you have internet on that thing?" Giulio asks.

"Yeah, but I also have a USB adapter with unlimited Wi-Fi."

The lumberjacks are back at work. At Bar Fuga, only Gerri has remained with his thirst and the hungry, singing slot machines, and Ghinozzi, who is rummaging around in a bag and lining up a long row of small coins on the counter to pay for his Campari with orange.

"You have to be careful with that one, Gerri. She'll use you and lose you," he says, counting a handful of five-cent coins. "You always need change, right? These coins are weighing me down."

"What are they saying about us?" asks the bartender, staring at the trail of heat left by his fingers on the cold steel counter.

"You can't imagine yourself?"

"They used to say the same things about my father, but they weren't true."

"I know, Gerri. People talk. I knew they weren't true. But the blonde . . . she's nothing like your mother. I hear she's always at the beauty parlor, the spa, the perfumery, leaving a trail of money behind her like a snail. I know it's none of my business, but you're going to end up in ruins if this continues. And I felt it was my duty to tell you, given the good relationship I always had with your parents." Ghinozzi puts on his hat, giving it a tug over his ears, and points to the row of coins on the counter. "Remember, I've never bribed a soul."

As the door closes behind Ghinozzi, Gerri thinks about his parents. About the rumors that circulated, just because his mother had been a beautiful woman. They said that Carmela knew all the secrets of chocolate. And that part was true. The house liqueur, the one made with chocolate that the lumberjacks drink to warm up, was her recipe. That morning she had left the house to go pick up some test results. Gerri had heard his father tell the story a hundred times. She was convinced she had some illness, but she had nothing of the kind. She was healthy as a fish. But she never found out, because the bus she took that morning to go hear the doctor say she was fine went over the wrong bridge. His father left the countryside a year later to go back to Sicily, to his sister's. He left Gerri the bar and some good advice on women that he didn't heed.

FOUR

"I was on my way to work at the practice room, but then I spotted the patrol car," says Viola, crawling through the window. "So I slipped behind the house. I was hoping it would go, but that idiot is spending his whole day here. What, are they scared you'll escape?"

"What do you mean you were on your way to work? Shouldn't you be in school?"

"Details. I was hiding here behind the house, then I saw the cat scurrying up the ladder and the open window." She spots the cat on the pillow and goes over to stroke it. "Thank you, little friend. You saved me today."

"I thought I saved you," says Giulio.

"You might save me from catching a cold if you close that window."

"Sorry, I'm not used to having visitors. You know how it is, I'm—"

"Under house arrest, I know. You keep saying that. Were you working?" she asks, gesturing toward the desk. Viola approaches the drawing pad. "What's this?"

"A tree. I'm working on a story that should start there."

"You make everything seem so easy. I'd like to show you my drawings one day. Maybe you can set me straight."

"Sure thing, if they don't put me away for life. Listen, about that Wi-Fi stick, could I borrow it?"

The girl looks at him. Giulio feels scrutinized, tested. Teenagers do it all the time, and their reactions can be unpredictable.

This girl in particular seems to be on the wild side. So many piercings, a tuft of hair over her eyes, heavy makeup. Always fidgeting with the long line of piercings in her left ear.

"What are you going to do with it?" she asks.

"What do you care?" But maybe a softer approach would be better. "Look . . ." He doesn't remember her name.

"Viola."

"Look, Viola, I have to look for something important, and I'll give it back as soon as I find it. And in the meantime, you can hide here."

"I don't think you should use it. You're not supposed to have any contact with the outside world, if you really are under house arrest."

"That sounds a little strange coming from the girl who just crawled through my window."

The girl looks like she's still figuring out the situation. She huffs, as if she's been forced to do something she's not convinced about. She places the backpack on the bed and rummages in one of the pockets, which seems to be full of stuff, until she pulls out a USB stick.

"Here it is. But if they catch you, don't sell me out."

Giulio takes his laptop bag, pulls out the laptop, and turns it on.

"Can you even use that?"

"Calm down. The ordinance says I can use the computer to work, but I can't go online. So they unplugged the Wi-Fi here at the hotel. That's why I need your adapter. Don't worry, nothing will happen to you. At most I could make some Skype calls if they haven't closed my account. But I doubt they have. Things never happen as quickly as they do in the movies."

The girl nods; she seems convinced. She takes off her jacket, stretches out on the bed, and scoops up the orange cat into her arms.

"So, what's this secret work you're doing?" he asks her as the laptop starts up.

"I'm working on a song, but I think it'll be an instrumental thing, so I don't know if I can even call it a song. Maybe I should call it a 'track,' right?"

"Sounds interesting."

"I have a band, like I was telling you the other day. It's called Lilith. We're breaking up on June twenty-first, but before that we want to record a track and put it on YouTube."

"What's it about?"

"No lyrics, it's an instrumental. I just told you."

"So you're saying instrumental songs aren't about anything? What kind of musician are you?"

"It's inspired by things that no one should ever forget. Maybe that's what it's about."

"It sounds like it was written for me."

"So is it true?" Viola lets go of the cat and sits up. "What's written in the paper, I mean. About how you lost your memory and everything else."

"I have no idea about everything else. But the part about losing my memory is true."

"What's it like?"

"That's what you want to know?"

"Yeah, why?"

Giulio turns. "Because you entered the bedroom of a suspected murderer. Now you're alone with him and your biggest concern is what it's like to lose your memory?"

"My mom says you didn't do it."

"Seriously? I hope she's right."

"What was she like as a kid?"

"A good girl, I'd say. Not really the window type," says Giulio, pointing to the one Viola crawled through. When he looks back at the screen, the computer is ready. He inserts the Wi-Fi adapter, and a window opens asking for the password. "What do I put?"

"You didn't answer me."

"We were classmates. It was twenty years ago, what do you want—"

"Not that. What's it like to lose your memory? To forget about something and to realize it was important."

Giulio looks at the laptop screen. The blank password field. All right, then.

"Once I was in a movie theater. They were playing a movie about dreams, by an Iranian director. In the end, I had this feeling they hadn't shown us the full version, so I went to the ticket office and asked if they were sure they had all the reels."

"What do reels have to do with it?"

"When the world wasn't all digital, they used to use reels. A movie usually had more than one."

"Go ahead." Viola takes off her shoes and crosses her legs on the bed.

"In the end, the ticket office told me they were missing a reel. They had shorted his delivery, and so he had projected what he had. Just like that, without telling anyone. I didn't know how the movie was supposed to go. And I can assure you that the narrative was the least of the problems that the director was dealing with. But my instinct that something was missing was immediate. And the hole remained. I have the same feeling about that night. I know things happened, but it's as if someone took them away from me. I know pieces are missing, but I can't put them back together again because it's as if I never had them to begin with. It's like that piece of movie I never saw. And I don't know where to look for it."

Strange, nobody had asked him how he felt. What effect it had on him. He had answered almost every question under the sun, but nothing like what this strange punk kid had thought to ask him.

"*Procolharum*, all one word. Do you know how to spell it?" Viola asks.

"What are you talking about?"

"The password you asked me for."

How this girl ever managed to know about that band is a story Giulio would like to hear, but there are more urgent matters at the moment.

He enters the password. The laptop connects to Wi-Fi.

Katerina burns off her salmon, butter, and prosecco as she rides the 999-euro computerized stationary bike in the front room, just forty-two inches from the bedroom where a cute, fit, nice girl has to sleep with an obese, lazy know-it-all who is as boring as all the books he says he's read, when maybe he's only read the plots on Wikipedia like everyone else. If they ever lost a reality TV bid, it's clear the blame would lie with that pretentious pig.

The golden iPhone resting against the bike display lights up. The name and face that appear reflect the boring guy. Gerri is calling her from the bar. Why does he have to be calling her constantly? Why can't he let her get on with her life without interrupting her every time she goes to do something important?

"I'm working out," she informs him with all the resentment she can muster.

"You have to help me with lunch."

"Do you need someone to explain how to warm up the sandwiches?"

"I need you to heat the sandwiches while I get on with other things."

"What other things do you have to get done in that cesspool of a bar?"

"Katerina, if you don't come now, I'll go over there and drag you here by your hair."

He's slurring his speech like he does after too much sparkling white.

"Are you drunk?"

"You're out of breath, what are you doing?"

"I'm on the bike, I told you."

"I'm calling the landline. I want to see if you pick up."

And he hangs up.

Katerina stares at the iPhone in her hands, mute, and wishes Gerri's face would reappear so she could break it against the bike.

The landline rings.

Suffocating the urge to scream, she gets up from the bike and picks up the cordless phone in the hallway.

"Happy?"

"Come to the bar."

"You're a maniac. And a drunk. You disgust me, I can smell the wine on you from here."

"If you don't get down here, I'll come and get you."

"Fuck you. Get over your hangover first, then we'll talk."

She slams the cordless phone back into its cradle, nearly splitting it in two. This was the last thing she needed. But if that asshole tries to ruin her plans, he'll take care of it. He'll sort him out for good.

"I don't want to spoil your party," says Viola, "but anything you do online can be traced, and sorry if my mother is a marshal, but I don't want to be up shit creek on your account. And this thing you're doing is making me a little nervous. I don't think you should do it, I'm serious." Giulio had opened a Google profile. When the page appeared, Viola immediately noticed that the username was Patrizia Alberti. "At least tell me what you're trying to do. You know how it is, I just lent my Wi-Fi stick to a guy who may have killed his girlfriend and hid her body, so I think it's normal to be a bit apprehensive."

Giulio turns, as if he's suddenly realized something important. "You can always say you lost it, maybe in the bar downstairs. I found it and here I am."

"Something more convincing?"

"I just have to check one thing. It might be useful. That deputy prosecutor already decided I'm a bloodthirsty monster, and if I can't put a single doubt in her head to the contrary, I'll be in a bad way."

"Shouldn't your lawyer be taking care of that?"

"I haven't decided if I'm going to keep him."

Giulio went through the contacts list. He found the one that he was apparently looking for. Leonardo Maccari. Blond, smiling, light-blue eyes. Like he just walked out of a 1980s chewing gum commercial.

"There it is."

"Can you at least tell me what you're doing?"

"Patrizia's office manages its email and messaging through a Google account."

"Which you've obviously violated."

"I'm a stalker, wasn't that in the newspapers?"

"I think I've made a big mistake coming here. Maybe you should give me back my stick."

Giulio turns to her. He takes a deep breath and tightens his lips into a worried grimace. "Listen to me, Viola, who writes instrumental songs for a group that will break up before summer starts. Grazia, your mother, may be right. At least, I hope she is. But they already have me for guilty, and if I can't find anything to help me, we'll never know if she really is right. Do you know what it means to live with that kind of doubt?"

"I'm going to end up in big trouble. I can already see it coming."

At Bar Fuga, lunchtime is approaching through an alternating rhythm of Campari and white wine spritzers. House prices are low, so most of the money shelled out ends up in the machines, which are in the other room, singing their songs, hungry as always.

Gerri is leaning with his arm against the counter. This morning he got into it with the sparkling white, and now he's a little out of it. He can't quite make out what the customers are saying. Especially the Kosovars, who just got off their carpentry shift. They go on and on and on in those loud voices as if they were at a festival. They raise their glasses and down their contents in a single gulp. And there's nothing to do but fill them up, those damned glasses. Watch how many they drink, because it's all fine and good that the prices are low, but if you get distracted, they'll only pay you for every other one. What if it were one of them? One of these young men with broad shoulders and hard muscles. First he screws Katerina and then comes here to have a drink. And he only pays for every other one.

Beasts.

The image that crosses his mind is that. The Kosovars with their wide shoulders, naked in the woods. Young, muscular, smeared with dirt. It's as if suddenly a light comes on in the trees and she appears, Katerina. Her long hair floats in the air. The white flesh of her naked body, covered only on the sides by a myrtle bush. Her red lips. Her round breasts and pert nipples in the cold air. The Kosovars look at her. They get excited. They start to move toward her. Like in a hunting ritual, they move in a pack. They surround her. She is beautiful and in danger. The first one is about to jump on her, but an arrow strikes his throat. The others look around. The one who got hit squirms on the ground, but only for a few seconds, before remaining motionless. The others are terrified. The second takes another arrow through his heart. He almost doesn't realize he's dying before he falls into a bush. They escape. They run away. And finally, Katerina smiles at him. Gerri slings the bow over his shoulder. She approaches him. He kisses her. A long, passionate kiss before laying her on a carpet of moss and kissing her again.

"Gerri, give me another Campari, I have a headache." Maglio is standing in front of him, big as a bison, his forehead glistening. Where did he come from? Why is he sweating? Is he the bastard who's screwing Katerina?

"Gerri, you there?" he says. "You seem a little out of it."

Giulio looks for messages from Maccari. He finds several. Work stuff. But there's more.

Let's meet tonight.

Just us, okay?

What's wrong with you?

I want to live this without fear.

Don't you think you should move on from this story sooner or later?

I realized you're special to me.

Don't blow me off again.

"This guy has a future as a poet," says Giulio.
"Did you find what you were looking for?" Viola asks.
"There's a lot of stuff. I need some time."
"Go ahead. I'm going to nap if you don't mind."
Giulio turns. Viola had slipped under the duvet as he was reading the messages. Her head is on the pillow, and she's putting in her headphones.
"You're sleeping? Here? In my bed?"
"You smell decent, I don't mind. If you're going to get me in trouble, I should probably rest up."

The girl who knows Procol Harum and writes songs about things that should never be forgotten closes her eyes. Giulio looks at her and seems to recognize her urgent need to seek a place of refuge. He decides to pull the curtains to give her some shade. As he approaches the window, he notices the patrol car is gone. And he suspects that Viola has noticed too.

Donato studies the tracks in the snow around the GeoService cabin. The Spirits had approached from the road. He traces them now in the daylight, and among those left by Magliarini Forestry Services and the patrol car, he thinks he can discern those of at least a few scooters. But around the cabin, the snow had been cleared by the lumberjacks who maintain the cabin, perhaps when they passed by this morning. And in the forest there are no footprints. Aside from his own.

Donato looks through the trees, trying to retrace their path from the other night, as they followed those greenish lights that, according to the website that documents haunted woods, were ignes fatui. As a rule, they're usually blue and organic, but in this case they were green and moved too fast to be a phenomenon of natural combustion.

A reflection. The only ray of sunshine he's seen here for a long time. Too many reflections for this officer ripped from his seaside village and transplanted into the mountains. The sun must have caught something metallic, or maybe some glass.

Donato looks in that direction. Again, a reflection in the woods. It takes off along the path he and the Marshal traveled at night. He follows it.

The reflection again. It seems to be hanging from a tree.

Grazia is back at the station. Her phone is charging, she's sent Donato to do surveillance at the Gherarda, and she's found the envelope where she placed the dirty handkerchief with the paint they found at GeoService. She opens it on her desk. She's only confirming, but if it doesn't turn out to be the same red, there's at least a glimmer of hope that things . . .

The color is the same. Grazia only sprays a few drops, but it's enough to remove any lingering doubts as to why Viola's boots were wet so early in the morning.

Donato has reached the object that was producing the reflection. It looks like a strange device: three propellers mounted on a nearly weightless metal chassis. It has a small eye that resembles a camcorder lens, and a second device that looks more like a tiny projector.

He's never held one in real life, but the last time he went to Euronics—to buy the latest *Call of Duty* for PlayStation 3—he saw the same strange gadgets lined up on a shelf.

The green light came from this flying object, which must have gotten stuck between the branches. Here, then, is the explanation for the Spirits of the Woods.

They're drones.

Viola opens her eyes. That guy is still in front of the computer. He's probably still reading all of his ex's messages. Is it even possible to be this obsessed with someone? Is there a way to get over it? Survive the past without feeling guilty? Will she manage to do it as well?

If it hadn't been for the patrol car, she probably would have already retrieved the drone that got stuck in the woods the other night. She sent a message to Diego so he'll do it. But she didn't mind the thought of staying here, even after she saw the car was gone.

She checks the time on her phone. It's almost time to leave Rodari's room and go home, since the Marshal decided to leave her some lunch in the kitchen. When it happens, it's usually a plate of cold pasta with tuna, tomato, and mayonnaise, which, together with toast, sums up everything in her mother's cooking repertoire.

"You still there?" she asks Giulio.

He turns and smiles. His eyes are red. He's been crying.

"Welcome back."

"You don't look good."

"That's the downside of memories. Sometimes they get stuck right where they hurt the most."

FIVE

Adele's Panda four by four has one specific purpose that keeps it running, inspection after inspection: a mile there and a mile back, every Wednesday afternoon. On this occasion, the passenger seat will be occupied by Mirna, her longtime companion in the Gherarda showdowns, the Buraco game held each week at the hotel that situates them opposite Barbara and that damned cousin of hers, Dorina the cunt.

Before getting in the car, Adele stops at the Novelli Pharmacy to buy a pack of tea biscuits to deliver to her rivals. No one has ever eaten one during the game, but Adele has noted that they contain castor oil and adores the thought of gifting them to Dorina.

When the time comes, Adele starts the Panda, whose engine faithfully turns with the key, and takes the road to Falconi's house, from which Mirna, noticing the car from the window, comes running outside with a tray of freshly baked cookies.

The trip there is silent. Full of tension. The mood on the return mostly depends on who wins the game. It's best of three, which, between tea breaks and some verbal sparring to heckle the other side, takes up the entire afternoon.

On the other side of the barricade, Barbara and Dorina wait side by side at the window, anticipating clean runs, pure Buracos, and above all, cold showers for their opponents. Because this is not about winning.

This is about humiliating the enemy. To close the game just before the other team decides to drop the points in their hand, because that's what hurts the most. "What a pity for that jolly, dear" becomes a triumphant song that every player of this ruthless game hopes to sing at least once every time.

The Panda pulls up. Mirna and Adele get out, closing the doors behind them in unison. They swagger over, almost arrogantly, like in an old western scene. Mirna with her tray of homemade cookies and Adele with her pack of tea biscuits. Barbara opens the door with a big, open smile that will disappear as soon as they sit at the table, which has been set with a green tablecloth and cups for tea.

"It's so cold today," says Mirna. "It seems even colder here than in the village," she adds, kicking off the hostilities.

Viola left the Wi-Fi adapter with Giulio. Her usage isn't controlled, and he can use it. Worst case, she can always say she lost it at the hotel and he must have found it. Violating his ban on contact with the outside world, even online, is the least of Giulio's worries.

He's filtering Patrizia's emails, not knowing exactly what he's looking for. It's like trying to satisfy his abstinence with small fragments of her. The ones about her new relationship are painful. And not because that douchebag tennis player may seriously have something to do with her disappearance, but because he makes Giulio feel as if he has been replaced, eliminated. Because this is what obsession does. It binds to something you can't have and stands by as you destroy everything you have to get it. And each time that same story comes to mind. The whale is white. And it repeats: "Do you remember the *Pequod*?"

The first time you read Melville, you wonder why Ahab can't just drop it and turn back. But he couldn't resist. And now there you are, on a splintered ship, a crew dotting the sea, defying your misfortune just to chase that white obsession that will sink you into the abyss once and for all.

You're the bad guy. And every story, from the bad guy's point of view, is exactly that.

Patrizia was seeing the tennis player. A smile in the office, lunch at the bar, Patrizia wants to start playing tennis and he's a total tennis fanatic, and what a coincidence, it was raining and they both had to hide under his jacket to get back to the office, running through the rain so close they could smell each other like in one of those romantic movies when the song plays at that moment that turns everything into a 1980s music video for some metal ballad. It's horrible, Patrizia. You're going to end up making out to Bon Jovi. It's surprising that you, the woman who never takes anything for a given, ended up living such a cliché.

"Do you think it's sunrise or sunset?" she asked him that day.

They're in bed. Naked, under the sheets. In Patrizia's apartment. She and Giulio have been seeing each other for a few months. On the wall is the Erwitt photograph he gave her, because he could not bear that her walls were so white and bare. He explained why, his white theory. The wall gave him a sense of the void, the impression that the place was soulless.

Now, instead, there's that photo of the kissing couple reflected in the rearview mirror of a car parked by the sea, which reflects the sun as it hovers near the horizon.

"Do you think it's sunrise or sunset?" Patrizia asks.

"Do you really want to know?"

"Is there a way to know?"

"You just have to know exactly where the photo was taken."

"Then I don't want to know."

"You change your mind quickly."

"Sometimes I'll see it as a sunrise, and others I'll see it as a sunset. And it will be beautiful just the same."

There are emails from colleagues, friends, personal and work conversations. Giulio can't stop searching her email messages. Each fragment becomes precious. Each glimpse of the whale, the white monster, is a step toward the end.

Toward the abyss.

"And why did you give him that ridiculous name?" Patrizia asks. They're walking along the tree-lined avenue that runs along the park. In the evening, she and Giulio often go there for an aperitif. The bar with the overturned tables and shattered glasses from the day he lost control for the first time isn't there yet. The beginning of his downfall. Not yet. It's a beautiful summer evening. They're talking about his job. About the gnome.

"Theophrastus Grimblegromble," says Giulio, as if he were introducing an old friend.

"Yeah. What does it mean?"

"It's a reference."

"I imagined. You're one for references."

"Philippus Aureolus Theophrastus Bombastus von Hohenheim, also known as Paracelso."

"Did he have a red beard and a green hat?"

"He was a fifteenth-century alchemist, the first person to talk about gnomes, tracing the name to the Greek root *gnosis*, for knowledge."

"A cultured reference, then. And the surname?"

"Grimble Gromble is the name of the gnome in a song by Syd Barrett, from Pink Floyd."

"Mystery solved. But don't you think that's the sort of thing the parents who buy your books for their kids would love to know?"

"That's why I find it fun."

Scrolling through her emails, he finds one whose subject catches his eye: "Reopening Bridge Collapse Investigation."

He didn't know Patrizia wanted to reopen the investigation. He clicks on the email. It's from a geologist. A professor Ubaldo Giampedretti.

Dear Patrizia,

As I mentioned, no new elements emerged regarding the calamity in question. In the sense that the recent discovery I mentioned to you does not relate to that specific event. However, it's still a notable finding and should be brought to the attention of the appropriate parties. I've attached the report and remain at your full disposal.

Kind regards,
Giampedretti

"But your stories about gnomes also have orcs. Doesn't that scare the kids?"

"Orcs exist."

"Is that how you do it, then? The gnome just serves to tell the children that the orcs exist?"

"It's a little like what Chesterton said about fairy tales. He was talking about dragons, but it's the same with orcs. Children already know that orcs exist. The stories about the gnome tell the children that orcs can be defeated."

SIX

The cold pasta with tuna, tomato, and mayonnaise had a coveted variation of capers. Viola hopes to be able to go back to Barbara's soon.

She leaves the house, her backpack and laptop in tow. She mounts the scooter and leaves the countryside behind. Just outside, at the mouth of the county road, there's a car on the road. A white Giulietta. The sound of gas in the engine, the wheels spinning. Viola stops. She leans her scooter against a tree along the road, leaves her helmet on the mirror and the backpack on the rack. She approaches.

Katerina is inside the car. With her mirrored sunglasses and her pink pop-star makeup.

"Do you need help?" Viola asks.

"Are you going to call someone?"

"Maybe I can do it on my own."

"Do you know how to drive?"

"Let me try."

Katerina gets out of the car. Viola walks a circle around the Giulietta and studies the situation. Her mother taught her to drive in the snow; she's obsessed with knowing all the tricks to driving in the snow. Viola compacts some under the wheels, where a mud pit is developing, so they adhere better to the ground.

"There was a black cat crossing the street," says Katerina, explaining why she's stranded. "And they say it's not true that they're bad luck."

"The most important thing, however, is to remain calm when it happens," says Viola, sitting in the driver's seat. "Just let the wheels turn very slowly."

The car, after a couple of motionless attempts, budges and finally leaves the pit.

Katerina thanks her but gets back in the car right away. She seems to be in a hurry. No time for small talk.

"If you're going to stay on the county road, be careful because the snow is loose this time of year and you can slip," says Viola, because it's clear that if she's taking the county road, she's not going to the bar, and she wants to see Katerina's reaction.

"Thank you," she responds, with a forced smile that she doesn't even bother to disguise.

Viola smiles as she waits for the Giulietta to leave. Katerina doesn't take the road to town: as expected, she takes the county road. Caught red-handed.

Viola walks back to her scooter, puts on her backpack, and drives off.

What she doesn't know is that four pairs of hidden eyes have witnessed everything. Two of them are human, while the others, glimmering in the light, belong unmistakably to two cats.

SEVEN

The first investigation into the collapse of the bridge ended after a year when the prosecutor shelved it. Seven lives swallowed into the abyss, what the deputy prosecutor had referred to as an "act of God," an unpreventable natural disaster outside of human control. No liability to be found.

Giulio is sitting at his desk with his legs stretched out, his feet resting on the windowsill. On the floor is the tray with the remains of his lunch and the bottle of bitter orange soda. On the bed, the envelope with the material he took from his mother. On the laptop, the browser is open to Gmail's record of Patrizia's last days and her conversations. Time stamps for what she sent, received, and archived, confirming that attorney Alberti was working nonstop. Giulio was her client and, from a certain point onward, her boyfriend. He can't deny that the time his lawyer was going back and forth with him and other clients had been the happiest. And if the gnome had asked him to focus on a happy thought to help a weary flower blossom, he probably would have picked a memory from that time, when everyone around them was in pieces, including his mother.

As a civil attorney, Patrizia had opposed the prosecutor's request and had asked the preliminary judge to open a new inquiry, summoning a hydrogeological expert from the area. The hearing and court decision took nearly half of the following year. Eventually, the judge listened to her, at least in part. He opened a new inquiry, remanding the case back to the prosecutor, albeit requesting general insights on only a few issues.

The second investigation lasted even longer. Twenty months. In practice, the deputy prosecutor repeated everything he had done the first time around and came to an identical conclusion. An act of God. Case closed.

One evening, Patrizia had told Giulio that, at that point, the only way to get a charge was to convince the preliminary judge to ask the prosecutor for one directly. "A coerced indictment," she had told him. But to persuade the tribunal to pursue this path, and not simply because of the "mutually beneficial relationship between the judge and the deputy prosecutor," Patrizia had commissioned a private expert on behalf of her clients, a geology professor of a certain renown, to conduct the expert assessment that the judge didn't order and that the deputy prosecutor never carried out (or at least not on the terms Patrizia was hoping for).

The amount of time the assessment would require, however, wasn't compatible with what the court could provide, which now, four years after Bridge Day, was suddenly in a hurry to shelve the case.

Giulio remembers the evening Patrizia met with all her clients in her office in the city. There was the head of the lumberjacks, Magliarini, and the old man from Bar Fuga, Torloni, both men having lost their wives. There was that distinguished lady who had lost her son. There were the family members of the plumber and the bus driver. Not a soul for the Kosovar. There were bottles of water and orange juice on the table, a bag of pretzels, a tray of sandwiches, and a set of copies of the binder with all the investigation files that had been released. The investigation had become Patrizia's professional obsession. And obsessions, Giulio Rodari is now in a position to observe, never bring anything good.

Obsessions are white. He has no doubt about it.

"I'm left with the conviction that a disaster like this can only be the result of negligence," Patrizia explained. "In the sense that if a bridge collapses, it can't be no one's fault. If that were the case, every motorist should be aware that whenever he crosses a bridge, there is a real risk that bridge could collapse. Because there are no specific legal liabilities in place to prevent it. And that, of course, is unacceptable." That afternoon, Akan had driven Amanda's old Ford to take Barbara to town to see the lawyer, and he had stopped by to pick up Giulio, who had never learned to drive. It was his first time back in the car he used to ride in as a child with his aunt, when she would take him out on her rounds, if she would only be a few hours. Those times she left for days at a time; on the other hand, no one ever knew where she was going. Among the many things that had been left unexplained was also why, on Bridge Day, Amanda had decided to take the bus. "Unfortunately, after years lost on paperwork, bureaucracy, and delays, which is certainly not the fault of the deputy prosecutor or the judge—nor is it ours—the court seems intent on closing the case and has upheld the prosecutor's request for the same. And we, because I delayed my decision about whether to order it, are not ready to present a report that might convince the judge—because at this point it really is about convincing him—to indict the parties under investigation, although I don't even believe they are principally liable." At that time, things with Patrizia were going less well. She was absorbed in her work. "All I can do at this point is continue my inquiry, which I've placed in the hands of a luminary in this field, and try to open the case again if new elements emerge."

Professor Ubaldo Giampedretti was the luminary in charge of said inquiry. Giulio had met him one day as he waited at Patrizia's office to speak with her. They hadn't seen each other for a while. He had shown up at her office without notice and had caused something very close to an uproar.

Remembering all this now is like opening a window on part of a story that had remained in the shadows. The period when Patrizia was carrying out her inquiry had been, for Giulio, the period of his own shipwreck, his progressive slide toward the abyss, his decline from human to predator.

"Do you get it now?" Patrizia would say, if she were there next to him. "Now can you can see what was happening on the other side of your barricade? I felt guilty for having miscalculated the investigation at times, and I was trying to make up for it, working into the night, because I couldn't take time away from my other cases. And in all this I had to endure your little scenes, because you didn't feel included, you didn't feel considered, coddled. You accused me of being an egomaniac, remember? You were so caught up in yourself you were incapable of considering anything but your own needs. And when I tried to keep you at arm's length, you showed me the worst of you."

"And the tennis player?" Giulio would ask her.

"Is that what this is about, Giulio? Your biggest issue is Maccari? If you ever found the time to be honest with yourself, as ruthless with yourself as you know how to be with everyone else, whose flaws you never forgive, by the way, then maybe you'll realize Maccari wasn't the reason I left you. But you won't do it, will you? You prefer to go digging around in my emails for answers, browse through all my messages, consoling yourself with the illusion that the explanation, the sense of it all, is hidden somewhere else."

Giulio angrily snaps the laptop shut.

I was only trying to understand, I don't need any consolation.

It's not the gnome that has the power to disappear; it's the forest that helps him do it. Because it's the forest that protects him.

Amanda had chosen the wrong day to take the bus. A bridge is like a picture hanging on the wall that comes down one day and ciao ciao. You turn away for an instant and the person you're talking to is gone. One day someone tells you that from now on your life will be completely different. And you can sink or swim. Adapt or die.

Giampedretti emailed his report to Patrizia three days before she disappeared. Three days before the night of that damned March 11, when a man who, according to the prosecution, answers to the name of Giulio Rodari attacked her in that alley without realizing that the image was reflected in a window in view of a surveillance camera. And maybe Patrizia really had been working all those times she didn't respond to his calls and brushed him off with a text: "I'm working, let's talk tomorrow." With the clarity Giulio believes he's put together in this moment, perhaps he might be willing to believe that they weren't just excuses, even if Maccari had been writing things like "Don't you think you should move on from this story sooner or later?" The story, the only story. Bridge Day. The investigation. Patrizia couldn't pull herself away. Persecuted by her ex, in his deranged stalker state, she kept working because she wanted to reopen the investigation.

Giulio feels a dim light come on in the dark.

Patrizia had commissioned a hydrogeological study to piece together elements that would convince the judge to reopen the investigation. Elements that were supposed to demonstrate the clear and objective responsibility for the deaths of seven people.

It's a weak light. But it's there.

Patrizia receives the report from the expert in charge. And after three days, she disappears.

Giulio approaches the laptop and opens it again. The Gmail screen reappears. The connection had been interrupted because he had let it idle. *Procolharum.*

The investigators' inquiries focus on her turbulent ex. The press calls it a "crime of passion," as if the feeling behind it made it better somehow. Sure, he killed her, but he loved her. But what if that's not how it went? What if her turbulent ex, whose memory sports a gaping hole of about four hours long, stayed home and the aggressor in question was not overwhelmed with passion for his victim?

An attorney wants to reopen an investigation into neglect and manslaughter. She commissions a study from a geologist. The report comes in, but the attorney disappears.

Giulio opens Giampedretti's email again.

Dear Patrizia,

As I mentioned, no new elements emerged regarding the calamity in question. In the sense that the recent discovery I mentioned to you does not relate to that specific event. However, it's still a notable finding and should be brought to the attention of the appropriate parties. I've attached the report and remain at your full disposal.

Kind regards,
Giampedretti

A discovery that had nothing to do with the event but still needed to be communicated to someone.

The new adventure of Teo the gnome would have to wait. Giulio decides he can allow himself to read the report. He takes the laptop, rests it on his legs, downloads the file, and begins to read.

EIGHT

Someone has decided to get involved.

Katerina has just gotten back in the car. She's emerged from the house of the man who promised her a better future without even one little gift. It's the first time her little puppy has broken a promise. But it's not his fault. Someone else has gotten in the way. Someone who obviously doesn't have anything better to do than trample people who are trying to realize their dreams.

As soon as she entered her little puppy's house, she dropped her purse on the floor and began to unbutton her jeans, when she realized that he was sitting on the couch, still dressed, with a yellow envelope next to him.

Inside, photographs that someone left in the mailbox. Photographs that captured the two of them, in the car, in a position that was truly impossible to mistake for anything else. And the real problem is that the account with all the money they were going to use to escape to Sosúa Bay, with its palm trees and the Caribbean Sea kissed by the Antilles sun, that damned account that burns like an ember of hope, is in his wife's name. The rest is rather logical, because if his wife ever found out about the little bunny and her puppy, they'd be in real trouble. Not so much because of the money that has already arrived, unbeknownst to the wife, in the account under her name, but because of the funds that are yet to come, whose destination can't be changed without setting up a foreign-to-foreign transfer, which presents its own challenges. Not to mention that the little wifey, according to the little puppy, is starting to suspect something. She's not sure what, but half a word too many could, at this point, be enough to make a big mess for them.

Katerina hopes that this someone with their photos and their request that could ruin the bunny's plans with her little puppy keels over with diarrhea. Also because, just as a precaution, they had to cancel today's appointment, and instead she's decided to have some fun without him, because that's how she keeps him in her power. And she needs to feel powerful, because she's tired of dreams that are never anything more than half-baked.

The inexperienced Buraco player makes their moves based on their hand. They think about their next play and plan which cards to drop. The expert Buraco player, on the other hand, moves according to the others: their companion and their opponents. The inexperienced player focuses on their own cards; the expert player considers the cards they don't hold. The expert Buraco player knows that the winner is the one who can understand and anticipate their opponent's move first. The inexperienced player is gullible and tends to keep all their good cards in hand in order to drop them at the perfect moment, to the dismay of their opponents. They think of their own move, always. They read the world from their own point of view. They might have six-card sequences in hand, one card away from Buraco, savoring the joy of their triumphal moment that sadly never comes. Buraco isn't a hard game. Technically, it's about ceding and attacking. But empathy with your partner makes for the difference between winning and losing. When two players sing the same song, the music is heavenly. But if everyone tries to play their own song, then it's a mess. And according to a Buraco player, experienced or not, the wrong song is always the one their companion chooses. That's why even the deepest friendships can be severely tested at the Buraco table. Because Mirna in this moment believes it's clear, as clear as a mountain stream, that if she throws down everything she has and remains with a single card in hand and a satisfied smile, it's because the card she's holding closes the game and she only wants her companion to have one chance to drop everything but her winning card, since the glutton has already taken two rejects and hasn't even dropped a run of three. And considering she needs two hundred points, only an idiot would snatch up the scraps instead of dropping their run.

But Adele does precisely that.

Mirna's first instinct is to send the table into the air and pounce on her companion. Strangle her. Or, even better, choke her by shoving one of those cards she's holding on to down her throat. But when Mirna realizes that Barbara has understood what she's thinking, she realizes she needs to be a better actress. The one who first understands their opponent's move wins. Never give your adversary the chance. Especially Barbara, who, with this committee, thinks she's more important than the mayor. Everyone in town hanging on her every word, everyone turning to her when they have a problem, when instead they should consult the mayor's wife. But nobody knocks on her door. Barbara's there when someone has a problem. It's Barbara who organizes the Evening of Bread. Because if Mirna fired up that gorgeous wood-burning oven behind her house, only demented Adele would show up to bake her bread. But the day of vengeance always comes for those who know how to wait. And when the old woods Barbara loves so much becomes home to a brand-new waste treatment plant, the Gherarda will finally close its doors forever.

Dorina closes. Adele pays three hundred points and concedes the second game to her two enemies. They're two and zero. A quick win.

Mirna tries to force a smile, but when she realizes she's only grinding her teeth, she takes to sipping her tea.

"I had all the game in hand, gosh darn it," Adele says. "Another turn and I would've dropped my whole run."

"Maybe you should have done it sooner, my dear," says Mirna, with all the venom she can muster without throttling her outright.

"We still have half an afternoon left," says Dorina, exalted by her winning move and the three hundred points her cousin had to pay. "How about a second round?"

Of course. Because when the wind is blowing in one direction, it doesn't just switch all of a sudden. Today Adele isn't fooling anyone; maybe she has a hint of Alzheimer's that disappears whenever she's at the card table. The second round would be worse than the first, and besides Adele, everyone knows it. That's why Dorina proposed it, and Barbara has muttered her unassuming "All right, why not?" leaving Mirna with no alternative but to say, "I need to get back, Eugenio's not feeling very well." A retreat. With dignity. When you can't win, it's the only alternative to defeat. And to enjoy vengeance, you must preserve yourself long enough to see it.

"I've noticed poor Eugenio has been a little worried lately," Dorina says. "Is it this business about the waste plant permits? I guess it's not easy for him to find a way to stop it."

"If it's not so easy to stop it," Mirna says, "maybe that's because it shouldn't be stopped." She understands too late that it's dangerous to expose her stance. She should have tempered her anger, but the recent card debacle, inspired by Adele's inadequacy, which after years of Buraco she hasn't managed to repair, has worn her down.

"What was that again, dear?" Dorina asks.

"Exactly what you heard, darling. Maybe we've been wrong about it from the beginning."

"You're not trying to convince your husband, are you?"

"Eugenio doesn't need to be convinced. He's the mayor, my dear."

"Yes, but what you're saying, Mirna dear . . . is that why you didn't come to the committee?"

"We didn't come because I had to buy a new electric oven, I told you, darling."

"But . . ." Dorina can't find the words and turns to Barbara. "Aren't you going to say something? Didn't you hear what she said?" And it's in that moment that her face flinches as if it had been hit with an intuition. "You have it out for her because people listen to her. You're jealous, and it kills you because you know she's the only reason you're the Misericordia president."

"Dorina, that's enough," Barbara interrupts.

"No, no, let her finish," Mirna says, crossing her arms.

"You know I'm right," says Dorina.

"Ladies, please," Adele says. "Let's try to remember that Buraco is how we distract ourselves from this kind of unpleasantness. Especially now that Giulio . . . well, in short, it mustn't be easy for you, Barbara. It's normal for you to be on edge."

"She's not that on edge," says Dorina, "if you haven't noticed."

"I wasn't talking to you, tightwad."

"Tightwad?"

"You know . . ."

"It seems to me we're all a little on edge," says Barbara. "Maybe we should put away the cards and have some cake."

"Have a biscuit, Dorina," Adele says, gesturing toward the unopened packet.

"I'm leaving," says Mirna.

Dorina will pay for what she said. Even if she has to eat every one of those disgusting tea biscuits Adele insists on bringing with her every time.

Farewells become a rushed formality. Mirna and Dorina don't even look at each other. Adele and Dorina stare each other down.

Outside the Gherarda, the temperature descends with the sun. Mirna gets in the car in silence. Dorina's words are still rumbling in her head, and she's too busy thinking about what she should have said to notice that Adele is crying. She only realizes once they're on the road and she hears Adele blow her nose.

"What's wrong?"

"No, nothing, I was just thinking . . ."

"Really, nothing's wrong? What were you thinking, dear?"

"I was thinking about Barbara. Her son up in that room, and we didn't even thank her."

"For what?"

"She hosted our Buraco game, Mirna. She has all these problems, and she hosted us all the same. It's so touching."

"Are you sure there's nothing else, Adele? You're not thinking about that thing, are you?"

"What if I did the wrong thing?"

"Adele, darling, nobody knows you did it, and the cards are so mixed up now that nobody will ever know. You don't have to worry about it, you don't have to worry about Barbara or her son, you don't have to worry about anyone or anything. Think about relaxing, and above all, come to me if you need to talk. It's not healthy to carry all that around in your conscience. Remember how you felt before you told me all those things?"

"But you didn't tell Eugenio, did you? I don't know if I should have told anyone. He said that—"

"Honey, we're friends, remember? Is there anything stronger than friendship?"

"No, Mirna."

Adele should be locked up in a home, that's the problem. By now it's clear that she's losing her mind. She would have been better off with the kind of quick blow that reduced her husband, Marcello, to a human larva. This is the first time they haven't spoken about the game on their journey home. When she gets out of the olive-green Panda four by four and walks up the driveway, Mirna realizes that she's still grinding her teeth. She doesn't know if she's more annoyed by the things Dorina said or by the fact that she was right.

From the window, a flickering light. Eugenio has lit the fireplace.

C1P8 is hidden on the other side of the street. Lilith, before starting its sound tests, has another job to do, and it's important that the drone, equipped with a video camera, patrols the area. Arturo's mother, Mrs. Assuntamaria Novelli, has never dropped her habit of popping in at random intervals with sandwiches and pizzas as if it were a twelve-year-old's birthday party. And there are certain things that Arturo's mother, Mrs. Assuntamaria Novelli of the Novelli Pharmacy, should not see.

"These are really good," Diego says of the images flicking across Arturo's twenty-seven-inch monitor. Diego is holding a long pipe that he puts in his mouth from time to time.

"We've got him," Arturo says. The camcorders had been his idea. Lilith was born from the myth of that forest. It was Viola who introduced the group to all those old stories about the spirits of the people in the country who went into the woods to find themselves, like the characters in *Spoon River*. It had something to do with that boy, Michele, who had taught her to play the guitar and who had given her the Fender she still played. Perhaps she needed to know that her friend was still there in order to feel safe. The whole idea of composing that piece, Lilith's first and last song, was born from the need to tell that story, because for Viola, telling it was the only way to make it last forever. The recordings, Michele's track, it all revolved around that magical place at the heart of the woods.

But then GeoService showed up. It seemed the story would proceed. Suddenly the locals knew that a part of the woods, right near the Crow's Rock, had been sold and would be destroyed so they could build a plant. They needed to rethink their strategy. The threat of the plant required targeted action. And after a quick consultation, the band decided that Lilith would create the Spirits of the Woods to defend it.

Born as the spin-off of the main project, the Spirits would avenge every tree, every bush, every fragment of that place. And since the first move in a battle is to know the enemy's first move, Arturo cooked up a video surveillance system that was connected to a central computer at their center of operations. They would spy on them. They would watch every move they made. And this would allow the Spirits to move safely during their sabotage operations. But those cameras had picked up a lot of things, all around those homes that, like all homes, hide the most inconceivable secrets, providing the Spirits of the Woods with an unexpected weapon.

"Of course we got him," Viola says. "As long as he doesn't go to the carabinieri and send my mother after us."

"You wanted to get him in trouble," says Arturo. "When we decided to do this, we knew we'd have to do dangerous things. Now he has to decide what he wants to do, and the committee will meet in a few days."

"But," says Diego, taking his pipe out of his mouth and caressing his long beard, "I don't really see him running to the cops and disgracing himself on his own accord. This material is great, seriously."

"Thank you, my associate," says Arturo. "But we have another issue."

The drone. The other night, when the Marshal and the other guy arrived at the GeoService cabin and almost caught all three of them, Arturo was the one who had flown it, doing a lot of tough maneuvers through the trees, in the dark, to activate the green laser and distract the cops. The plan went better than he thought it would, in the sense that he had planned to distract the cops long enough for them to get away, but Diego and Viola acted quickly and found the composure to complete the mission. The only problem was that the drone got caught in a tree and lost its connection with the tablet Arturo was using to control it. They couldn't go back and get it that night, as the device no longer emitted a signal, and so they decided to postpone the retrieval to the next morning. Viola had been on her way to get it when she spotted the patrol car and had to change her plans, taking refuge in Giulio's room. Arturo was the only one out of play: no child of the Novelli family, of the famed Novelli Pharmacy, could ever dream of skipping a day of school. That left Diego. But when he went back, the drone wasn't there.

"We have others," says Diego.

"Yeah, we do," Arturo says, "but that's not the problem. The drone has our recordings on it. That's the problem."

"Do you think they could trace it back to us?" Viola asks.

"I don't know how long it would take, but I wouldn't count it out."

"Cops," says Diego, pointing to the monitor.

C1P8 has captured an image from the road. The carabinieri patrol is approaching Lilith's bunker.

"Shit," says Arturo, "this place is packed with stuff they can't see."

"Can we make it disappear?" Diego asks.

"It's not like throwing your weed in the trash. This takes time."

"Try it again with the drone. We'll hide the others with the hard disks in the duffel bag and put it behind the woodpile," says Viola.

Arturo opens the window and places a drone on the windowsill that's identical to the one from the evening before. He takes the tablet and starts to maneuver it, directing it toward the woods. Making sure not to repeat the same mistake, Arturo slips it through the trees, lands it gently, and launches its signal. Green light. The "ignis fatuus," as the carabiniere called it the other night.

On the monitor, the patrol car stops just a few feet from C1P8. Viola sees Donato step out and look into the woods. He's alone.

"He's casing us again," he says.

"Let's hope," says Arturo.

Donato looks toward the woods. He has seen the green light. He's walking toward the trees.

"Get ready," says Arturo. "As soon as he moves, get the stuff out."

Donato is in the woods. Arturo moves the drone back, managing to dodge the trees. He lands it again and launches the signal. The green light. The monitor switches from C1P8 to the drone's view. Donato is walking through the trees. He can't see the shed anymore.

"Go," says Arturo.

Viola and Diego pick up the duffel bag. They open the door.

And they find themselves face-to-face with the Marshal.

"And what does that mean?"

Maglio is thinking aloud. He's accompanied by three other lumberjacks. Their shift just ended, and they've arrived at Bar Fuga for their usual drinks. Chocolate liqueur is the only medicine that can banish the pain that arrives with their fatigue and the cold. But there's a sign taped to the door of the bar. The message, scrawled in pen, says: CLOSED FOR THE HOLIDAYS.

"Donato, you can come back," says Grazia, speaking into her radio. "The Spirits of the Woods are having a rough night."

In the living room the fireplace is lit. Katerina's scent still lingers in the air, even though he had to send her away. Someone is spying on them, and if his wife finds out, they'll be in serious trouble. He needs to wait. Wait to pick the fruit when it's ripe.

Eugenio Falconi takes off his cowboy hat and decides to take a shower while the fire destroys the photographs they left in his mailbox.

Again. The first time it had been a single photo, but this time there were at least a dozen. What if Mirna had made it home first? The envelope had been addressed to him, fine, and usually his wife doesn't open his mail. But what if she had? It would have been a pretty big mess.

In the living room the fire is devouring the evidence. In the air is Katerina's scent, but the fire will devour that too. There's only one thing that the fire can't erase.

Certain things can only end one way. All it takes is a moment. You're focused on your own problems, so absorbed that you don't notice the one small detail slipping by. You pick up a stack of photographs in your hand, you think about what would happen if you hadn't been the one to find them, and while you drink a glass of your favorite scotch to blunt your fears, one of those photos slips away under the coffee table in front of the sofa.

You can't know it, not in the moment. You're sitting by the fire with the taste of your favorite scotch in your mouth. You already feel more relaxed than you did a few minutes ago, now that you are watching the photos turn to ashes. You remind yourself that you're always a step ahead of the rest, and your convictions return, the certainty that everything will go as expected. And you can't know it, but a crack has appeared in your plans. A tiny crack. A crack no one could ever discern, at least not now. But soon. Very soon.

And while you're in the shower, Mirna comes home and walks over to the sofa.

NINE

I'm the white cat. I'm the evil one.

I'm the one who feels certain things before the others. Especially bad intentions. It's amazing how many people have bad intentions. How many people, if they were really free to say whatever they think and do whatever they want, would be ready to hurt someone. Everyone believes that evil people are crazy, people who suddenly lose their sense of reason and stop being normal people. But that's not true. The fact is that humans, with all their clothes and everything else that makes them so different from us, are no better than we are in the end. They also get excited at the thought of blood; they just don't show it. I know these things and I accept them. And then they say I'm evil. A beautiful paradox.

But there are some people I like. There are some, in particular, who give me great satisfaction. There's that guy, for example. The one who's always behind the counter at his bar, drinking like a sponge. Sometimes he's so soft he has to cling to the counter just to stand. I say he's cooking up something interesting.

Today my associate, the black one, made the guy's wife, what's her name, the blonde, get stuck in the snow. He knew that if he ran into the middle of the road she would skid. And so she did. Then he sat off to the side and enjoyed the scene. I was near, but no one noticed me. No one ever notices me.

The blonde is really stupid. When she can't do something, she just keeps doing it in the same way and never realizes she'll just keep making the same mistake. If humans didn't help each other, they'd already be extinct. Someone like the blonde, for example, wouldn't have a prayer. Lucky for her the girl came and got her out of it. I enjoyed watching them. But the really funny thing was that both of them, the girl and the blonde, were being watched by two other people who, unbeknownst to each other, observed the scene from their own positions, just like me and my associate.

The first was the Marshal. She was following her daughter. And I think she kept following her even after the girl left the blonde behind. But I was more interested in the other hidden observer of the scene. The guy from the bar.

He had squeezed in through the trees with one of those sweatshirts that should, as a rule, help him hide in the foliage. Of course, it doesn't have quite the same effect when everything is white, but I don't even think that the guy was completely sober when he planned it. He was using one of those things that they put over their eyes to see farther. Humans don't have good eyesight, poor creatures, and they need those ridiculous things to see. Survival of the fittest gave them a major break, that's the truth.

In short, that guy stayed for the entire scene. When the blonde left, so did he. He has a snowmobile. That's right. He came through the woods on a snowmobile and left on it too, shielded by the trees, to follow the blonde. I followed him without him knowing. And we arrived at the house where the blonde pulled up.

The guy from the bar stayed there, hiding in the trees, with that thing in front of his face, while his wife went in the house. When she came out again and left, he got back on the snowmobile and continued to follow her. But I stayed there. Because I like houses. I like to spy on them from outside and see what the others can't see. Because I can see things. I can hear them. And houses are places where strange things happen. Everything happens behind those closed windows. Some people succeed in showing the worst of themselves only when they're inside. You would think that a den is a safe place, but for humans it isn't necessarily so. If only some walls could talk, they would have stories, so many things to say. And in that house, in particular, by the twitch of my whiskers, something happened. I tried to tell her too, but lately she's been a bit distracted. If someone would just pay attention to me, they would understand that all the seemingly inexplicable things that have happened since old Peter's disappearance didn't happen by chance. But they're all so caught up in themselves they can't even see a hand in front of their own eyes. Then they're so surprised to have understood things too late, so convinced as they always are that they know everything beyond a shadow of a doubt. The more stupid they are, the fewer doubts they have. They think they know what everyone else is doing, but they only know what others want them to know. And everything, for them, ends in tragedy.

Just like the person who was just killed only understood when it was too late.

PART FOUR

THE ESCAPE

"Viola? Viola!"

ONE

A flare of sunlight announces the arrival of dawn. Silence. Everything is still around the Gherarda. But the air is different, spring is near. In the coming weeks the snow will begin to melt, and little by little the grass will return with the flowers, the leaves, and all the colors of the forest. What is left buried under the snow will come to light, and the hawthorne will blossom.

Barbara walks around the hotel. She is holding the damp cloth where she tucked the ashes from the other evening, collected from the oven that had been lit all night for the Evening of Bread. It's an ancient ritual.

The ashes are supposed to surround the houses, and then they must be brought to the heart of the old woods and offered to its inhabitants, who once lived in those same houses and after death found shelter among the trees. This is so that the ashes used for the rite of the bread, from the shared dinner, become earth, and from the earth life springs anew.

She opens her hand and lets the ashes fall. There's no wind. Not even a breeze. Four years have passed since that day. The ashes she held were different then. In the heart of the woods. That day, she had done it for her sister. The ashes had been a body and a soul, dreams and weaknesses, the days they spent together, her childlike hands, the embrace of eternity, the voice she would never hear again. That day, she had dropped the ashes in the heart of the old woods so that what had once been her sister would become earth and life would blossom from it again.

She's been away from the Crow's Rock for too long. She'd like to return, one night, to listen to the moon. But she can't right now. But she can wait for dawn. Walking alongside the snowy meadow and watching the white become illuminated little by little, as the sun invades the sky with its vanity, reflected in the mirror of ice. Welcome back, daylight. He who heals the wounds of darkness.

He could sell everything and leave. Take her away with him. Just for a while, enough time to make up for the hurt she caused and, when the money runs out, end it for both of them.

Gerri hasn't slept a wink. He's sitting in his armchair, next to the window, where he always makes the most important decisions of his life. The trip out East, to meet someone he met on Facebook with a great love for the Italian sun. And even before that, the decision to take over his parents' bar, quitting archery, which didn't offer half the security as a business in town. Maybe the problem with all the bad decisions he's made is just that—the armchair. It's crazy to realize only now that the damned armchair might be to blame for all the mistakes that have brought him to this point, meditating on whether to sell everything and pocket enough to take his wife on a luxury vacation for a few months. With a one-way ticket. It's not a bad plan in theory. But he isn't entirely convinced he should have to die because of that slut.

Gerri gets up and looks out at the sky, which is growing light. He made a whole pot of coffee because even when he was still drunk he had decided that by dawn he'd have decided what to do. But he doesn't know yet. Everything else, however, he knows. He knows who his wife's lover is, and the thought of it is like a hungry dog gnawing at his stomach. Tearing away mouthfuls of his flesh.

Gerri gets up. He stands next to the window. The sun is about to rise. It's the chair that's mistaken, Gerri. It was a bad advisor. Try changing this one habit. Choose a different point of view. Choose a place where it's easier to aim.

He opens the sliding door. Outside it's cold and he's in his pajamas. No matter. He goes out on the balcony and feels his body contract in the frigid morning air. He fills his lungs with a deep breath. From here it all looks different, wouldn't you know. Perspectives change. By now everything is illuminated, the sky, but not just that. And it comes. From behind the woods, in the lower part of the village, the sun escapes the line of trees along the horizon, and the reddish light shines on the roofs of the houses, through the chimneys and the satellite dishes. Along the balconies, through boxes of herbs and flowers, and clothes hung out to dry. Through the church bell tower and, above it, the castle tower. And on the soccer ball abandoned under a canopy in Adaster's yard, where no one has bothered to shovel the snow. There it is, the ball. It's far away, but Gerri can see it. He always had a good eye. And he knows now. He's sure, in this moment. He doesn't have the slightest doubt. He'd be able to nail it.

The tree has taken shape. The shutters don't close well, and sunlight pierces Giulio's room, coming to rest on the drawing he has been working on the whole night. He loves to draw at night, because that's when everything disappears except for him and the gnome. The story begins there, in that tree house with the ladder that goes down to the ground. The owl, the butterflies, the birds.

They spoke for hours before collapsing.

Viola told her about the plan with the Spirits. To defend the forest, the place that holds the memory of those who are gone. It had been years since she had seen Viola so fragile. Since she had seen her daughter in tears as she talked about Michele, the boy who had taught her to play the guitar and who died on Bridge Day.

"Wounds heal, Mom," she said, "but when they're deep they leave a scar." You don't know how right you are, little one.

Viola had never forgotten that boy, but Grazia hadn't realized how attached she'd been. Everything had happened during a time when they'd stopped being friends, so a great deal had been left unsaid between them. Voids. And in the face of the void left by an absence, Grazia knows, people need to cling to something so that they don't fall in. For Viola, that something was the heart of the woods. The Crow's Rock. That place she had known to be wonderful and magical since she was a child. And the real wonderful and magical thing was the way this place had taken root in her daughter, growing into something of such importance. So strong. To hear her story was like getting to know her all over again. But the enchantment was a luxury Grazia could only afford herself for a short time. Because, in addition to listening to her daughter, she had to think fast about how to act. What to do about the report she had to file, the pressure from Scalise to solve the vandalism case, the whole story about the Spirits of the Woods that GeoService wanted to get to the bottom of, along with any sabotage operations against its precious plant. They'll try to come down as hard as possible, those assholes, to discourage copycat resistance. And for Viola and the other two, it will mean serious trouble. And then there's the whole story of the photos and blackmail. The worst part. The good thing is that if it all goes that way, without any other hitches, that pig may not file a complaint to avoid outing himself.

Her job, her daughter. If she had to choose which side to take, the choice was already made. She knows it. That's why Scalise doesn't like women. All those boys who abandoned the station after she was appointed had been right. Friguglia had been right to get sick, because it makes no sense to have a commander who, when choosing between her role as commander and her role as mother, will always choose the latter.

Viola is asleep next to her. It has been years since they have slept like this, together, in the "big bed," as Viola had called it as a child. A big bed that was always half-empty because the Marshal and mother never left any space for the woman. And God only knows how much the woman wanted to be part of that life.

Grazia turns on her side. Toward Viola. Her breath is heavy. She's sleeping in the kind of deep sleep that she'll soon grow out of. Grazia passes her hand over Viola's hair, above her pierced ear, where it's only a few millimeters long. When did her little girl get so big? She knows every inch of that body. She finds the cut on the nape of her neck that she got when she was eight and fell off her bike. And she wondered when she got so distracted. It's as if she turned away for an instant and someone snatched away those ten years that she had hoped to spend with her.

Outside it's suddenly dawn. Her shift starts soon. Donato knows everything. It was only fair to tell him how things went. He listened, he understood. He already told her that he's fine with any way she chooses to resolve it.

"I get this feeling that command has abandoned us here, chief," he said. "At this point, we might as well do what we want."

Donato isn't someone who's inclined to think this way. Grazia knows it, and it makes her feel even more in his debt. If the Spirits of the Woods disappear, people will soon stop looking for them. She has to think about this, first of all. She has to convince Viola to understand that it's not worth it to get in trouble just to protect Michele's memory. But in the end, after all is said and done, perhaps not even Grazia, Marshal and mother, is totally convinced about that. Because if Michele's memory isn't worth fighting for, what is?

Barbara is back. She's taken off her jacket, settled into her heavy wool shawl, and prepared herself a cup of herbal tea. She's sitting at the table in the barroom. The sound of the pipes, that roar again. Akan must be up, taking another shower. He's constantly washing himself, at least three showers a day.

On the table in front of her is her phone. The conversation that just ended went as badly as she could have imagined.

TWO

Katerina leaves the house early. Gerri has been acting strange for a few days, and she doesn't even want to know why. He's probably drunk as usual. There are people who keel over because they drink too much, and maybe he'll be one of them. A nice heart attack and a big "fuck you." Today, however, is her day of pampering, and she has to relax; otherwise, her regenerative massage and exfoliating treatment won't reach their fullest potential.

She walks quickly to the parking lot where she left the Giulietta. The thermal spa where she booked her appointments is twenty kilometers away, enough time to listen to some music, sing as she drives, and not think about anything else. These are the last days she'll spend in this shithole before she waltzes off into the Antilles sun over Sosúa Bay.

> *Yo quiero que este*
> *Sea el mundo que conteste*
> *Del este hasta oeste*
> *Y bajo el mismo sol*

Álvaro Soler's voice emanates from the Prada crocodile bag on her arm. She checks her iPhone display. She had hoped for Sara, the code name for her little puppy. Instead, it's that odious pig again. She swipes the display to respond.

"What now?"

"Try not to get too excited. Your husband is acting strange, I don't want him to catch on."

"But who—what? He drinks. It's clear."

"Gerri's been drinking since he discovered he had a mouth. In my opinion it's something else. Looks like he's trying to get us in trouble. We have to keep our heads on straight, because if not, it'll all go to hell and we'll be in deep shit."

"Yes, I understand. But what can I do about my husband being a good-for-nothing?"

"You'll figure it out, but try to make him behave."

"What a pain in the ass! I can't today, I have stuff to do."

"Then I haven't been clear. Yesterday afternoon the bar was closed."

"What do you mean, closed?"

"Where was he?"

"How the hell should I know? But why is it suddenly so important what that asshole is doing?"

"It'll all be over in a few days, Katerina. But if it doesn't end as I say . . . well, you get the idea, don't you?"

Katerina ends the call and buries her phone in her purse.

"Fuck you too," she says, and strides off toward the car. After a few steps, she stops. She stamps her feet. The massage, the treatment, the hot water. "Goddammit, what a pain in the ass," she says, turning back.

Maglio slips his phone into his coat pocket and observes Katerina from the window of the Fioralba minimart. He had seen her walk by while they were making his sandwiches and knew she was on her way to take care of business.

They need to keep her husband under control, because he is acting strange. There's that story about the photo someone sent to Falconi that they still have to figure out. Gerri doesn't seem like the type, but if he finds out his wife is sleeping with Falconi, he could go ballistic and jeopardize the whole thing. And he couldn't afford to let that happen. Not now that he was in so deep.

"You'll never believe this," Dorina says as she bursts into the Gherarda barroom. She takes off her coat and hangs it up on its usual spot, then plops down at Barbara's table. Those words usually precede what Dorina considers to be breaking news.

"What?" asks Barbara, who is still sitting with her phone out, her ears filled with the echo of what Giulio's attorney has just told her.

"Mirna didn't even show her face at the Misericordia market. Adele said she went to her beach house for a long weekend. She said she ran into Eugenio and he told her so. Can you imagine? Going to the beach on the same day as the Misericordia market? If you ask me, being the president of the committee drove her to the brink, and now what does she go and do on the most important day of the year? She runs off to the beach for a long weekend, that's what. Are you listening to me? What—"

"Colletti called, Giulio's attorney."

"Did something happen?"

"One of his friends from the prosecutor's office called just before six. Apparently, after the interrogation, Lorenzon became convinced that Giulio should go back to prison. She says he's dangerous and that if he really did what they say he did, he could do it again. Colletti thinks she's wrong, but he thinks the judge will side with her."

"When will we find out?"

"I'm waiting for the phone call."

"I'm sorry, Barbara. Sometimes I forget about the hell you're going through."

"Don't worry, sometimes I need to forget about it too."

"Love?" Gerri is getting dressed when he hears the door open along with Katerina's voice. "Love, where are you?" What on earth is she up to? Why did she come back? "Love, are you home? There you are. I was thinking about something. Why don't you take the morning off from that pack of drunks and come to the spa with me?" What kind of game is she playing?

THREE

David Bowie's face on the cover of *Space Oddity* disappears and is replaced by Tom Waits on the cover of *Blood Money*.

The laptop's screen saver is set to randomly reproduce album covers from the iTunes library. Two windows remain open behind the screen saver: the PDF with Professor Giampedretti's report and Skype, with the phone call he's just managed to make, using Viola's Wi-Fi adapter and his account, which still has some credit left.

And while Tom Waits stares him down, showing him the hand of cards that he's about to play, he thinks about how Patrizia never would have been able to reopen the investigation with her hand—that report.

He had to stay up all night drawing to get his thoughts off the report and try to sleep. Then the good news came, this morning, about his likely return to prison. And so he went straight back to work, because if he could find something to hand off to Colletti, he would feel more relaxed, even in the face of the less than appealing prospect of seeing the world from behind bars. And the only thing he was able to cling to was the slim chance that the attack on Patrizia and her disappearance—what, according to the investigators, couldn't be anything other than a homicide—are in some way linked to attorney Alberti's decision to reopen the investigation into Bridge Day.

But by the same admission of its author, the report in question wouldn't have led to the desired outcome. Not counting the final coup de grâce that Patrizia's hydrogeological luminary shared with her.

The new element the geologist referred to in the report was, in fact, something entirely different. That is, the presence of a small aquifer never seen before just inside the old woods. Full of water and everything.

To better understand the scope of the thing, Giulio got on Skype and called the number in the margin of the report. This led him to Professor Giampedretti's office in Milan, and he presented himself as a friend and colleague of Patrizia Alberti.

"Of course, attorney Alberti, how is she?"

I guess it's possible somebody on the planet still hasn't heard the story, Giulio thought.

"I haven't heard from her in a few days," he replied.

He immediately asked the professor about the report, and why he had insisted that the finding of the aquifer was so important.

"You see, attorney, the issue with these underground deposits is that their mapping is usually entrusted to the municipalities," he explained. "But the municipalities, who can't even afford to cry with their own eyes anymore, don't do it. One solution could be to form consortia to hire geologists, splitting the expenses, to map a more vast area. Of course, it would take some time, but believe me: there's no other way to find out where the aquifers are and take the necessary steps to protect them. We drink without thinking about the water that leaves the tap, you know? We take it for granted, but we shouldn't. We're made of water, did you know that?" Giulio couldn't help but think of the fact that water had pulled down that bridge and taken the lives of seven people on it. But an alarm bell, inside him, was starting to sound. "They used to think the human body was between seventy and ninety percent water. But according to recent studies by Gerald Pollack, a professor of bioengineering at the University of Washington, the real water content could be up to ninety-nine percent. In practice, we are made almost exclusively of water. This is because water is the number one chemical constituent of muscle tissue. And this implies that to understand the diseases and functioning of the human body, we have to study the components of water. So the next time you stick a glass under the tap, think about how you, your life, your body, are all made up of that water. Looking at it that way, don't you think it's important to know where it comes from? But tell me, why didn't your colleague call me? She seemed so interested in this case."

"Well, Professor, the point is exactly that. Why do you suppose she was so interested in this thing?"

"I can only venture a guess."

"Please."

"But I should point out that this is a very personal theory."

"I see. And what's that?"

"Attorney Alberti is a Pisces."

"A what?"

"Her zodiac sign. Do you believe in astrology, attorney?"

"Astrology?"

"The position of Earth in relation to its axis influences water. Think about the tides. Their relationship with the lunar phases. And we're made of water, remember?"

This stuff about the lunar phases is what Giulio remembers with greater clarity, now that he is staring at Professor Giampedretti's report. Patrizia was a Pisces, the explanation for everything. How obvious. He can hear the gnome chuckling. He can only imagine what kind of effect this information would have on deputy prosecutor Annalaura Lorenzon: "You see, ma'am, we can't overlook the fact that Patrizia Alberti, the woman you accuse me of murdering, was a Pisces." He wants to be the one to tell her just so he can see her face. Maybe the incompatibility of their signs could help his case. Or the tides, lunar phases. How his aunt Amanda would have been able to contribute to his defense.

It's over. This is all Giulio can think. It's game over with this astrology nonsense. To keep looking for a way out at this point would be like taunting himself. His memories, if they ever return, will wait until after the judge's ruling. And then maybe he can appeal.

Akan had promised to make him mushroom and chestnut soup. His last meal before jail. Now he has to find the courage to face the future with dignity. Because it's important, dignity.

Tom Waits disappears and is replaced by Paul Simonon, playing his bass on the Palladium stage in New York on the cover of *London Calling*, by the Clash.

FOUR

Talking with Arturo's parents was painful. The Novelli family, of the Novelli Pharmacy, quickly tried to bury the case "for the good of the kids," and Marshal Grazia Parodi has never taken well to that kind of request. Some people believe they're above the law, and it's a great pleasure to remind them that they're not. This time, however, she had to nod along, because one of the three kids was her daughter. The Novellis land on their feet again.

"First of all, I need to understand how things went," she had told the Novellis the night before, delivering Arturo under a sort of unofficial house arrest.

With Diego's parents, it had been less humiliating. His mother had taken a few sick days and would stay home with him until they decided how to proceed.

The problem is Viola. And remembering it in these terms doesn't help soothe her veiled sense of guilt that is absolutely unfair but also inevitable. The dirty dishes in the sink, the house that's an explosion of clothes and shoes, her daughter who is in trouble up to her neck with no place to go.

And so Grazia took her to the Gherarda, where she just discovered that Rodari would likely be sent back to prison, that they would come get him that day, meaning she might have to confront a certain Scalise, who will be anxious for an update on the vandalism case attributed to the so-called Spirits of the Woods.

"I'm sorry, Barbara," Grazia tells her.

"The truth will come out," says the Gherarda's owner.

"If it's too much trouble for you to take Viola, I can figure out something else. I don't want her to be alone right now—I'll fill you in later."

"It's no problem at all."

As she walks back to the patrol car, Grazia feels someone watching her. Just before she gets in the car, she stops and turns. Giulio is standing in the window. He had opened the blinds and was staring right at her. He waves. He knows they're coming to get him and that he'll be leaving soon. Back to jail. His stay at the Gherarda lasted just long enough for his interrogation, where the deputy prosecutor got what she wanted, and for them to smoke that cigarette together, reminiscing about better days.

Grazia waves back. One of those cheerless, tight-lipped smiles that people use when times are bad.

Giulio hunches over, crosses his eyes, and peels back his lips, baring his teeth. And he says something. Grazia can't hear him, but she can read his lips.

Degenerates!

FIVE

No massage. No exfoliating treatment. No thermal spa. No oligomineral water that smells of sulfur. No bill to pay by flaunting her exclusive credit card.

Katerina's eyes are wide with anger. Next to her, Gerri sleeps. And he's snoring. He didn't feel like going to the spa. He had that strange look in his eyes. He approached her without taking his eyes off her. Excited as a sixteen-year-old boy. He stripped her. One garment at a time, slowly, without saying a word. First her jacket, then her sweater, her shirt, her boots, her jeans, her socks, her bra, her panties. And then he just looked at her, not uttering a single word. And she almost didn't mind. It was strange. He touched her naked body as if he were seeing it for the first time. Katerina thought that alcohol had fried his brain. Then he suddenly grasped her. An almost violent gesture. But not like back when they pretended to hurt each other. This time he was serious. He slammed her facedown on the bed. And he kept staring at her. She tried to flip over, but he stopped her. Katerina heard the sound of his belt loosening. She waited to feel him inside of her. But nothing. She tried to flip over again, but he stopped her. And then she understood, as soon as she heard his breath growing heavy. And finally the hot jet of fluid on her back. She lay there, trying to figure out what was going on in his mind, as he went to the bathroom to wash up. When he came back, he was only wearing a shirt. He lay down beside her on the bed. His eyes were bloodshot. Katerina understood that Maglio had been right: Gerri is out of his mind and needs to be controlled. So she took off his shirt, gently, and kissed him on his chest. She let her hot tongue glide over his neck. His ear. His lips. She helped him with her caresses and guided him between her legs, lying back for him. Slowly, almost sweetly.

But when Gerri fell asleep, she started thinking about the spa again. The smell of massage oil, dead cells rubbed away to make room for new ones, everyone sucking up to her because they know she knows no limits with her credit card.

She gets up and looks for her shirt, and as she slips it on, she grabs her phone and goes into the bathroom. She sits on the toilet and opens WhatsApp as she pees.

He really is acting strange. Do you think he knows?

A gray check mark.
Two gray check marks.
A few minutes pass.
Two blue check marks.
A speech bubble.

I don't know. Keep an eye on him.

I don't want to stay home

Don't you fucking leave that house

Asshole

Whore

Don't call me a whore

Stop it and concentrate on Gerri, don't blow it now

I said don't call me a whore

Fine, but you need to calm down

She gets up, flushes the toilet, and returns to the bedroom to find her panties. Gerri is sleeping. And snoring. She can't stand it when he snores. She goes to the kitchen and opens the fridge. There's still some salmon left. "I can't stay here all day," she mutters, looking for a butter knife.

> *Yo quiero que este*
> *Sea el mundo que conteste*
> *Del este hasta oeste*
> *Y bajo el mismo sol*

Álvaro Soler is going to wake up Gerri. Katerina pounces on her iPhone.
It's Sara.

Grazia arrives at the station. She gets out of the patrol car and opens the trunk, where she placed the duffel bag that the Spirits of the Woods were trying to hide. Hard drives and memory cards containing hours of video recordings made by the drones. Better check everything before formatting. Better understand what's behind the blackmail story. She grabs the duffel bag and enters the station.

As soon as she opens the door, she hears, in this order, the squeaking of the bed, the clasping of a belt, and boots being pulled on, one by one.

Donato bolts out of the room where the cot is, his hair disheveled and his eyes puffy.

"You can sleep," says Grazia. "One of us will have to sooner or later."

191

"Any news?"

"The list is too long. I'll give you a quick rundown of the main things. I need you at the Gherarda. I think Scalise will be there soon—they're revoking Giulio's house arrest—but they won't warn us, and they'll arrive out of nowhere. So we have to be ready. Viola's there too. I saw Diego Chessa, and if nothing else, I think I figured out who's selling weed to my daughter. The good news is the genius doesn't have anything to do with Solfrizzi. Meanwhile, I have to go through these hard drives, because like I said, the Spirits of the Woods were also spies and blackmailers, as well as vandals. I just hope I don't get you in trouble, because you're the only one I know at this point who doesn't deserve it. I wanted to tell you that after this case, I'm resigning, so the sooner you know, the better. If you want my advice, I'd say put in for a transfer."

Without waiting for answers, Grazia enters the room with the cot where they've set up a laptop for investigation activities. And she connects the hard drive, hoping to find no other surprises.

Seven lives swallowed in the collapse of the bridge. Giulio is stretched out on his bed. He no longer wants to do anything else. He took his mother's envelope and reread all the old articles. The headlines. The photos. More or less all of them were taken from Facebook. People's obsession with putting all their photos online was a manna from heaven for newspapers who wanted to find photographs of the dead to publish. The only blurry photo is old Peter's. He didn't have a Facebook profile. He appears in an old shot that someone must have taken of him in the woods, crouching behind his belongings.

The roar of the pipes. Giulio looks around. Akan has to do something about this noise; it's enough to drive any normal person up a wall. It's just strange that it doesn't happen every time. There must be a hydraulic problem somewhere.

Water.

The photo of old Peter.

It's just a hunch. The next dead end.

But what if it isn't?

Giulio looks for Peter's picture. He rummages through his mother's clippings. There's a photo of his aunt, Amanda. Photos of all the others. Finally he finds the article about Peter. It's a sidebar, the kind at the bottom of the page, because officially his disappearance was not related to the collapse of the bridge and the river flooding, even though he disappeared more or less around the same time. Four years ago. He finds the photo of Peter. He's holding those strange sticks he used to walk around the woods with. He was a water diviner.

He was looking for water.

"A water diviner looking for water underground," says Giulio.

"And what if he'd found it?" Giulio asks the gnome.

The laptop. Space bar. Giampedretti's report. The aquifer. Skype.

"Professor, it's Patrizia's colleague again."

"Hi. How can I help you?"

"I absolutely must ask another question."

"I'm all ears."

"Can they grant permission to build a waste treatment plant over an aquifer?"

"Of course not. That would be crazy. There's a huge risk of percolation, not to mention any other kind of infiltration would jeopardize not only the aquifer but its whole network. Why do you ask? Hello? Can you hear me? There must be a problem with the line . . . hello?"

Giampedretti's voice resounds in the room, but Giulio isn't there. The door is open.

Technically, he's a fugitive.

SIX

The alarm clock has Mickey Mouse's smiling face on it. Gerri has a habit of sleeping on his right side, in the fetal position, and the first thing he sees when he opens his eyes, since he was too small to even have memories, is Mickey Mouse's smiling face. It was this way in the home where he spent his early years, a farm where his parents lived with his mother's parents for a time. And it was this way in his second home, an apartment in town, with a television and colorful plastic furniture that looked like the future. The alarm stayed through his adolescence, when he'd close himself in his bedroom with some porn procured by his most enterprising friends, the ones who had the nerve to go to the newsstand and buy it. It was what he saw during his archery years, when he woke up at dawn on Sunday to claim his trophies. And it remained that way even after, when he dropped his bow, his arrows, his desire for change, and his dreams in favor of an indefinite sentence behind the counter at Bar Fuga, a mortgage for the apartment with a garage and an attic, a daylong drive, and a date with the gorgeous woman who was supposed to brighten the life that was already becoming identical to his father's. And even though Mickey's smile never changed over the years, it's as if something in that smile had changed its tone. As if it had a different meaning. What used to be a "good morning" smile lately seems to be one of mockery. Mickey's face is becoming derisive, increasingly difficult to bear. That cursed rat in clothing continues to smile, even though there's no longer any reason to. Because Gerri's life has collapsed into a shithole that he's been able to smell for years, a smell he chose to ignore. Day after day, behind the counter of that bar, while his wife became more and more demanding and distant, while the mortgage rate for the house mounted with the loan for the car, and the payments for the television that filled up half the wall, and the stationary bike, and the hydromassage, and the clothes, and the shoes, and the spa treatments, and the hair treatments, and the manicures, and the hot springs. It all funneled into a bank account belonging to someone who couldn't afford the lifestyle but who couldn't say no to his beautiful wife, because it would be like surrendering to the fact that she made his life no brighter. And while he's sinking in his own shithole, she's off with someone else.

The image in his mind is always the same. It's as if a light suddenly comes on among the trees and she appears, Katerina. Her long hair floats in the air. Her white flesh, her naked body, covered only along the sides by a myrtle bush. Her red lips. Her round breasts and pert nipples in the cold air. And now Falconi appears. His body is strangely young and muscular. He sniffs at the air like a beast and moves toward her.

Gerri gets up. He knows how the story ends.

He goes to the bathroom. He turns on the tap to rinse away the image. But to let the water flow, to let the water rise, to let the river swell—it's dangerous.

Maybe that's what happened with the bridge. Maybe that's why his mother is gone, why his father went back to Sicily, and why he tried to save himself by marrying a beautiful woman he didn't know anything about. He says it all without speaking, looking into the mirror as the water flows into the sink. That's how it all happened. A day comes when you can't turn back. And you recognize that day because everything around you gets distant, meaningless, irrelevant. You no longer care about your damned mouse in the alarm clock that laughs at you every time you open your eyes. When that day comes, there's only one thing to do. That's why there's no turning back.

Because once you do that, there's nothing to turn back to.

SEVEN

Barbara has gathered everyone at the table in the bar. Viola, Akan, and Donato. A community cobbled together by a combination of emergencies, loneliness, and mistakes. Dorina had also been there until recently, but she left after Viola arrived, saying she'd be back in the afternoon. Barbara told her not to worry about it, but her Buraco companion had taken out her hearing aid and couldn't hear a thing.

The hostess took out a pie with cream, pine nuts, and hazelnuts and set the table with small plates, coffee cups, spoons, and napkins. There is no better way to spend time together than eating at a shared table. People today seem to have forgotten this, and sometimes it's good to have someone around who can remind them. Plus there was no other way to keep them all happy at once.

"You're a great cook," says Donato, checking that he hasn't stained his uniform.

Even the orange cat is thankful, sitting on his windowsill just above the radiator.

"I need a phone." Everyone turns to the new person who has just spoken. Giulio. "And Grazia's number."

"Excuse me, Rodari," Donato says, "but you can't use the phone. Actually, you can't even leave the part of the structure designated for—"

"They killed her because she discovered an aquifer." There's a clock on the wall, battery operated. Never has there been a moment in this bar when it has been silent enough to hear the mechanism that moves the hands. "That German, Peter, was a water diviner, wasn't he? They probably got him too."

"What are you talking about?" says Donato.

"I have to call Grazia before they bring me in. We have to talk to the mayor, tell him that GeoService is behind this. They could be dangerous— they could be mafia. It's happened around here before. Do you remember when those guys wanted to buy the Francini vineyard and he refused, and the next day all of his vines had been cut with lasers? Maybe it's the same people. I have to talk to Grazia and Falconi."

"You have to calm down, first of all," Donato repeated.

"Skype the station," Viola says.

"What? Skype? What are you talking about?" says Donato.

"Giulio, start from the beginning," says Barbara.

"Rodari, go back to your room," says Donato, "or I'll be forced to intervene."

"Mom has automatic forwarding to her cell phone," says Viola.

Giulio snaps his fingers and sprints up the stairs.

Barbara still doesn't understand what's going on, but there's something to that story about the aquifer. Something too small to know if it's anything, but that has been imprinted in her mind nonetheless. Peter. The German told her one day he was convinced of it. He had heard about it from some old man, and he was trying to find it. But what does Patrizia have to do with it?

"Excuse me, but I have to go put an end to this," says Donato.

It happens in a flash. Just as he gets up, the orange cat leaps into the center of the table, knocking over cups, cakes, creams, and, oh, how it spins everywhere like a washing machine. And before he leaps away, leaving the devastation behind him, he tips over two cups of boiling coffee onto the trousers of the carabiniere, who instantly begins to shout and scream, as he tries to save his balls from near certain incineration, stripping down to his underwear in front of everyone.

"Shit!" he shouts. "It's burning!"

"You need to get some ice on that right away," says Akan.

"What on earth was that?" Barbara asks the cat, who has paused in a corner to enjoy the scene, licking at a paw.

"Hi, Grazia? It's me, Giulio—"

"Giulio?"

"Don't ask questions and listen, I think I know what happened to Patrizia. We have to go to Falconi and make him tell us how to contact GeoService and who these people are, because they might be behind Patrizia's disappearance."

"But what are you talking about? And why? How did you get a phone?"

"I told you, no questions. We have to—"

"Look, Giulio, I assure you my day's already going shitty enough. Hang up the phone immediately and hand it over to Donato."

"You don't understand. They're coming to get me today and—"

"And if they find you with a phone in your hand, it'll be an even bigger mess for me to clean up, which is the last thing I need."

"At least give me Falconi's number. It's not online, and I have to call him."

"Online? Do you have to call him? Giulio, you can't be online or use the phone. Where is Donato? I'm hanging up now, and I'm calling him right away. Let's put an end to this story once and for all, please."

She actually hangs up.

Now what?

Akan has gone to get ice. Barbara is helping Donato take off his uniform jacket. The officer has dropped his underpants and is covering his still-sore groin with a towel as he stands in the bathroom door. In the confusion, only Viola hears the phone ring.

"Mom," she says, answering.

"Viola? Why are you answering?"

"Because Donato can't answer right now."

"Why is that?"

"A cat spilled some boiling coffee on him—you know where."

"What on earth is going on? Pass me to Donato, please."

Donato has to unfold the towel to put more ice inside, and Barbara looks away. And that's when her eyes widen.

"What the . . . ?" she says.

Viola turns in the direction Barbara is looking. Through the window she sees Giulio out on the terrace, looking down. Giulio seems to be assessing the height. Down below there's a snowdrift.

"Nothing's going on, Mom," Viola says into the phone. "But you should talk to your friend. Rodari. I think he has something important to tell you."

"Put it there," says Akan, passing Donato the bag of ice.

"Viola, when exactly did you speak with Rodari?" Grazia asks. "Because it suddenly seems to me that Rodari is talking to a whole lot of people."

Giulio launches himself off the terrace. Onto the snowdrift. Barbara and Viola are agape. The snow, in fact, is almost iced over, and Giulio takes a hard hit before rolling to the ground.

"Oh shit," says Viola.

"What was that?" says Grazia.

"No, nothing, just that . . ."

Viola and Barbara look at each other. Barbara is about to leave the carabiniere, but Giulio gets up. He looks stunned. He touches his back. He bends over and takes a deep breath. Barbara also takes a breath.

"Now what's his plan?" she asks, thinking aloud.

"I have no idea," says Viola.

"What?" says Grazia, still on the phone. "Look, Viola, can you pass me to Donato, please, so we can put an end to this before it goes too far?"

Giulio enters the garage.

"Fine, here he is. Just one sec, he's icing his balls."

Viola is about to get up but sees Barbara's eyes widen again to the point where they might fall out of her head. She turns to the window to figure out what's going on. Amanda's old Ford emerges from the garage, in reverse, finally drifting across the road.

"I don't know what he's trying to do," Barbara says, "but he won't make it if it involves getting behind the wheel."

"He can't drive?" Viola asks.

"Who?" asks Grazia. "Who can't drive? Who are you talking about?"

"No, he can't drive," says Barbara.

"Maybe you could go out and sit in the snow," Akan tells the officer, who has his eyes closed in an expression of bliss.

"Viola? Viola!" Grazia's voice comes through the phone that her daughter abandoned on the table before slipping on her jacket and leaving. "Viola, if you're up to trouble, I swear to God I'll make you pay for it with interest! Do you hear me? Viola? Viola!"

Her mother continues to call her while Barbara watches Amanda's old Ford whiz past the window.

PART FIVE
THE HUNT

"But there's blood everywhere."

ONE

The patrol car pulls away. The carabinieri had come to GeoService's office for surveillance after they got a report of vandalism. There's the fox head that the younger carabiniere, the driver, had lingered to inspect. As the car drives away, Falconi and Maglio remain.

"Go ahead," Magliarini says to the lumberjack who has just seen what happened at the cabin and called everyone. "I'll catch up with you in five minutes, I have to talk to the mayor for a minute."

The lumberjack walks away, whistling.

"Maybe we shouldn't have called the cops," Falconi says. "We shouldn't have too much traffic in this area."

"The boy found it. He came to do maintenance. What could I do?"

They look around. Then their gaze ends at the same point. Among the trees. "Do you feel guilty?" Falconi asks.

"I thought I'd feel worse."

"There was no other way. If we want to go all the way, we have to pay the price, you know."

"You don't need to convince me. I just want to get out of here." They both look toward that point in the trees as if they can't help themselves. "Sometimes I think of Teresa. I don't know. If she were still around, all this . . . I mean, I don't know if I would have done it. But the best part of me died that day. That's why I don't feel as guilty as I should. Because the part of me that should have felt guilty died that day the bridge came down."

Falconi looks away from the woods and turns to him. "We've come this far, we have to finish it."

"I know, you don't have to keep telling me that." Maglio turns to look at him, his eyes dark, deep.

"There's another problem," Falconi says.

"What's that?"

"I got a photo the other day."

"A photo?"

"Of Katerina and me. If Mirna had found it, I would've had a mess on my hands."

"Do you know who could have . . . ?"

"No, but keep your eye out, okay?"

They say goodbye. Maglio catches up with the lumberjack, who is waiting for him in the Magliarini Forestry Services pickup truck. Falconi returns to his car. He turns on his engine and takes the road that leads back home.

TWO

One of the worst Buraco days of all time. There's no doubt about it. Adele has forgotten how to play, no doubt about that either. And she's still burning up over Dorina's play.

Mirna has just gotten out of Adele's olive-green Panda four by four. She can see the flicker of the fireplace through the living room window. Maybe this is the night of the big announcement. Adele had said something about a job Eugenio is working on. She told her she couldn't say anything about it, but something did manage to escape her. It had to do with that land of Marcello's that Adele sold to those gentlemen through Eugenio. She doesn't know how, but Marcello managed to sign off on it.

Eugenio was the kind of husband who knew how to provide for his wife. A beautiful house, a seaside apartment, two grown daughters who have made their own way in the world. Eugenio traveled with her all around the world, on organized trips, cruises, all documented with stacks of photos that she sometimes pulls out when her friends drop in for tea. Eugenio is a respected man, and everyone turns to him when they need help. He will always be a central figure in this community, as he always has been. And she wanted to take on the corresponding role of First Lady, but Barbara Tantulli was always in her way, contradicting her husband at every turn, taking the attention away from her. But victory as Misericordia president is only her first step toward redemption.

And soon Eugenio will tell her everything. She could have made Adele spit it all out, but if she had, Adele would have eventually told Eugenio, ruining his surprise. We are in the game, then. He must be hiding something big. And this time she will send a nice postcard to her dear old friend Barbara. *Barbara, darling, I'm sending you some postcards to hang in that sad hotel of yours.*

Mirna goes inside. She takes off her coat. A fire is burning in the fireplace, but Eugenio isn't there. She can hear the sound of the shower. It feels good to be home. Mirna loves her cozy living room. She's back just in time to relax for a while before she makes dinner. She takes off her shoes and sits on the couch. She massages her feet through her stockings.

On the glass coffee table, in front of the fire, there is a glass and Eugenio's bottle of scotch. He'd had a drop. He deserves it, he works so hard. Who knows where he thought of taking her this time, what he's been working on. Maybe South America, where it's hot now. Or to some little island in the Pacific, the kind where they put a beautiful flower garland on your neck and serve you a fruit cocktail with a straw, where they play music on the beach and you can dance barefoot in the torchlight with the sound of the surf lapping at the shore. Let's just hope he didn't book it at too short notice, because Eugenio sometimes doesn't realize that it takes time to pack if you don't want to risk forgetting something essential. First, you prepare a nice list of things to bring and then you check them off as you place them in the suitcase. Nothing can ruin a vacation like forgetting something important and finding yourself, for example, without a hair straightener on a Pacific island where you certainly can't buy another one, which, in any case, could never match your own. She just needed to know where they were going so she could start preparing, and she could even pretend she didn't know anything yet, but at least she could start on her mental list.

Mirna relaxes on the sofa and thinks about the Pacific. She'll have a lot of postcards to send. Do they have postcards in the Pacific? She should probably find out so she can at least pick up a few at the airport, because she can't very well waltz off to the middle of the Pacific without even sending a postcard. It would be as if she hadn't gone at all.

There's something under the table. A leaflet. Hmm, maybe it's a brochure. No, it's a photo.

The combination of hot water and scotch works wonders. Eugenio lingers in the shower, letting the jet massage his neck. It's the place where he stores all his tension. He's had too much on his plate for a while now. Everything on his shoulders, as usual. They would not be able to dig a spider out of a hole without him. But he pays for it, in terms of stress and tension. He's entitled to a little extra, that's right. Extra helpings for his extra work. And then he'll be gone, off to start his new life in the Antilles. Far away from everyone. Away from his bloodsucking daughters and their respective husbands, a pair of bankrupts who pound on the door every Christmas. If it's not the renovation of their house, it's a car. And they don't even have kids yet. Enough, the ATM is closed. He has given so much to others, now it's time for him to take a little something for himself. And Katerina is all he wants. He could do anything for that body moving over him. For those lips that know how to do things that are downright otherworldly. And look at the effect they have from afar: without even a caress, the flag is up.

He turns off the water, opens the shower door, and puts on his bathrobe, white and fragrant.

Katerina the sex goddess. To have her there, beside him, from morning to evening on a wonderful beach. Far away from this cold, dark place. From this dreary life. From Mirna, who is getting old. Of course he's not, he feels younger. He wants to dance. And he wants to fuck, more than anything else. He looks at himself in the mirror. He's not so old, in fact. When he gets a tan he can grow a nice white beard and look like Paul Newman in that movie, *The Life and Times of Judge Roy Bean*, with Ava Gardner, who Mirna resembled when she had been young. And now he plans to stretch out on the sofa in his bathrobe, in front of the fire, with another glass of the good stuff.

He dries his hair under his cap and goes into the living room.

Gerri arrives at the hut. He calls it that, but in fact it's a solid structure, with all due heating, insulation, reprieve, and habitability. Once, it had been a real hunting lodge, but now it's a magical hideaway that only he can enter. It's where he keeps his snowmobile. And not only that.

He is wearing his insulated camouflage. It's a cold evening.

Katerina has just left Falconi's place.

Gerri turns on the light and looks around. All of his treasures. Including a wooden box containing a magnum of Dom Pérignon that he's been saving for a worthy occasion. Until recently, he thought he'd pop it open to celebrate some news, like becoming a father. But Katerina had changed her mind about that just after the wedding. And then the bottle stayed there, waiting for another great opportunity. Next to that wooden box there is a case that contains one of his other great treasures.

A leather case.

He takes it. A few words are embroidered on the lid. He passes his fingers over it to wipe the dust away. He pauses to read the words, then pulls at the zipper and sits down on the snowmobile to enjoy the spectacle he pulls out.

A black DymondWood riser. The spine is a light maple, coated on both sides with high-resistance black fiberglass. Handmade white and black fiberglass tips.

His bow. A masterpiece, with his name engraved at the top.

He grips the handle. He stands upright. A wonderful feeling returns to him. He imagines the arrow.

He imagines the shot.

We'll figure it out tomorrow. Falconi repeats it like a mantra. But what a pity about the evening, which had begun under such different auspices. He was supposed to see Katerina, but instead . . . first the photos screwed up his plans, then Mirna. As soon as he walked into the living room, he spotted her big gray head over the back of the sofa. She was just sitting there, motionless, staring into the fire. It was a habit of hers—one that would annoy a saint. Silent, with a pissed-off expression on her face, waiting for you to guess why she's silent with a pissed-off face. Always with an attitude of judgment, condemnation, the belief that she's always right. The attitude of an old ballbuster who makes everything look older than it is. It makes you wonder what you did wrong, if you finished off her cranberry juice she insists on drinking before she goes to sleep, if you forgot to put out a new roll of toilet paper, if you moved some object because after using it you simply put it down without thinking about its proper place in the world, if you forgot a date or some other circumstance or commitment, or if you've been caught with some shortcoming that a normal person wouldn't even notice. But Mirna notices. She doesn't always tell you, but she has her ways of letting you know. In that suffocating world where everything has its place—nice Eugenio's is in a golden doghouse with a good-night boner. But the old Falcon got stubborn and decided to resume flying.

So Eugenio walked to the other side of the sofa to see what kind of storm was awaiting him. And then he saw the photo. It was resting on Mirna's lap. A beautiful display. That goddamned photo just had to fall from the stack before he threw the rest into the fire. So the situation proceeded quickly. But there is a solution for everything, Mr. Falconi said to himself. So, in a matter of minutes, he solved the problem. And in those few minutes, Mirna's squawking tortured his eardrums for the last time.

And then, after he did what he had to do, he realized that the arrogant bitch hadn't even made his dinner.

Falconi goes into the kitchen. He rests the still-warm hunting rifle on the counter, in front of the new electric oven they'd bought with points, a real deal. His white bathrobe is splattered with blood. He'll have to put everything in the washer—maybe Katerina can do it—and then take another shower. Relax. Not a bad idea. First, however, he needs to eat. Stuff his gullet. It's impossible to do anything, including think, on an empty stomach.

He opens the fridge, takes out a packet of prosciutto, a jar of artichokes in oil, a piece of aged cheese, and a nice cold beer. He cuts two slices of homemade bread, pours the beer into a glass, because only boys drink it from the can, filling their bellies with foam. Then he goes back to the living room. In front of his beautiful, lit fireplace.

He puts another beautiful log on the fire and sits down on the sofa. Next to Mirna.

His wife hasn't even changed position. She's still holding the picture she kept waving at him. If it wasn't for the fact that she's missing half her face, this could be like any other night they used to spend there, with dinner in front of the fire, a plate balanced on their legs, thick socks on their feet, which they always propped up on the table. Mirna always preferred a good fire to television during dinner. They always kept the television in the bedroom, where there hasn't been much else to do over the last thirty years.

Eugenio places the prosciutto on a slice of bread and takes a bite. He chews slowly, the old Falcon, because it would be a shame to ruin a crown just before he's about to leave. Who knows what kind of dentists they have in Sosúa Bay. Best not find out.

The sofa is covered in blood, a real mess. The bathrobe might have to go in the garbage, but who cares. The fact is, she was too caught up in disgracing him, hurling at him years' worth of threats and insults. She was going to take his name off their bank account. She was going to ruin him. She was sitting there with that photo in her hand, babbling on like a lunatic about lawsuits, attorneys, and carabinieri, with her loud, know-it-all voice rubbing his face in everything. She was out of her mind. And that was that. He implored her to calm down a few times, and then it was "Mirna, my God, you're going to ruin everything," and then "Mirna, there's money in it for you too," and Mirna, Mirna, Mirna. But Mirna didn't want to hear it. She just kept saying "You disgust me," and "I'll never let you do it," and then even more things he didn't really understand, like "That bitch is going to be so happy," and "That bitch is going to love his," and "I will not let you embarrass me like this in front of her."

The problem, for Mr. Falconi, is tension. When it gets to be too much, then it's just too much.

Mirna wouldn't stop shouting. She was in a real fury. That fucking voice of hers was growing more unbearable by the day. And so he opened his lovely mahogany English display case where he kept his rifle, loaded it with wild boar cartridges, and just as she was screaming, "You overestimated yourself, you old pig," he shot her in the head. Holy silence. Just what he needed to think through the situation.

Mirna had to disappear.

The prosciutto isn't bad. The prepackaged stuff isn't as good as the hand-cut, which is another thing entirely, with the drawback that it dries out too quickly, becoming hard and salty, while this, presliced and stored in an airtight packet, is always fresh, soft, and tasty. Now he takes a long sip of beer and a nice oiled artichoke. Too bad there aren't any chives.

Eugenio continues to chew slowly to protect his crowns as he sits next to his wife with her skull blown open and her muddy blood still dripping onto the floor. It will take a while to clean it all up, that dark mush that must be her brain, spread over the sofa and splattered on the back wall. But he already has an idea about how to make the body disappear. He should inform the others of this unexpected development, but tonight he needs to relax. Eat his dinner, drink his beer.

And have a nice sleep.

THREE

The unexpected developments regarding Mrs. Falconi required a meeting, but apparently the man who should have convened it was taking his time. First he wanted to clean up everything and put the cushion covers back on the sofa to cover his tracks, even if there was still a huge stain on the wall.

Maglio was the first to arrive. He had been in the woods for a shift with a couple of coworkers, but when he saw the caller ID on his phone, he knew it was something big and took his lunch break an hour early. The second to arrive was Adele. When she got Maglio's call, she'd been in the kitchen wondering what to prepare for lunch—a nice minestrone or a chicken breast with fennel in the microwave. And five minutes later, after her usual imaginary conversation with her husband, she was already at the wheel of her olive-green Panda four by four. The last one to arrive was Katerina. She left a note for Gerri, who was still in bed, telling him she was going to buy something bubbly to drink. It took her a while to get there.

"You told me to stay with Gerri, remember?" Katerina says, turning to Maglio, who commented on her delay. "It's not like I could just run out. I have no idea what he's doing right now. Maybe I shouldn't have come at all."

"You could have at least left your car in the woods," says Maglio. "Anyone who walks around the house could notice it out back where you left it."

Falconi tries to calm the waters. "Why would someone walk around the house?"

"This hussy doesn't give two shits," Adele says, pointing to Katerina with as much index finger as she can muster. "She shouldn't have been a part of this at all, that's the problem."

Katerina crosses her arms. "If this one starts, I'm leaving."

"Don't start, Adele," says Falconi.

"Where did you put Mirna?" asks Maglio, trying to get straight to the problem.

"Downstairs in the freezer."

"Why the freezer?"

"Because when I moved her, a bunch of blood poured out, so I froze her. At least then it'll be easier to cut her up if we have to."

"Are you hearing this?" Adele says. "You're talking about Mirna, for the love of God. Your wife, Eugenio. Your wife!"

"I told you to let it go, Adele," Falconi says again.

"I will not let it go. You'd better believe I'm not letting this go. When this whole thing started, I accepted because you said it would make Mirna happy, my friend Mirna. And now you've changed everything around, that hussy's in the picture, and I wasn't even able to tell Mirna, my dear friend Mirna, what we were doing. Don't you understand what this means for me?"

"Poor woman . . . ," says Katerina, contorting her lips into a childlike grimace.

"Shut up, whore," Adele says.

"You insult her one more time," Eugenio says, "and I'm sending you off with your dear friend Mirna forever."

"Do you hear him?" Adele stretches out her arms, as if talking to an imaginary audience. "Don't you realize it's all his fault that we're in this mess? An old pig who—"

"Don't exaggerate, Adele," says Maglio. "Don't forget that we did everything ourselves. You just agreed to sell a piece of land that fell into your husband's hands. We did the rest. So just think about the money you're getting and hush."

"Exactly. And if she didn't need to get involved," says Katerina, "she could have stayed home."

"And you could have stayed at home too," Adele replied. "It would have been better for everyone if Gerri had left you where he found you."

"Adele!" Falconi's eyes are bulging. "She's with me, and it's none of your business."

"But you shot her! Do you realize?" she continues. "You shot Mirna! The woman who cared for you when you were sick is sitting in a freezer so you can cut her up into little pieces! The woman who shared all the joy and pain of your life! The woman whom you swore to God for! The mother of your two daughters who—"

"Two needy brats!" Falconi screams. "And now that they're married, I have four needy brats. They sucked away all the money I had. Was I supposed to just stand by and watch while they sucked my blood? Was I supposed to sit here and give my life to this circle of spoiled brats until the day I died? Everyone makes their own choices, Adele, remember?"

"Good choice you made, congratulations. At sixty-five, you're with a hussy who the first chance she gets will—"

"What? What will I do?" Katerina interrupts her. "Come on, tell me what I'll do, say it! Do you know what your problem is? You're just jealous there's someone else your age who still likes to fuck, that's what!"

"You take that back!" cries Adele.

"Enough!" Maglio raises his voice and stands still, his arms open, his breath quickening, in an attempt to calm himself down. "Stop it, we have a real problem to solve."

"Yeah, a big one," says Adele. "Because I'm out, do you understand? Mirna was supposed to be in her place. And in any case, you told me there'd be something for Mirna, but that we weren't going to bring her in until the end so we didn't have issues with the bank. 'Problems with signatures,' that's what you said. And I thought she might be able to join me later, my dear friend Mirna. And now you tell me she can't join me anymore, and I'm not exactly okay with what you've done here, do you understand? I'm not okay with it at all! And I don't know what to do now, I don't know. I have to think about it, because I don't like what you've done to my friend, and I don't think this bitch should have her share. I don't want this whore—because she is a whore—to have Mirna's share. I don't want her to. And if she ends up with Mirna's money, I swear—"

The shot hits her right in the gut, opens a hole you can almost see through. Adele's eyes are open in a look of surprise, and they stay that way as her legs surrender and her body collapses onto the glass table, shattering it. A large splinter slices into her neck. The blood spills out, forming a puddle on the carpet.

The double-barrel in Falconi's hand is smoking. No one noticed that he had picked it up again.

"What the fuck are you doing?" says Maglio, who can't take his eyes off Adele's body.

"I warned her. If she insulted Katerina one more time, I'd reunite her with her friend. So now they can catch up with each other, the bitches."

"Don't lie, Falconi. You did it because she didn't want you to give Mirna's part to your girlfriend."

"Well, now we don't have to give anything to Mirna or Adele, so we divide a bigger pie into three pieces."

"I'm not so sure it's fair to split it three ways."

"The cartridge in my gun says it is."

"Are you threatening me?"

"The deal was that Katerina would get her share."

"The deal was that—"

"Someone's here!" Katerina interrupts, pointing to the window.

"What?" says Falconi.

"A car stopped there, near the gate."

"Oh shit."

Maglio approaches Adele's body and assesses the situation. "Quick, wrap her in the carpet so I can drag her into the closet."

"But there's blood everywhere . . . ," the mayor says, looking around.

"Why do you figure?" asks Maglio. "Anyway, genius, your car's out there. If they ring, open the door and pretend you don't feel well so they go. But at least get Adele out of here."

"It's that guy, Barbara's son!" says Katerina, who's looking out the window.

"Oh shit," Falconi repeats.

"Stop saying 'oh shit' and give me a hand, okay?" says Maglio. "Pull from that side. Did you really have to shoot this cretin? Couldn't you have given her a kick upside the head? Look what a mess you've made."

FOUR

"Where are you? What's going on?"

Grazia is sitting in front of the laptop at the station. She's browsing through images of the Spirits of the Woods on an external hard disk so she can figure out how to make the Falconi blackmailing story disappear. She's finally managed to get Esposito on the phone.

"Nothing, boss, everything's fine. I was just in the bathroom because that big cat knocked over our breakfast and spilled my coffee all over . . ."

She scrolls through the images quickly, as the time stamps in the lower right-hand part of the screen speed forward.

"I had Viola on the phone before, but she must've cut out. Where is she now?"

"She's in the bathroom, boss. Ms. Barbara said she ran to the bathroom."

Each hard disk contains footage shot by a drone. Apparently, the Spirits of the Woods had good equipment.

"She ran to the bathroom? Is she okay?"

One hard disk shows footage from the front of Falconi's house. It looks like a scene from a play: Adele's Panda arrives, Mirna leaves, the Panda drives off, Katerina's Giulietta arrives, Katerina goes inside. On another hard disk there's footage of the GeoService cabin. The patrol car appears often. That's how they didn't get caught: they kept everything under control. It would take months to watch everything the drones had filmed. But what Grazia's looking at now is something else.

"Ms. Barbara says she's fine, it's Rodari that has me worried," says Donato. "He was raving about some aquifer."

"Let's calm down. One thing at a time."

"Rodari thinks the whole story has something to do with attorney Alberti's disappearance, and if they put him back in jail, he's afraid no one will care."

Grazia was looking at the recordings on one of the hard drives when she realized that something was out of place. She knew that car, and she knew it shouldn't have been there.

"Boss? Can you hear me?"

So she began to follow its movements and noticed other cars. It took a few hours, but in the end she managed to trace a whole series of movements.

"Esposito, I can't do so many things at once, and I'm watching this footage now. Have him tell you every last detail of this story and then report back to me, okay?"

She has to know what she's looking for. Because every drone has recorded a piece of its path. And not only that. It's clear that over the past few days there's been a lot of traffic on these roads, between all the scooters, patrols, snowmobiles, and private cars. And the range of the drones is quite wide. They reach the county road that leads to the city. And isn't it strange that the car in question moves on the very night and at the very time that Patrizia Alberti disappeared?

"You really don't know how to drive?"

Viola is at the wheel of the old Ford that Giulio used to leave the garage at the Gherarda. He is in the passenger seat and is holding a handful of snow to his forehead, right where he slammed his head on the steering wheel, which was the moment he remembered he didn't have a driver's license.

"I take after my mother. She can't drive either."

"So whose car is this?"

"My aunt's. She did all the driving."

"Do you want to tell me about the aquifer?"

"In the presence of an aquifer, there are important reasons not to authorize the construction of a plant like the one GeoService wants to build in the woods. It's actually strange that they were able to buy that piece of the woods, which apparently lies within the reserve but isn't part of the reserve. But the fact is, the presence of an aquifer could send their plans down the river. And those people have no scruples. I mean, you read the papers, right?"

"Refresh my memory."

"They open these establishments in the middle of nowhere, in secluded places, where nobody realizes what they're storing. They take a lot of money from people who need to get rid of dangerous waste but don't want to go through costly legal channels to do it. So they accept bins of all kinds of stuff and find a way to change the names on them, to make them disappear. Sometimes they even sell them as agricultural fertilizer or leave them out until they decide they've made enough money and find a way to close the whole thing down. Do you know who these people are? The mafia. The kind of people who think nothing of getting rid of anyone who steps in their way. And that's exactly what happened to old Peter and Patrizia. GeoService might be registered under aliases, but once the story comes out I'll no longer be the only suspect. No more crazy guy who offed his ex because he was obsessed with her. It wasn't me, do you understand? This whole story is all about money and illegal interests, not a crime of passion."

"What about the pig?" Viola asks.

"The pig?"

"Falconi. Why are you in a hurry to talk to him?"

"As far as I understand, he was looking for ways to deny the permit. He'll be excited when I tell him something that will give him the upper hand over GeoService. If I could just get the tiniest detail out of him, like who owns the company, I could give my lawyer something to start on. I need to talk to Falconi. But why did you call him a pig?"

"Long story, I'll explain later. We're here. See? That's his house. So go."

"Wait for me in the car. I'm officially a fugitive, so you shouldn't get caught hanging around me. In fact, get down so no one can see you at all. I drove myself."

"Okay, but don't take too long. If the Marshal catches me, she might arrest me for real."

"I'll just be a few minutes. I know Falconi, he's quick on the uptake."

"Donato, it's me again."

"Chief, at your service."

"I have to talk to Rodari."

"Now?"

"No, after the summer holidays. I called you now because I wanted to ask you in advance."

"The holidays?"

"Esposito, go get Rodari."

"Right away."

"Falconi, first of all, I'm sorry for barging in on you like this, but I absolutely must talk to you."

"But aren't you supposed to be under—"

"House arrest, yes, I shouldn't be here. But, you see, I have to tell you something really important."

"Honestly, I'm not feeling very well at the moment."

"It'll just be a few minutes, then you can call the carabinieri and get them here to pick me up. If you want, I'll call them myself."

"You want to call the carabinieri?"

"To pick me up."

"Just a second, maybe you don't have to go that far . . ."

"Give me five minutes. I've discovered something important: there is an aquifer in the woods."

"A what?"

"Right where GeoService wants to build that plant. Do you realize? Patrizia Alberti discovered it and that's why she disappeared. Do you understand? You have to help me find a way to—"

"Are you alone?"

"Excuse me?"

"Did you come here alone?"

"Yeah. I came in my aunt's old car, see? They've kept it at the Gherarda ever since—"

"Come in, sit down. We can talk here where it's warm. You don't want to catch a cold, do you?"

"Boss, Rodari's gone."

"Esposito, what on earth are you saying?"

"He's not in his room."

"What? Is Barbara there?"

"Yeah."

"Put her on."

. . .

"Hi, Grazia."

"Barbara, what's going on?"

"I think Viola is helping Giulio discover something important—"

"Viola is a little girl, Barbara! I left her with you so she wouldn't make any more messes! Tell me where she is this instant."

"I think they went to the mayor's house."

"Oh my holy God! Put Esposito back on."

. . .

"Hi, boss."

"Hi, my ass! I leave you to watch my daughter and Rodari, and you don't even notice they've both gone out for a drive?"

"What do you mean, a drive?"

"Get to Falconi's house, move."

"All right, but . . . I walked here."

"Barbara has a car. Have her give you the keys and take that."

"Negative, boss. Apparently, the car is already in use."

"What are you talking about?"

"Viola and Rodari have it."

"But Rodari can't drive, everyone knows he takes after his mother and—"

"Rodari can't drive, boss. But Viola can."

FIVE

Look, Mirna, I know you still have something to do with this. You've never been one to give up, have you? I don't know how you've managed to create this whole other mess, but while this guy is standing in front of me telling me a story about an aquifer that might put an end to everything, I can feel with absolutely every bone in my body that you're behind it. I knew that moment Rodari said he'd call the carabinieri. And this isn't exactly a good time for him to do it, with you in the freezer, Adele rolled up in a carpet, and blood all over the living room that this ballbuster here will notice soon enough.

And then what?

Only two days to go, Mirna. In two days, the committee votes on the GeoService permits, and more money than you can even imagine will pass from one account to another to another to another. Bouncing from one country to another, making it virtually impossible to trace the source of all that money, because it would require the collaboration of governments who know very well how to protect the interests of those who make their fortune. Do you understand, Mirna? Do you know the game I'm in on? You broke my balls if I didn't put my underwear and socks in the laundry basket, or if I left my dirty coffee cup in the sink, or if I didn't spray that nasty, wood-scented deodorizer in the bathroom after I did the "big one." You couldn't even bring yourself to say "poop," do you realize? You had sex out of duty, with the light off and without saying a word. Sometimes I thought you were a repressed lesbian. And I still didn't want things to end the way they did. Not that I didn't experience a certain amount of pleasure when I opened your skull, darling, but my plans were different. The Falcon just wanted to go off on his own and let you live undisturbed in this house until the end of your days. You could've had the same routine you'd always had, or you could've gone off with that wench, Adele. But no, you had to get in the middle of things again. And Adele followed you into it. But you can't stop the Falcon. The Falcon is a hunter. That's right. Mr. Falconi has had enough of this life, and he'll be damned if he stays in his place while the leeches attached to his balls suck away the rest of his life. Fuck you, Mirna. What you never understood was that life is short but it can be big, that no one can force us to be someone we're not, that if you like dancing and having fun, you don't have to quit because it's not okay, that if fucking were only for having kids, then no one would have a dick for life, that you can wipe your ass with what others think of you, that you only have one life, Mirna, and since no one can give it back to you, it doesn't make sense to live it the way everyone else wants you to, according to what they think is good, what they think is right. I have the right to that beach, to Katerina, to those magical pleasure pills, to all the money they promised me in exchange for my signature. This place has no future, Mirna. The people who left, did, they're gone, and that was before the damn bus went down with the bridge. So why not put all that money in your pocket? Do you really believe the spirits of the dead live in the woods? Why get bogged down in the murk of nostalgia, memories, of what is no longer? That's not living, it's just a conditioned reflex. It's like a heart that only beats from an electrical charge. An involuntary muscle. How did you feed yourself with what was in the house? A precooked microwave dinner, day after day. Come on, Mirna, admit it. Admit that wasn't what you wanted. Admit that settling down for so long isn't all it's meant to be. So let me go. Get out of my head. Stop shouting all those bad things through me like you're doing now. You didn't even suffer. You didn't even know it was coming. Leave me alone. Stop screaming like this.

"Falconi? Do you understand what I'm telling you?"

Eugenio looks at Rodari and thinks about the shotgun in the kitchen, leaning against the table with the coffee machine. And then he thinks about how there's still one shot left in there, after what he fired at Mirna and Adele.

The three red, bean-shaped candies disappear, and a group of purple, grape-shaped bunches appear in their place, which then disappear into a pair of orange, ovular candies that she can never figure out what they're meant to be. Seeds, maybe. Or dates. Who knows? Date-shaped candies. Viola is in the car, lying on the seat so no one can see her, passing the time with a game of *Candy Crush Saga*. Every now and then, she checks the time on her iPhone and looks at Falconi's house, a pretty, two-story little villa, almost hidden among the trees, with a snowy roof. What a disgusting pig. If only the Marshal had given her two more days . . . but she's too stubborn. And now he's off the hook. If Rodari can get him on board with this aquifer story . . . but he's taking a long time. When Esposito starts to catch on to how long it's been that she went to the bathroom and goes looking for her, she will officially be in huge trouble. And it's not so easy to explain why she decided to help Rodari. The fact is, that guy has something, maybe he reminds her a little of Michele. Or maybe he reminds her of someone who could have been the father she could have had. A scenario confined to a past conditional tense—as the Italian professor says—indicating events that are no longer possible. So, when she saw that expression in Barbara's eyes, she remembered the line from "Heroes" he told her about, her favorite part of the song, and from there, going out to give him a hand

226

was nothing. If they really could save the forest . . . They say things done without too much thought are usually the best. But when people say "usually," it means they're not really convinced of what they're saying. Anyway, five red beans. But the game stops and Mussolini's face appears on the display. The image that corresponds to her mother's number. The Marshal is calling her. Viola looks at the image but doesn't answer. Because the Marshal, of course, is onto something, and Viola certainly can't tell her where she is. She pretends she doesn't hear it. She silences the phone. Looking back at Falconi's house, she thinks that Rodari really needs to get moving.

Donato runs like a madman. He's made a big mess of things this time. The Marshal will lose her mind. He runs along the road when he hears a noise. It's in the woods.

A snowmobile, through the trees.

Falconi seems distracted. They sit on the sofa. Giulio is talking about Giampedretti's report, but the mayor has a strange expression on his face. After inviting him in, Falconi kept looking around as if he were looking for something. He didn't even seem to be listening to him. Every now and then he shakes his head as if to drive off a fly buzzing around him. But there's no fly in the room.

"Falconi? Do you understand what I'm telling you?" Giulio asks.

"What's that?"

"You seem . . . a little distracted."

"Distracted?"

"Did something happen?"

"Oh yes. You can't even imagine how many things have happened."

"But right now you should focus a little on this thing, Mayor. Look, I have the report. I can send it to you right away, if you believe me."

"Would you like a coffee?"

"A coffee?"

"Yes, a coffee. I have a great machine, the kind with the pods. You know. It makes a nice coffee."

Falconi moves away toward the kitchen. Giulio turns to look at the unlit hearth. Inside, there are still blackened logs, a sign that there had been a nice fire there the night before. It's strange, though. In front of this sofa, there was usually a coffee table, and instead there's just an empty space. It's even stranger because the rest of the house is packed. Furniture in every corner, the sign of a home where life is lived. That's what people do: over the years they fill up their homes with a ton of stuff that one day someone else will have to take away and throw out, and they pay a lot of money to do it. There are so many little ornaments, photographs, objects. There's also a big dark stain on the wall. Indeed, there's one on the sofa too, coming out from under this horrible towel that's been thrown on top of it. There's a strange odor too. Giulio couldn't say what it is, but it makes him think of hunting. And there's a strange dark trail that leads to the door next to the kitchen.

The gnome has a sixth sense for things that aren't right, and in this living room there is something that isn't right. A strange feeling. As if something had escaped him. Maybe it's better to skip the coffee.

Giulio gets up from the sofa. He looks around and then turns back to the kitchen.

And he finds himself face-to-face with Mr. Falconi holding a shotgun in his hand.

"Falconi, what . . . ?"

On instinct, he throws himself to the side, and this is the only reason the blow doesn't hit him straight on. Giulio can't tell if he heard the gunshot first or felt the sudden burning at his side. He hardly has time to realize that his legs no longer support him. And he feels a sudden sleep that grabs him and carries him down. Into a dark place.

The orange ovals burst at the same moment Viola hears the shot. She sits upright. She looks toward the mayor's home. What is going on?

Grazia feels her car skidding. She's driving too fast for these conditions. But she's in a blind rage over her criminal daughter, who went from joints to harassment to aiding a suspected murderer who has escaped from house arrest. And she's not answering her damned phone. The worst part is that she may be in over her head, given the drone footage, and that the Spirits of the Woods, too concerned with looking for photos of Falconi with Katerina, failed to notice. All they had to do was put it together, check the times. To use reason. Which is exactly what Viola never, ever does.

Grazia feels like a character in a video game, one of those desperate men who dodge dangers knowing that they'll have to keep doing it until someone brings them down and then sayonara.

At the edge of the village, she arrives at the turn onto the county road and sees someone running like a damned maniac down the road. It's Donato. She had told him to get a move on, and that poor soul has been running all the way from the Gherarda. She turns onto the county road. Then she puts the car in reverse and goes to pick him up.

"Boss, I ran as fast as I could," he tells her, collapsing into the passenger seat.

"Do you have your gun?"

"My gun?"

"Yeah, hello? That thing you shoot . . ."

"Yeah, of course. What's going on?"

As soon as Rodari goes down with a thud, Maglio and Katerina burst out of the door of the room where they've arranged Adele.

"Don't you ever learn?" screams Maglio.

"Puppy, my love, did you really need to shoot this one too?" says Katerina.

"You heard him, didn't you?" says Falconi, the shotgun still smoking in his hand. "He found something. I told you we needed to take the lawyer's computer. If we'd done it, maybe he wouldn't have had to die."

"Why didn't you take it then?" asks Maglio. "Since I had to do all the rest."

"What do you mean, the rest? What exactly did you do? Are you still whining about that lawyer? You're the one who had the bright idea to bury her up there, you and your obsession with American movies."

"DNA tests on corpses don't just happen in the movies, idiot. And when they get here it'll take them five minutes to figure out what happened. There are tracks everywhere. How do you plan to get out of this one?"

"What's the problem? Do you think anyone will show up around here in the next two days? Mirna went to spend time by the sea. Adele? I have no idea, why would she come here if her dear Mirna is by the sea? Maybe she went with her, right? This idiot here? Just take his car and put it somewhere in the woods. We need two days, do you get it? In two days it will all be over and you'll be rich. You could leave today, since you don't have to sign. Pick up tonight and go, and in two days the money will be in your account."

"Like hell I'm leaving. Because if the money doesn't show, how will I be able to find you? No, my friend. The agreement was that we only go our own ways once everyone has their share. And speaking of shares—"

"Someone's here," says Katerina, pointing at the window.

"Again?" says Maglio.

Falconi turns. The Marshal's daughter is at the window. Wild-eyed. Rodari's body is on the floor, practically in front of her. She saw it. And now she sees Falconi with the shotgun in his hand.

"Oh shit," Falconi says.

"What now?" asks Maglio. "You can't . . ."

Falconi looks him dead in the face. "You guys try to clean up a little around here."

He walks over to the glass case where he keeps his shotguns. Next to it is the door to the stairs that lead down to the basement. The knob is smeared with blood. He'll take care of that later. He opens a drawer and grabs a handful of cartridges. He loads two and slips the others in his pocket. Then he takes his cowboy hat and goes to leave.

"She's just a girl," says Maglio.

"My puppy . . . ," Katerina calls to him.

Falconi turns to her. The sun from the outside now illuminates her angular features. "Tell me, my little bunny . . ."

"Think of the Antilles."

Falconi smiles at her. He puts on his hat. And he goes hunting.

The double wooden door of the shed is open. The shed is hidden in the woods. There's still some smoke in the air left by the snowmobile that had been there.

Inside, there's a coffee table on which some items have been arranged. There's a wooden box, its lid sitting off to the side. There's a magnum of Dom Pérignon, whose cork lies somewhere in the woods, and next to it is one glass, which is empty. Champagne bubbles still dance just above the neck of the bottle. And there is one last object. A leather case. It's open. It's empty. On the top is a hand-embroidered phrase.

AN ARROW NEVER TURNS BACK

SIX

Viola runs. As she opens the door to the old Ford, she can hear the door to Falconi's house slam.

"Viola, stop! I can explain!" the mayor cries.

But as she starts the car, she notices he still has the shotgun in his hand. Someone who wants to explain something does not do it with a shotgun. It had been Giulio on the floor. He shot him. And there were other people there. Katerina, surely. And maybe Magliarini. They shot him. She turns the key, the car starts. But it doesn't move.

The wheels slip on the snow, which is melting in the radiant sun.

The important thing is to stay calm. Remember, Viola? You have to be calm.

"Get out of the car and we'll talk," says Falconi, who has almost reached her.

The car doesn't budge.

The forest.

The story of the gnome. The woods protect him.

Viola opens the passenger door and, hidden by the car, runs into the trees.

"Stop, just one thing!"

But Viola doesn't stop. Instead, she throws herself into the trees, just as the shot sprays a beech tree behind her. Falconi actually shot at her. The pig killed Giulio and now he wants to kill her too. Acid rises from her stomach to her throat.

She slips in the snow. She has to get over this ridge, and if she falls again, she'll end up right in this crazy man's mouth. But once she's over the ridge, she can run and look for a way to hide. She has to call her mother. As soon as she gets over the ridge, she'll do it.

Another shot. This, too, ends up in a tree.

Viola runs. She's about to fall again. She grabs a root. She can't slide downhill, because she'd be going backward, where he is waiting. The tears she didn't even notice she was crying cloud her view. Somehow, she has to get over this ridge.

A distant voice. The voice of a woman. It's Patrizia. Giulio stands up, finally light, and turns to her. Patrizia isn't there. Giulio runs, without fatigue. He looks around. A long corridor full of rooms. It's his old school. *Why am I here?* Then that voice again. It's not Patrizia. He's not running. His body is heavy and unmoving. He's wrapped in darkness. *I have to move I have to move I have to move.* They shot him, he can feel the pain. But everything is dark. *I have to open my eyes I have to open my eyes I have to open my eyes.*

"Let's put them all in the freezer," says the woman.

"Do you think they'll fit?" another voice says, a man.

"He has two down there, huge ones, for wild boars."

What are they putting in the freezer? Where are the voices coming from? Am I dead?

The first thing you have to do is open your eyes.

The gnome says it's easy, just open them one at a time. Courage. You have to lift the gate. Opening an eyelid is such a simple thing that you never imagine that it could become such a difficult undertaking. You have to be able to unstick it from the bottom lid. As if it were glued.

But the gnome says once you unstick it from the bottom one, you've done it. You'll see. Once you unstick it, the rest is a piece of cake.

There she is. Falconi has spotted her. The girl is in the trees. *The Falcon's eye has always been sharp,* he thinks. But it's just a glimpse before she disappears beyond the ridge. That little girl runs like the devil, and maybe he should have taken more than one gun so he wouldn't have to stop to reload so often.

He has to catch her. He may not even have to kill her. He could tie her up, gag her, close her away somewhere. But if she knows about the aquifer, it's a problem. And it would be a problem even after he takes the money. Because if for some reason the permits were to be rescinded, or revoked, they would come for him. And those people don't need international warrants. No, he needs a few years at least. Then his tracks will be covered and it won't matter if they find the damned aquifer. But he needs time. And if the girl knows that story, then he has to keep her from telling anyone. Just one more woman he has to get out of the way. Having scruples at this point would be self-defeating. She's just one more interruption, like all the others. The attorney, Mirna, Adele, Rodari, and now this little girl. Women always make trouble, that's how things are. And the men who don't know how to keep them in their place are to blame. Women have too much freedom. That is a fact. In his father's days, Falconi thinks, this whole mess never would have happened. The men would have come to an agreement among themselves. Even a man like Rodari could be compelled to compromise in the end. But no. Women are envious, jealous, greedy, selfish. If Katerina were to become like that, he would get rid of her just as he did with all these others. But the important thing right now is to get rid of the girl.

Falconi arrives at the top of the ridge. The old woods span out before him. The girl is here. She's close. He can see her tracks through the trees. It won't be hard for this old hunter to sniff her out.

The patrol car pulls up in front of Falconi's house right after Falconi disappears behind the ridge. The carabinieri didn't see him, but the black cat hidden in a bush did.

Heave-ho. Come on, pull up the eyelid. Heave-ho. The gnome is there with the rope in hand, pulling, pulling, pulling, pulling. He gives it all his strength. Heave-ho. The important thing is to unstick it from the bottom lid. Heave-ho.

Viola is running in the woods. She reaches into her pocket for her phone to call her mother. The phone is not there.

Grazia and Donato get out of the patrol car.

"I don't know who it was, boss. I just saw the snowmobile through the trees. It was heading toward the woods, but I didn't see the driver."

They approach the mayor's home.

Grazia tries to call Viola. She hears her daughter's phone ring. She looks around. She follows the vintage ring that Viola chose because she detests the modern ringtones. As she approaches, the sound gets louder. It's coming from Amanda's old Ford. That's how they got here. Grazia peers inside the car. The iPhone is on the ground, next to the open door on the passenger's side. Mussolini's face is on the screen.

"They're in the woods!"

Grazia turns in the direction of the voice. There's someone in the trees near the mayor's house.

"They ran into the woods right there! The mayor has a gun!"

Heave-ho. The gnome is pulling with all his strength. His face is as red as his beard now. Heave-ho. Almost there, just one last pull and the eyelid will open. Courage. Heave-ho. A glimmer of light. Finally . . . the eyelid moves and . . . nothing. It's useless. It falls back down. It's bolted shut. The voices return.

"The carabinieri?" says the woman.

"Don't move, let's pretend no one is home," says the man.

"I left my car out back . . ."

"Yeah, stupid move. Now be quiet."

"They're coming closer . . ."

"Shut up! Look. Maybe we got lucky."

"But what is she doing? Tell me what's happening, I can't see a thing . . ."

"The Marshal is holding the phone . . . but what's going on? She's looking into the woods. There's someone out there."

Viola should go back on her own footprints, like that little boy in *The Shining*, but it takes too long and the old woods is a labyrinth. She keeps running, hoping an idea will come to her. She has to hide. The Crow's Rock. The cave. They're not far. And the woods protect the gnome.

Grazia looks toward the trees. Dorina comes out.

"Dorina, what on earth are you doing here?"

"What now? Maglio, tell me what's going on." The woman's voice sounds worried. Very worried.

"The Marshal is running into the woods." The man's voice sounds worried too.

"What about the other carabiniere?"

"He's here. He has his gun. Shit, someone warned them. We're fucked. Let's hide. Come on. Get in there. We can't let them find us."

The front door is open. Donato holds up his gun. It's the first time he's had to think about using it. To be sure the safety is off, he'd normally fire a test shot, but something tells him that wouldn't be a good idea. He grips it with both hands, one hand with a finger around the trigger and the other hand underneath the first to support it, like he practiced at the firing range. He can hear his heart pounding in his head.

He enters to find himself in the living room. Nobody there. Traces of blood on the ground, leading to a closed door. Maybe he should say something like "Come out with your hands up," but it sounds like something out of a movie; and anyway, Donato's throat is so dry that if he talks, he would probably just stammer.

He slowly approaches the door. A few steps. A light-brown wood door. The traces of blood disappear underneath it. Another step. The light-brown wood door.

Grazia follows the tracks in the snow. In glimpses, through the trees, she thinks she can see Falconi. Or maybe it's an illusion. Her gun is drawn.

She can feel the sweat down her back. Her thighs are burning. She's gasping for breath.

"The Crow's Rock is over there!" says Dorina. She had managed to keep up to this point, but now she has to stop and lean against a tree.

Grazia takes off running through the snow again.

The snowmobile emerges from the woods at the back of Falconi's house.

The white Giulietta is parked there.

Donato is standing in front of the door. He moves his left hand from the gun to the knob.

He opens the door.

SEVEN

"Please stay here tonight." Patrizia has appeared in the ethereal form she always assumes in his memories. But this time there's a background. It's as if he were really with her. As if the storm were over. His memories return to their places. It already happened this way once before after that time when he walked all night and didn't remember a thing. It took months, but in the end a lot of stuff had returned to its place, if not all of it. They're at her house now. They've just started dating. He has to go to one of those group sessions with the psychologist and his mother, but he doesn't want to. He can't think of anything other than her. Patrizia. They closed themselves up in her apartment for two days. He arrived at her place on a Friday night with one bottle of Barolo and another of apple juice. They made love, ate spaghetti with garlic and chili in bed, wearing only their shirts, they watched one of those Jane Austen–type movies that may have been adapted from a Jane Austen novel, they made love, they had coffee, they showered together, they made love, they thought about where to go on vacation, maybe somewhere hot, they made love. Now it's Sunday afternoon and he has to leave. And then she says, "Stay here tonight. Please."

"I can't this time."

"But that's how it went, don't you remember? I asked you to stay, you said yes, and then you stayed. All of this already happened. You're remembering it now."

"I know, it's funny. I do remember it now, but I have to go."

"Is it because you know it wasn't you?"

Giulio searches for the answer. Everything has already happened, it's just a reflection of the past.

"Maybe. I was afraid I really had killed you."

"And now you want to leave?"

"You decide. Decide whether to let me go or not."

"You never did want to decide anything for yourself."

"Is that why you asked me?"

"You have to want it. From now on, you'll have to remember that."

The man getting off the snowmobile is carrying a quiver with twelve reinforced fir wood arrows.

"No more time, you have to decide," Patrizia says.

"I'll stay."

"I know, but not now."

"What does that mean?"

"You have to open your eyes. You have to go back and talk to her."

"Why?"

"Because she needs you."

"But how do I go back?"

"Ask for help, yell."

"But I can't even open my eyes, how can I scream?"

"You have to, come on."

"Let's try to stay calm, okay?" says Aurelio Magliarini. Donato opened the door to the closet and found the lumberjack inside. Donato takes a step back and puts his left hand back on the gun.

"What are you doing here?" asks the carabiniere.

"I came to see Falconi, but he's not here . . ."

"And so you hid in the closet?"

"Aggggh . . ."

As Magliarini tries to find an answer, a strange moan comes from the darkness of the closet. It sounds like a lament.

"What's that?" asks Donato. "Is there someone here with you?"

"Aggggh . . ." The moan again.

Donato looks at the floor; there's something in the corner. It looks like a rolled-up carpet. And next to it . . . is Rodari's gray fleece.

"Step aside, Magliarini, and turn on the light. Look, I—"

A sharp pain.

Then darkness.

Katerina is holding the cast-iron skillet she took from the kitchen. As soon as she realizes it has blood on it, she shrieks and drops it to the ground.

"Calm down," says Maglio. "Help me drag him inside and we'll figure out what to do with all of them. What a mess. We need to get the fuck out of here. Now."

"As it is we're all in for it. Get a gun and go help him in the woods, what are you waiting for?"

"Shit, shit, shit!" Maglio's screams crescendo. "What a mess! I'd love to see how we get out of this one."

"You have to go help him."

"I don't have to do shit! Just stop it. Don't you know it's all gone to hell? Don't you see what a mess this is? I'm getting the fuck out of here, that's what I'm doing."

Maglio goes to the cabinet and grabs a shotgun. He opens the drawer and takes some boar cartridges. He loads two, then shoves the others in his pocket.

"You can stay if you want, wait for him to come back," he says. But when he turns to speak to Katerina, he sees her there, petrified.

Her husband is standing in the living room. He's holding a bow and arrow.

"Gerri, what the fuck are you doing?" asks Maglio.

"You've been having some fun here, haven't you?" says the bartender.

His eyes are wide, his expression rigid.

"Look, Gerri, we have a big mess on our hands," says Maglio. "But if we stay calm, we can still get out of it. Now lower that bow and let's talk it out. Right, Katerina? Tell him that everything is fine and that we need to talk."

"My love . . . ," Katerina tries to say.

"Shut up, slut." Gerri's voice has a finality to it.

"Don't say that, friend," says Maglio. "It's not what you think . . ."

"You had an orgy, didn't you? You had your fun. Dirty perverts."

"Gerri, you're mistaken, look, I—"

"Shut up!"

Maglio responds by pointing the shotgun at him. "Gerri, I'm telling you, that language isn't necessary . . ."

"I say it is."

The arrow leaves the bow. An instant later, the shotgun fires.

Viola arrives at the Crow's Rock. It's covered by trees. She only has a few seconds to do what the kid in *The Shining* did. She jumps on the rocks.

Now her tracks lead him there. If she manages to climb up the Crow's Rock, she can go down the other side and into the cave.

Maglio's eyes are crossed. They are looking inward in a grotesque attempt to observe the arrow that has traversed his skull and nailed it to the English mahogany frame of the broken display window. His body jerked like a mad puppet at first. Then he was still. His mouth wide open. Katerina turns to her husband. Gerri is hurt. He's losing blood like a busted beer keg. But he's still standing and is loading another arrow onto the bow.

"My love . . . Gerri . . . you can calm down now. It's me, Kati, your Kati. You're hurt, let me take care of you. Let's forget about everything. And everything will always be like it was this morning. We had a nice time, didn't we? We stayed in bed. I . . . I didn't want to leave you." She moves toward her husband, very slowly, with her hands outstretched, to calm him down. "You were upset when you didn't see me, weren't you? It's that . . . I had to come here because . . . let's leave it all behind us, my love. We can pretend it never happened. You'll see, everything will be fine." She steps past Maglio's body. "Remember when we stood in front of the priest? Remember the honeymoon? The cruise? The two of us, alone . . . let's start again from there, let's leave right away. As long as it takes for your wound to heal. Can't you see? You're losing a lot of blood, my love." She's standing just a few feet from her husband. "We'll say that you came to save me, because these people wanted to hurt me. You came here and he pointed the gun at you and you saved me. And then we'll go off on our cruise, like back when we loved each other so much. And we can love each other again. I've never stopped loving you. Let's leave this all behind us and go, what do you say? Let's go off together, the two of us alone, what do you say?"

Falconi is exhausted. The girl had wanted to run. But enough now. She's here. She must be here. The tracks lead to the rock, and the snow around it is pristine.

"You're here, aren't you? I know you're here. And here's what's going to happen. I'm going to find you. And after I do, no one else will ever find you again, you fucking little bitch." Falconi starts to walk around on the rocks. She must be here somewhere. "I worked hard on this project. And you keep getting in the middle. I deserve that money, do you understand? I deserve to leave this place. Was that so wrong? In a few years nobody will even live here. Only old people. What then? Was it so wrong to make a little money for ourselves? I was going to sign, take the money, and leave. But no, first that lawyer bitch. She called me and told me she could give me a hand. She could help me reject the permit. I told her to keep it to herself, but she refused. I offered her money, but she refused. It's where he grew up, she said. She wouldn't be able to sleep at night, she said. But she sleeps now. That lumberjack didn't even mean to break her neck when he grabbed her. But that's how it went. And then that ballbuster, Mirna. She wanted to send everything to hell because I wanted to be with someone thirty years younger than her, who makes me fuck like I've never fucked in my life. Hard choice, don't you think?"

A noise. Viola gives herself away.

Falconi walks around the rock.

Run, Grazia, run! You're almost there and you have to reach Viola.

The slightest sound was all it took. The floor of the cave is covered in brush, and Viola would have been safe in there, had she not stepped on a wrong stone and fell, making a rustling noise. And then suddenly Falconi stopped talking. In a second, he will be pointing his shotgun at her. Viola is frozen with fear. She sees him coming around the rock.

But then on the other side of the rock, a bush moves. Viola sees something like a black spot. And Falconi turns. Viola takes advantage of the distraction and slips into the cave. One shot. A cat sound, something like a scream. It was the black cat from the Gherarda. He had saved her.

Viola stays in the hole. She can hear Falconi's footsteps around the rock. She sees him. He's less than three feet away from her. When she entered the small cave, she damaged the bush that covered the entrance. It was all mangled. If he turns, he'll see it.

Falconi turns. His eyes are on her. For a moment he seems to be looking at her. Yet he doesn't see her. It's as if Viola suddenly became invisible. The forest. The gnome. Can it be?

"Falconi, drop the gun and put your hands in the air." Her mother's voice. She's here.

Falconi approaches the rock. He's right next to Viola. She can smell his sweat, his rotten breath, his breath heavy like a beast's. And she can see he's smiling, a kind of satisfied smirk, as he takes the rifle and raises it. He's seen her. He saw her mother and now he'll shoot both of them. She has to do something. Falconi has his finger on the trigger. He's about to shoot.

"No!"

Viola moves the rifle, the shot misses. But Falconi grabs her by the arm and drags her out.

"Well, well, Marshal!" he screams, satisfied. "We have a surprise for you."

He's clutching her arm hard, he's hurting her. And now he presses the double-barrel against her throat.

Grazia comes out in the open.

"I'm here, Falconi! Let her go," she says with her hands in the air, showing him the pistol she's no longer pointing. "Let go of my daughter, please. She doesn't have anything to do with this."

Viola is scared. She's crying.

"Hush, my love. Mama will make it better, you'll see."

"Put the gun at my feet," Falconi orders.

"What are you going to do? Don't you know it's over?"

"The fuck it's over!" he screams. "Place the gun at my feet, or I'll have you picking your daughter's head off a tree, you understand?"

Grazia throws the gun at his feet. She's no longer armed.

Falconi drops Viola's arm but continues to press the shotgun into her neck. He slowly bends down to pick up the gun. He takes it and points it at Grazia. Viola pushes past the barrel of the shotgun and runs to her mother.

Grazia embraces her. She presses her head against her chest, as if she were a little girl.

"Everything will be all right, baby. It's okay."

But she doesn't know how everything will be okay. Her only hope is that Donato reaches them.

But Donato is lying on the floor, his head split open with a cast-iron skillet. His eyes are closed, fixed on a distant void, blood streaming down his forehead. A few feet from him, Maglio is nailed to an English-style mahogany cabinet with an arrow through his brain.

Yo quiero que este
Sea el mundo que conteste

Álvaro Soler's cheerful voice emanates from the crocodile Prada bag by the sofa, filling the room with its melody.

Giulio is on the floor of the closet. Not moving. Next to him, Adele is wrapped in a carpet soaked in blood. Downstairs, Mirna's body is in the freezer.

Del este hasta oeste
Y bajo el mismo sol

The crocodile Prada bag is open, and the phone is resting on top of her other things. The caller ID shows the spa where Katerina would have gone this morning. Massages, exfoliating treatments, thermal water, white towels, relaxing music, aromatic and detoxifying tea.

But now there's no one to answer it.

Katerina's blue eyes are devoid of light. They will never see Sosúa Bay, lined with palm trees along the Caribbean beach kissed by the Antilles sun. Her head is drooping onto her shoulder. She looks like a wax statue, frozen in her expression of stupor. She's nailed to the basement door.

The arrow went through her heart. Her husband shot it right through the center.

And the Latin song about sunshine and love keeps on playing, as blood pools everywhere on the terra-cotta floor.

Outside the house, the snowmobile's tracks form a meandering path. It seems that its driver slipped a few times, leaving behind a stream of blood.

"Falconi, what are you going to do? Are you going to bury us in the woods too?" Grazia tries to stall for time. Donato is her only card left to play. She has to make Falconi talk; in his place people usually need to justify themselves.

"Why would I stop now?"

"The footage. It won't take long for my colleagues to put this together the way I did."

"What are you talking about?"

"Do you remember those photos of you and Katerina?"

"How do you know about those?"

"Someone was spying on you, Falconi. And they also got stuff they didn't know how to read. Like certain movements of you and Maglio in your car the night Patrizia Alberti disappeared. You made a few trips that night. And you ended up on GeoService's land. The spies also picked that up. The Spirits of the Woods had eyes everywhere. The footage shows you carrying something. I would have gone to check myself, but someone else will do it. And the mystery of Patrizia Alberti's disappearance will be solved."

"Where are the recordings?"

"At the station."

"So your daughter will stay with me while you go get them."

"Why would I do that when you've already decided to kill us?"

"You're trying my patience, you know that?"

"I'm just trying to make you see reason, Falconi. You plan's gone up in smoke."

"Well, isn't that nice to know!" Falconi screams, as Viola clings harder to her mother, and Grazia hopes she's getting him on the right track. "Nothing's gone up in smoke here." There's a hiss in the distance. It sounds like an engine is approaching. "What's that? Who's with you?"

"It's my men, Falconi. You're trapped." Grazia has no idea what the noise is. But it sounds like a snowmobile. Maybe it's the one Donato said he saw in the woods.

Falconi slings the shotgun over his shoulder and grabs Viola again with his free hand. He pulls her to him and points the pistol at her throat. Viola is crying.

"What do you want, Falconi?" Grazia asks.

"I don't hear anything anymore. Where did the noise go?"

"They're surrounding us. It can only get worse from here."

"Why can't I hear the noise?" Falconi screams. He looks around. But there is something he fails to notice. On the rock behind him. In the white snow there is another white shape that's moving. His thick ivory coat. His fierce red eyes. His slow, light stride of an albino tiger, his muscles tensing the instant before he pounces. The white cat.

The engine is off. The snowmobile came to a stop against a tree, just a few feet into the woods. Gerri is hunched over on the handlebars. His eyes are open. Empty. From his left hand, stretched out in front of him, red blood drips down onto the white snow. He's holding something between his fingers. It's his gold medal from the 1999 regional archery championships.

The white cat pounces. In a moment, he's on Falconi's head. The cowboy hat falls to the ground. The white beast claws at Falconi, looking for his eyes. To get rid of him, Falconi lets go of Viola. Grazia grabs her and throws her to the ground and then throws herself on top of her for cover should Falconi let a shot escape. Still gripping the pistol, Falconi tries to grab the cat, screaming from the pain of being scratched in the face. The cat digs into his flesh: he's looking for his eyes. With a scream, Falconi finally wrests the beast from his head, throwing it toward the rocks. His face is bloody, twisted in an expression of anger, hatred, and sorrow. That cat almost ripped one of his eyes out. His breath is shallow, like a wounded animal's. He points the gun at Grazia, but blood drips into his good eye, and he hesitates for an instant. An instant too long.

The sound of the shot comes from the trees. Falconi looks up. His mouth wide open, a face of surprise. He tries to figure out where the shot came from, as a bloodstain blossoms like a red rose across his jacket at chest level. He drops the gun, takes a step back, and leans against the rock. Now both of his eyes have gone black. He's afraid. His surprise has given way to consciousness. He tries to catch his breath, maybe to get more air or maybe to say something. But the second shot doesn't give him a chance. A new red spot appears across his chest, next to the first one. Falconi's legs give way, and his back slides down the Crow's Rock until he arrives to his final resting place on the ground. His breath becomes heavy. His eyes still see nothing but blackness. And in a matter of seconds, they assume the unnatural stare of death.

Barbara lowers the rifle. She looks toward the clearing by the Crow's Rock. She hands the semiautomatic Remington with its steaming cannon to Akan, who is still sitting on the Gherarda snowmobile, and starts off toward Grazia and Viola.

PART SIX
HAWTHORNE SEASON

"Remember that photograph?"

ONE

Carabinieri, forestry, rescue vehicles, lumberjacks, journalists. The GeoService area is buzzing with people. Viola is sitting in the back of an ambulance, sipping on a cup of hot chocolate. Akan holds a blanket over her shoulders.

"That'll do it!" yells the guy on the excavator. Grazia walks over. Scalise is next to her. Two men get out of the gray van owned by the Misericordia Funeral Parlor. Their job is to take away all the bodies, arranged in plastic bags, and leave them at the deputy prosecutor's disposal. They're working overtime today, and they're going on their third journey.

TV crews and photographers also approach the pit.

The excavator stops, and men gather round with their spades in hand. It doesn't take much digging.

There's a big bag in the ground. Scalise gestures to one of his men to open it a little, and there is Patrizia Alberti's face. Gray and sunken, but recognizable.

"We found her, Marshal," says Scalise.

"There's something else here," says one of the men pulling out the body. "There's another bag."

"Old Peter," says Grazia, while the others pull him out of the ground. "My daughter told me Rodari's theory, which seems to be playing out."

"Eight dead, Marshal," says Scalise. "I hope it won't be ten. Never seen anything like it. A massacre, that's what it is. An explosion of madness. Two buried corpses, one in a freezer, one wrapped up in a carpet, two nailed with arrows, one driving a snowmobile holding his own guts, and one shot down in the woods by the hotel owner. Good thing the hotel is near enough for them to have heard the shots that lunatic fired at your daughter. I'll need a detailed report, Marshal Parodi. I urge you to give this matter your complete attention and give me a first draft in the next few hours. Needless to say, we need to enhance the force around here."

The colonel clears his voice, adjusts his coat, straightening his buttons and lapels, and then prepares to address the journalists. To make himself look taller on TV, he has constructed a little podium near the GeoService cabin, where he is headed when Grazia stops him.

"Colonel . . ."

"What, Marshal."

"I wanted to let you know that the report will be my last task as commander of this station. I intend to hand in my resignation immediately after I deliver it."

"What are you talking about?"

"I don't think I've handled the job in the best way, there are things that . . ."

"Listen to me. There are always things. Our job is to do our best, Marshal. And you did. Besides, I'm having a terrible time finding men who want to move here for a job. Resignation rejected, Marshal. Expect a raise instead."

"For what?"

"For catching on to what was happening, saving your daughter and maybe Rodari, solving the case of attorney Alberti's disappearance and someone else we didn't even know about, for having stopped a criminal plan from being put in place by a group of covert assassins and perhaps even saving this whole place from the clutches of a company that will soon be summoned to court to clarify their involvement in the whole mess. Marshal, you did what you were supposed to do. And with regard to the footage that led you to your conclusions . . ."

"Colonel, I . . ."

"I think we can set that aspect of the matter aside, Marshal. Resignation rejected, you can keep it along with all your things. When you're finished with the paperwork, take a week of leave. Friguglia called out of the blue to express his wish to return to service. Some unfounded rumors may have reached him about transfers to special units against organized crime. Anyway, his health conditions have miraculously improved and so—" A sneeze interrupts him. The colonel digs around in his coat pocket. He's looking for something. He finds it. He pulls out a chestnut. He looks at her, his contracted eyebrows suddenly severe. "Do you know what I think, Marshal? I think the only thing that can fight a cold is aspirin." He launches the chestnut into the woods. They both watch it disappear between the trees. "So let's get this press conference started, the spotlight awaits us."

TWO

Giulio opens his eyes. She's still there, close to him. She has her usual shawl on her shoulders, gathered tight at her neck, her hands gripping the thermos as she looks out the window. She doesn't have her usual cup of tea with her, which she was forced to leave back at the Gherarda.

Outside, the sky is gray. But the last time he opened his eyes, it was sunny. He must have slept a lot. The effect of the morphine. He immediately asked how bad it was, and they told him that everything went well but that he'd be medicated for a few days so he could get through the pain. The yellowish light in the room is annoying. The bed next to him has been turned down. Maybe they were letting her sleep in his room. He had the feeling that she had been nearby when he was sleeping. They explained everything to him.

Grazia had stopped in to see him. They'd managed to save Donato. He'll have a bad headache for a while. He and Grazia spoke alone. Comparing the footage of the attack on Patrizia with what the drones had captured, arriving to the theory that it was Maglio who killed her and then buried her, with Falconi's help, near the GeoService cabin. They're testing the DNA on Patrizia for a match with Maglio's, since she had apparently tried to defend herself. Is that supposed to make him feel better? Maybe in time. But not now. Giulio is no longer a suspect, this absurd and terrible story is over, but the truth is that Patrizia was killed in a dark alley so a permit could be authorized. The gnome is right: evil lurks where you least expect it. Where you wouldn't think to look for it, where everything seems completely normal. And yet it's not.

"Did I sleep a lot?" Giulio asks.

She turns. In a moment her eyes tear up. She smiles at her own weakness and wipes at her tears as she approaches the bed to take his hands in hers.

"A bit. How are you now?"

"I don't know. I think it will take a while for me to be able to tell."

She sits in the chair next to his bed. "Now that this whole thing is over, you'll have all the time you need."

"And you won't be able to sell the hotel, I imagine."

"What?" A rainbow of emotions crosses her eyes. First, it's almost a kind of disgust, which transforms into surprise, then guilt, and then almost relief, as if the weight of something hidden has suddenly vanished.

"He blackmailed you, didn't he? That's why you were about to sell the Gherarda. Falconi discovered your secret."

She looks down, as if it were too much to look him in the eyes.

"Don't you have anything to say?" Giulio asks. "Grazia told me how things went. You took a big risk with that second shot. Falconi was already down when you shot him again. You weren't just trying to stop him, were you?"

"Try not to judge me," she says, looking up, as if she had found the courage to look into his eyes. "There are a few things you still don't know."

"Where should we begin? The woods seem like a good starting point."

"The woods? What do you mean, Giulio?"

"Your accomplice, Dorina. She did a great job. I saw her as I was stepping inside Falconi's house. She was spying on him. I suppose she was there for Adele, right? Maybe she wasn't wearing her hearing aid, as usual, so she didn't hear the shots. She had no idea what was happening. But when she saw Viola run into the woods and Falconi chasing her with a shotgun, she called you."

Dorina takes out her hearing aid just outside the Gherarda and stashes it in her purse. She doesn't like people seeing her with that thing behind her ear. She can always pretend to be distracted. And anyway, she feels good, so to hell with what other people say. It's just the damn wax that settles over her eardrum that she'll wash out one day or another. The hearing aid is just helping her for the time being; she doesn't even need it, which is why she doesn't want to wear it and have people think she's deaf.

Fortunately she always keeps a pair of snowshoes at the Gherarda so she can take the trail home, which veers into the woods but cuts a lot of time off the trip to the village. And there's nothing better than walking on fresh snow in comfy, fur-lined boots on a sunny day.

The trail slopes slightly downhill. Nonexperts believe that going downhill is easier, but that's not true. Uphill is a matter of breath, downhill is a matter of muscles and joints, especially the knees. So at Walker's Reprieve, a clearing with benches and a fountain, where people usually have barbecues in the summer, she stops to rest awhile.

She sweeps snow from a bench. Her coat will get wet, but the invitation to sit is impossible to ignore. What a wonderful day. Dorina looks around. She takes a few minutes to breathe and massage her legs. How the fresh air helps. There isn't a living soul around, aside from some cold little birds and the occasional squirrel running through the snow to its nest. She slips her hand into her handbag, moves aside her hearing aid, and fishes around for her pack of Chesterfields. She's been sneaking them ever since she was a little girl. She's managed to make it to sixty without anyone ever discovering her little secret. It's been enough for her to keep mints around and wait to go back inside after she's done. That's the mistake that secret smokers make most often because they can't smell the smoke on their clothes like others can. She lights one up.

The woods really are splendid. They should be ashamed of themselves for wanting to build that thing. And yet some people know no shame. They distract you with a beautiful smile while they sharpen their knives. And they do it for the sole purpose of ambushing you. Sell the Gherarda to those cretins. Blackmail people by leveraging their little secrets, their weaknesses, their sorrows. And they keep smiling. Some people deserve their comeuppance. You just have to have courage, find the right time.

After finishing her cigarette, Dorina pops a mint into her mouth and starts walking again. But having resumed her path, she notices something. There's a car in the trees. It would be impossible not to recognize it. Adele's olive-green Panda four by four. What's it doing there?

Dorina approaches the car and sees it's not the only one parked there. Behind a row of trees there's also the Magliarini Forestry Services pickup. But what are they doing here? They're parked in a clearing off the county road. The classic spot where kids come to mess around. A concealed place, near a curve. And behind the curve . . . is Falconi's house. The cursed blackmailer. Maybe she's even blackmailing them. Go figure that Adele owns the land where the monster will rise.

Dorina wants to find out more. She leaves the trail and walks along the curve of the county road, hidden in the trees. After the bend, she reaches Falconi's house. A beautiful stand-alone villa with a snow-covered roof. Is that Amanda's old Ford parked in front? What on earth is going on? She'd better put in her hearing aid, which she'll need until she can wash out that damned wax in her ear.

She puts it in her ear and turns it on as she walks, and out of the corner of her eye, she can spot a dark shape entering the woods.

"Stop, just one thing!"

It's Falconi. He's running out of his house with a shotgun in his hand. That bastard is chasing someone who came here in Amanda's car. Dorina digs around in her purse for her cell phone.

"And so she called you," Giulio says. He reaches for the sugar water on the bedside table. She tightens the shawl around her neck, as if she suddenly feels cold. She seems to be unable to speak, still uncertain whether to admit that Giulio was right or to embark on a last desperate attempt to deny it. Giulio drinks a sip and resumes talking so she doesn't have time to make the wrong choice. "Because if you had waited to hear the shots from the middle of the woods, as you said to the carabinieri, you wouldn't have had time to get your rifle, load it, and have Akan drive you on the snowmobile to Falconi's exact location. No, you followed him almost immediately, as soon as Dorina called you. The instant that crazy chase in the forest began."

"I didn't know about what he and Maglio had done to Patrizia. If I'd known . . ."

"He was blackmailing you. He wanted to make you sell the Gherarda, I assume, as part of his agreement with GeoService. I'm sure we'll find out about that part soon enough, when we discover who owned the company. But nothing will come of your relationship with Falconi besides a letter of intent for a sale that never materialized. You can always say you were thinking about it but that you weren't convinced. But I know that unless someone had blackmailed you, you never would have sold the Gherarda to anyone. And then it hit me."

"What?"

"Falconi discovered the secret you've been carrying around for four years. Did you seriously think I wouldn't have figured it out? That you could fool me like you fooled the others? Because you did fool the others, didn't you? Didn't you fool them, *Amanda*?"

She stays silent. Only her sad smile hints at an admission.

"The funny thing, Aunt Amanda, is this," Giulio continues. "It would have been a big shock for me, don't you think? The kind of discovery that would have left me speechless. But no. It's a bit like accepting something I already knew. The fact is, I never understood why you took the bus that day. You'd never taken it in your life. You loved to go out for your spins in the car, even when you didn't have to go anywhere. You even brought me with you sometimes. 'Let's go for a spin,' you'd say, remember? And then one day you take a bus, and the only bus you take in your life ends up going down with a collapsed bridge. And then the photograph that disappeared. The one that shows the scar on your neck, these shawls you always wear, the ashes you carry into the woods. Did you think I didn't see you? I was at the window when you went to spread the ashes as you always did. Amanda, the witch. The final piece fell in place when I got in the car and the keys were in the ignition. When I reversed I saw the tracks from the snow tires. But the seat was too high up for Akan. So I knew then, even before Grazia told me the drone had captured the old Ford going up and down the county road in the middle of the night. You couldn't resist going for your spins, could you? Mom didn't even know how to start a car. And she had terrible aim. She wouldn't have been able to hit Falconi from a foot away. But you had no problems hitting your target. And you solved a lot of problems when you did."

"I saved Grazia and Viola."

"And the Gherarda, which you'd promised to sell to GeoService. You weren't doing seasonal work. You'd closed the hotel because you were about to sell it."

"I have to be more careful where I leave things, apparently."

"You wanted me to find it, didn't you? You wanted me to understand everything, to spare you having to explain. You've always been that way."

"After four years I began to doubt your powers of observation."

"Falconi made you sign it. He knew about you, somehow he knew. He was more observant than I was."

"He knew from the beginning," Amanda says. "He approached Barbara that horrible day as she waited for the bus and they spoke."

"Had he already tried to make her sell?"

"Apparently. GeoService's plan had been in the works for a while. You can imagine your mother's response."

"So when he realized what you were doing after the accident, he waited for you to take your sister's place, and when it was time, when it was too late for you to turn back, he threatened to reveal your identity to everyone. So the other day you decided it might be the right opportunity to put an end to the whole story."

"You sound like an assassin."

"Says you."

"I saved those two girls. Do you think I would have shot Falconi if they hadn't been there? Do you think I would have killed someone over a contract?"

"It wasn't a contract. It was your secret."

"Do you think I would have killed him over that?"

"Let's put it this way, Aunt. I don't think you would have done it if Grazia and Viola hadn't been there. But I think you probably couldn't believe your luck when you saw Grazia and Viola, right there, in that situation, in need of your good aim. And then there was that second shot. Grazia says you didn't know if Falconi had been disarmed or not, that you were in shock, that you didn't know how to use the rifle and the second shot just happened. But my dad was a hunter, so I do know a thing or two about it. And I know that was a perfect shot. I think it almost scares you to think of it now. To the point that you need someone to remind you of who you are. But at this point you'll have to tell me who you are yourself. Otherwise, I can't help you. You have to tell me why you wanted to take my mother's place, her life, to disappear inside of her, to willfully imprison yourself in such a huge secret. Why did you do all of this?"

"Do you know what they say about twins? About how one can feel it when something happens to the other? It's all true." Amanda takes a deep breath, as if she were preparing for a confession that had been pending for a long time. "I was cleaning artichokes that day. I had just returned from a trip to Egypt, remember? I brought you a little mummy." She smiles. "The TV was on. I was running the knife under the water, humming, when I heard it. It was like a punch, right here, in my heart. I understood everything. I dropped the knife and looked for a chair because I couldn't stand. Barbara was dead. I knew it. An abyss opened at my feet. I felt like I was falling. I stayed frozen for hours. I was terrified. I thought if I didn't move, I could somehow stop time and prevent the nightmare from happening. I could hardly breathe. Then the phone call. The carabinieri. I didn't understand it right then and there, because I was so out of my head. But apparently they thought Amanda was the one who had died. Your mother and I had the same purse. We didn't do it on purpose, but that kind of thing always happens to twins. Or at least it did with us. And that morning she had taken my bag. So when they recovered her body and read her papers, they thought I was dead. It's hard to explain, but when that guy on the phone called me Barbara, it was as if she wasn't dead. As if I could choose not to accept it. As if I could keep her with me for a while. But the really amazing thing happened later. All those people, thinking I was her, made me feel so close that I didn't have the courage to admit the truth. I know it's probably hard for you to understand. But over the next few days, I realized that all these people needed Barbara as much as I did. The owner of the Gherarda. When we heard about the waste plant, everyone came here to ask me for advice. They never would have asked Amanda, the witch. Amanda, the globe-trotter. Amanda, the unreliable one. This place . . . everyone, we all needed Barbara."

"And Dorina . . ."

"I needed an ally. Especially after Falconi blackmailed me into selling the Gherarda. She didn't flinch when I told her. I suspect she already knew. But what we were defending—the Gherarda, the woods—were precious, too important to go back on. She helped me understand things about my sister that maybe I didn't even know. And so, over the years, I've been a bit of her and a bit of me. I didn't have to get rid of Amanda entirely, in the end. Good aim, a certain knack for Buraco, and a good relationship with the three cats that have watched over the Gherarda like brave guardians. But it was Barbara that everyone wanted, always. It was the first time I felt like that. After a lifetime, I became the good sister, the one they all loved, and so I left the other me behind, the person who had only been able to entertain a little boy with her stories about gnomes and magical forests."

"Those stories were important to that little boy."

"But they were just stories. And even if that little boy grew up and didn't come back so often, I like to think I helped to keep his mother in his life awhile longer."

Giulio feels an emotion that has been welling in him for a long time. Tears fill his eyes. He smiles and doesn't try to hold them back.

"Are any of those stories about spirits?" he asks his aunt.

"All stories are about spirits."

Amanda smiles. She stands up, wincing slightly. She looks out the window.

"Spring is coming, the hawthorne will blossom soon. Remember what your mother always said? The winter snow hides so much, but when hawthorne season comes, the snow disappears and everything resurfaces. I always think about that." Her eyes are still moist. She wipes away her tears and turns to Giulio. She reaches into her pocket.

"I still have a few coins for that machine out there. It makes tea. I mean, not real tea. A 'tea-flavored beverage,' whatever that is. But it's not bad if you like lemon and sugar. Only I refuse to drink out of those plastic cups that melt and leave a nasty aftertaste. If you want I can talk to the nurse, maybe they have other cups we can use."

"Great idea," Giulio says.

Amanda approaches the door. She opens it and then stops.

"Akan told me to say hello. He said something about a storm." She closes her eyes so she can focus and remember. "He said you shouldn't look back, because when you do, a part of you will stay stuck there. And you have to be willing to lose that part of you in order to survive. He said you'd understand."

She smiles again. She also understands what he means.

"Does Akan know the truth?" Giulio asks.

"You can't hide anything from that man. And then he went and told everyone I was the one who'd taught him how to make wild boar ragù, since it was the Gherarda's signature dish. Fortunately your mother had a recipe book, because I don't have the faintest idea how to make ragù."

When Amanda closes the door behind her, Giulio opens the drawer in the nightstand and takes out the thing Grazia left him. His phone. Now that he's no longer under arrest, he can use it. He puts on his headphones and opens WhatsApp. There's a message waiting for him with a file attached. The number isn't stored in his contacts, but he knows who it is. Viola.

> It's weird, you know? Remember what the gnome says? That the forest protects him? I think your little friend is right. I think that when you need it, the forest really does protect you. It will be hard to forget what happened, but some things aren't meant to be forgotten. And I want to remember what happened during one of the worst moments of my life forever. He was there, less than a step away from me, I was right in front of his eyes, yet for some reason he couldn't see me. It's strange. At that moment, I thought about my friend. His name was Michele, and he died on Bridge Day. He plays the keyboard in the song. It's a long

story, an old recording I held on to for no reason, and now it's as if that reason arrived. There's also another track of something besides the instruments. I think it somehow has something to do with what happened, even though I still can't explain why. It's a sound, I think, but you can't hear it. I can't understand what it is, and yet it's there. It sounds like a pulse, a whisper, or maybe it really is the breath of the woods. Or it might be the water running underground that no one knew about. The fact is that I somehow know the sound is there, even if I can't hear it. A bit like your gnome, who no one ever sees. And maybe there's something to be understood in all this. That we're surrounded by so much more than what we can see and hear. Things that have been there forever and that we have to learn to recognize. Maybe someday I'll pass by your window and we can talk about it in person, but in the meantime I wanted to share the song with you. It's not done yet and we don't have a title, but at least now you know what it's about.

Giulio downloads the file and presses play.

A keyboard. That boy, Michele, is playing a slow blues in a minor key. A hypnotic music that carries him away. And after a few bars, Viola's guitar enters. A dissonant arpeggio that reminds him of certain dark wave moods, a little psychedelic.

Giulio closes his eyes and listens.

Music, especially some music, has always had the power to carry him far away. The gnome approves, because he knows that travel is good for understanding the bigger picture and the meaning of going back.

"They say people who survive a tragedy usually feel guilty." His first encounter with Patrizia. One of the first things she said to him. In her office, after Bridge Day. "It's natural, and they suggest people process it with a psychologist."

We all survive something, Patrizia. Every day. Now he'd be able to tell her. Now that the storm was over. Now that he'd always live his life *from now on.*

"Remember that photograph?" Patrizia asks. Now that day is unanchored in time, they're in some place, in a before or after, it doesn't matter anymore. "The one you gave me with the reflection of the two lovers kissing in the rearview mirror, with the sun near the horizon."

"Yeah, I remember. You liked it, but you never cared if it was a sunrise or a sunset."

"That's what I wanted to tell you. It doesn't matter which one it is, Giulio. They're two lovers. For them, sunrise and sunset are the same thing."

THREE

"Did you give it to him?" Viola asks. She's in the car in the passenger seat.

"Yeah, I gave it to him," says Grazia, sitting beside her.

It's raining. All around them, by the hospital, the gray of the cement blends with the gray of the sky. Viola checks her WhatsApp and sees the two check marks change color. From gray to blue. It means Giulio read her message. Now he'll download the file.

"Did you remove Mussolini's face from my contact?" her mother asks.

"Yeah, I took it off."

"What do you have now?"

"Pinochet."

"Look, Viola . . ."

And as she turns, Viola snaps a picture of her.

"I'll put this instead. It flatters you, don't you think?"

"I look pissed off . . ."

"You always look pissed off."

Grazia turns the key in the ignition. The engine starts and the windshield wipers activate.

"I have an idea."

"What?" says Viola, putting away her iPhone.

"Let's go to McDonald's for dinner, fill up on crap, and then go to the movie theater to watch a bunch of movies until it closes."

"Okay, but no movies with people kissing."

Grazia hits the turn signal, glances in the mirror, and puts the car in drive. "What do you have against people kissing?"

"It's a great thing, but I don't see why they have to make movies about it."

"Well, because it's a great thing . . ."

"It's also a great thing to go to the bathroom when you need to, but I'm not going to make a movie about it."

"Okay, no people kissing."

The car slowly begins to make its way to the exit of the hospital parking lot. All around there are other parked cars, people running under their umbrellas, a bus stopping in front of a sheltered stop.

"And . . . one other thing," says Viola.

"Mayo for your french fries?"

"I was thinking more like a little smoke."

"A what? You don't have weed on you, do you?"

The car becomes smaller and smaller, joining the other traffic that flows into the ring road. The lights along the avenues are already glowing in the unnatural darkness of the leaden sky that hangs over the entire city.

"Let me remind you, Mom, that I'm still in shock, and you can find more than one study online about how weed helps with relaxation and trauma management . . ."

"Viola, I'm a carabinieri marshal. You can't tell me you go around with weed in your pocket."

"Well, I don't have any . . ."

"Yeah, right."

From here, the city is a puzzle made up of tiny, faded pieces. In their continuous motion, some join together for a moment, only to part and connect with others.

"I meant I don't have any in my pocket. I usually keep it at home . . ."

"You keep weed at our house?"

"Only a little . . ."

"That's the first thing every drug dealer says when I stop them."

"Have you stopped a lot of dealers?"

"Don't change the subject."

And all those little puzzle pieces seem to be part of a movement that is both random and perfect.

"I love you, Marshal. But look, McDonald's was back there."

"Where do you keep it?"

"Seriously, Mom, you missed the turn. You're going the wrong way."

EPILOGUE

And that's that. More or less. The fact is, in lending order to chaos, in looking for the right connections between facts, something always remains unexplained. Something escapes. There's the feeling that something else lies in the folds of the story. A meaning that hasn't been captured in full. Maybe it's really like that guy says, that evil doesn't always have an explanation. And in fact, when people lose something in their lives, when they can't explain the things that happen, they always have this sense of emptiness, of absence, of loneliness, which they have to reconcile and learn to manage before the void fills up with the wrong things. Because when you lose something, you can't just go back to being what you were before—you have to become something else, something that hasn't existed yet. And if you don't, you're lost. Think about it, as someone who was spared this time around: What else would have killed these people?

As for us three, she put us here to defend the Gherarda and its inhabitants, and we did our job. We took and we gave, without saving anything for ourselves. So now we just want to have a good sit in front of the fireplace and lick our wounds, being the good house cats that we are, and wait for someone to offer us a nice treat to munch on.

Soon the snow will be gone. The whiteness will disappear and everything else will come back. Meadows, flowers. And the Gherarda will reopen. She always trusted it would. She never stopped believing that the Gherarda would reopen in the spring. That's how it works. You have to believe in what you do, because if you don't, how can you convince others? It's one of those things that the gnome always says. And he's right. He's always right.

Oh yeah, the gnome.

He never stopped believing in them. Of course at first, they didn't really look like the best candidates to accomplish such an important task. They were all so alone and scared. But he, the gnome, always knew they'd do it. That they would learn. He always knew they were the right people and that somehow they would find a way to save their old woods. So if things went as they did in the end, he deserves the credit. You don't really think three cats and an old witch could have done it alone, do you?

There are places that aren't like all the others.

The woods had to be saved, and so they were. The ones who had to be stopped were stopped, and the ones who were lost found their way home. If one day you ever decide to believe in these things, to believe in them for real, then you'll understand that this was exactly what the gnome wanted. Think about it. Certain stories really only begin after they're over.

Don't go, please stay
The snow will stop tomorrow
And the love between us will return
In hawthorne season

Fabrizio De André, "Inverno"

ABOUT THE AUTHOR

Riccardo Bruni is an Italian journalist who writes for newspapers, maga-
zines, webzines, and blogs. Two of his previous novels have been translated into English: *The Night of the Moths* and *The Lion and the Rose*.
His other novels include *La lunga notte dell'iguana*, *Nessun dolore*, *Zona
d'ombra*, and *La notte delle falene*, which was nominated for the Premio
Strega 2016. For more information, please visit www.riccardobruni.com.